THE MIDWIFE'S TALE

The Midwife's Tale

Gretchen Moran Laskas

The Dial Press

THE MIDWIFE'S TALE

A Dial Press Book / April 2003

Published by
The Dial Press
A Division of Random House, Inc.
New York, New York

BOOK DESIGN BY GLEN EDELSTEIN

Library of Congress Cataloging-in-Publication Data
Laskas, Gretchen Moran.
The midwife's tale/ Gretchen Moran Laskas.
p. cm.
ISBN 0-385-33551-2
1. Midwives—Fiction. 2. Mothers and daughters—Fiction. 3. Appalachian
region, Southern—Fiction. I. Title

PS3612.A85 M43 2003   2002041010
813/.54 21

Manufactured in the United States of America
Published simultaneously in Canada

BVG 10 9 8 7 6 5 4 3 2 1

To Karl

For promises kept

THE MIDWIFE'S TALE

PROLOGUE

Mama always said that most of being a good midwife was in knowing the family history. Not just the birthing story of any given woman—although that was a good thing to keep in mind—but the whole history. The Teller family, for instance, runs to twins, though this may skip a generation or two, like it did for Shirley Teller Meroe, who had twins after her mother and grandmother going without. Her twin girls went on to have twins of their own.

Mama called this "the history of the body," as there were a lot of folks, family and otherwise, who had gone before this person, and remembering those people was nearly as important to a midwife as anything we might do with our hands. Mama knew I would understand, seeing as how I was to be a midwife, too. I come from a long line of midwives, from my great-granny Denniker to Granny Whitely to Mama to me. This is our own story—a history intertwined with more than a thousand babies we've brought into these hills of West Virginia.

Women would find their way to our clapboard house, set against the lowest ridge along Denniker's Mountain, on the banks of Kettle Creek. You could see the roofline of our square front porch from the road in winter and early spring, but come summer we lived back inside the woods like deer. Even in the trees, women found us. Mama always said the women liked being out of sight. Nothing like a little privacy to make a body talk.

These women would come, hello the house or rap quietly on the door. The very youngest shy, their bodies full of life both inside and out.

"So let's sit and talk a minute," Mama would say to the woman, handing out tea as though this were a social call.

"Talk about what?" the woman would want to know.

"Whatever you want to," Mama would answer. She would smile at the girl, and at that moment you couldn't help but feel that the only thing that mattered to Mama was this woman and the baby she carried.

Many were hardly older than myself, at least from the time Mama started insisting that I listen in. They would come, sit there with my mama on my own front porch while I waited just inside the door, peering at them with their round bellies and shiny-bright hair, mouths talking up a storm. "Why can't I sit out with you?" I asked Mama once. I was fifteen.

"You will," Mama promised. "In fact, someday you'll be talking to women like this all on your own. For now, you need to learn how to listen."

I would try, but often, the talk seemed so silly.

"I don't know where I'd start," the girl would say.

"Just talk about what is on your mind, as it comes to you," Mama would answer, her voice warm and kind. A voice that made you want to tell her secrets.

Such prattle might seem idle, but it wasn't. I learned that soon enough. The girls would talk at first about their men— about being courted, whether by one they loved or one who loved them. How people seemed to change after words had been said over them, or not, as the case often was. As the girls' bellies grew and they realized now that they were to be women, they spoke less about their men and more about their mothers. They spoke of sisters, or the wives of brothers. Grandmothers and aunts. Cousins who had had hard births.

No matter what they talked about, Mama always said the same thing at the end. "Your family has a good history of births, and I expect you'll do just fine."

I had no reason to think Mama wasn't doing right by these women until Missy Janicor came down, walking all the way from Little Laurel Mountain. I'd known Missy from when she was still going to school, so I knew her mama and her grandmother. I had sat in their house listening to the story of the awful night Missy was born, and how her mama had nearly died when the doctor couldn't stop the blood. So I knew Mama was lying when she told Missy things had always been all right.

"You told a falsehood," I chided Mama, watching Missy disappear through the trees. Mama was still sitting on the porch, her hands folded in her lap, looking off in the direction of Kettle Creek. My cheeks burned with heat, as this was August, hot and sticky as grease inside the house, and I was glad to come out into the cool air.

"How so?" she asked, but I saw the corners of her mouth twitching. I wondered if she was laughing at me, yet I couldn't see why.

"You know very well that Missy's mama had an awful birthing time."

Behind Mama's eyes, light sparked and caught, making her appear lit up from the inside. Her red hair seemed to flame, and she was suddenly very beautiful. I knew I had done something to make her happy, and I wished I knew what it was so I could do it all my born days just to see her look at me like this.

"Very good, Elizabeth," was all she said.

I wanted to ask what I'd done that was so good, but before I could figure out my own words, she had taken my hand and was pulling me around our house, past the great maple that shaded us all summer, stepping lightly through the neatly weeded garden rows until we'd reached the creek. "My feet are baking, after sitting so." She hiked her skirt above her knees and waded in the water, her legs white and straight, dappled with light. I waded out, too.

After we'd stood there a long minute, feeling the mud between our toes, Mama turned to me and said, "A woman who thinks things will go well often makes it so."

"But it wasn't true," I told her, as if she didn't know.

"Missy needs to think so," Mama said. "Sometimes the truth isn't found in the story itself, but in the telling—telling what you know, not just what is real."

Still, I didn't fathom it, standing in the creek water at the age of fifteen, just all that she meant by that. I stood there on that hot August day in 1913, thinking that the story of my life was easy enough to tell. Would always be so simple. I knew I was expected to follow Mama, follow Granny, follow Great-granny. In the end, I didn't disappoint them. Or perhaps I did. After all, I was the last midwife. There were no more midwives after me.

ONE

If you were born in Kettle Creek or hereabouts on our part of the Tygart River Valley, your name was written in the ledgers that lined our shelves. They were tall black leather books, shiny and thin like the ones Greeley MacIntosher used over at the store in Philippi. With a good birth we came home and wrote the baby's full name, the mama's name, the daddy's, and the date. All those lists of names should tell you that our family was good at what we do.

We never talked about the ledgers to anyone but ourselves. Not that we were ashamed—these were just names after all, but on account of the babies who didn't come through—and the pain that such knowledge brought. Most babies like that didn't even have names given them, and when Mama thought me old enough to know, she showed me the lists of Baby Girl Teller, or Baby Boy Switzer, if the woman was far enough along to tell. No matter what, we recorded the names and anything else we could recall about the birthing itself.

"Write it down," Mama told me. "Everything." She was the first to do this, marking little things about the birth that weren't so important in and of themselves, but might be later, when you needed to see the history of the family. Granny Whitely and Granny Denniker had kept most everything in their heads—all but the names and dates. "A written record is more reliable," Mama taught me. And she was right. Kettle Valley is full of Teller, Meroe, and Switzer families, and writing things down kept names and families straight. For a midwife, confusing a family history was one of the worst things you could do, as confusion might make a bad situation worse if you needed to choose the right tonic, or know just when to make a cut.

I learned to read looking at those ledgers. Mama taught me herself, using the family Bible once the black books were mastered. Given the number of Hezekiahs and Micahs and Ruths and Mordecais I read about, it was often difficult to remember which ones were biblical wonders and which lived along the Philippi road. Sometimes, even when I read the scriptures now, I can't be sure I didn't once hear that King David's wife Abigail had given birth to a little girl weighing more than twelve pounds. Fortunately, around the turn of the century, fashionable names changed—Henry, Otis, Maurice.

Mama didn't tell me about the little red book, which she kept hidden until I was seventeen and had been attending births for more than three years. I suppose she thought I wasn't ready for it, and that was truth, for I wasn't. Don't know when I might of been ready, natural-like, but I found out about it because Sarah Meroe went into labor right at the same time as Old Lady Whipple. Old Man Whipple was a justice of the peace and was known for making things rough for people who didn't please him, so when he came, Mama went with him, leaving me to handle Sarah's birthing all alone.

"Ain't like Old Lady Whipple needs the help," I muttered to Mama as she gathered her things and helped me prepare my bag. I'd never had a bag packed just for me before. I was scared to be attending Sarah, who was a little bitty thing known for her snorty laugh and big brown eyes—eyes that had nearly swelled shut during her confinement.

"Hush, Elizabeth," Mama told me. Her face looked white, the deep red of her hair shockingly dark against her skin. I wondered what Mama knew about Old Lady Whipple that I didn't. That high-and-mighty woman had brought out fifteen children, and I couldn't see that one more would make much difference.

"You'll have to make do," Mama told me. Then she smiled, reached out, and smoothed my hair. "You're a fine midwife," she said. Already her voice had that birthing tone—as strong and sure as a bell ringing in winter. With that voice she called to women through the fiery pain of childbearing when there was nothing more she could do with her hands in their bellies. I coveted my mama's voice more than anything she owned.

"I'll try," I said, my own voice weak as well water.

So I did, and everything went fine. I came home, my steps almost dancing on the path before me. My body hummed and stirred like one who has witnessed a great joy—and I had, as Sarah's baby had been a big boy who looked just like his daddy. A good dose of black cherry tea had calmed what trouble Sarah had suffered towards the end, and I was feeling proud and happy. I could hear the sound of Kettle Creek bubbling over rocks as I went into the house.

Mama was already home, sitting in her chair, staring into the fireplace where she'd built a roaring fire. She didn't greet me when I arrived, but I didn't pay her any mind, so busy was I writing down Ernest Meroe's name in the black ledger. The first I had ever recorded in my own handwriting.

I noticed then that Mama had written nothing from her own birthing. "Didn't it go well?" I asked.

"Well enough, I guess," Mama said, her voice flat and wearied.

"Didn't they name it yet?" Sometimes families couldn't

agree upon a name, but usually this was only over the first baby, when the father was still interested, or if the mother-in-law was living with them. I'd seen families squabble about a name for weeks. "Did they just run out of names?" I asked with a laugh. "After sixteen babies, surely no one cares."

But Mama didn't laugh with me, and this bothered me, seeing as she was a great one for laughing, even when no one else could see the joke. "Come sit down, Elizabeth," she said. She was clutching a red book, her knuckles so white around the edges that I wondered that they didn't snap. There were traces of blood and afterbirth rimmed around her fingernails.

"What is it?" I asked, curious now.

She reached out and handed me the little book, but she did not look at me. I turned the strange book over. The red leather cover was dusty and hard. When I opened it I saw a list of names, most familiar to me—names of folks living in Kettle Valley, just like those written in the black ledgers on the desk. There were family names, followed by a letter, a B or a G, sometimes followed by the letter D. I figured B was for boy and G was girl, but I wondered why we didn't just write the names in the black ledger as we always did. At the very end was the name Whipple, with the letter G. There was no D.

"What's the D for?" I asked, seeing it written after about every third name. The dates went back for more than fifty years, and I saw in the beginning names written in Granny Denniker's handwriting—names that I had never heard tell of in all of Mama's stories.

"Mama?" I asked, flipping the pages, filled with B's and G's and D's. "What's the D for?"

"Deformed," Mama said. She covered her face with her hands, leaving bloody smudges across her freckled skin. "Means the baby came out and there was something wrong with it."

I glanced over the pages again. "And if there is no letter D?" I asked.

"Then there was nothing wrong," Mama answered. The hands left her face and settled again into her lap.

"Meaning?" I asked, but somewhere inside of me I began to understand.

"The baby wasn't welcomed. Whether it was deformed or not." Her hands tightened into fists, fanned out, and were still again.

I stood up, shaking, the book falling to the floor. "How?"

"Pillow, normally." Mama pushed some hair out of her eyes. I couldn't seem to stop staring at her hands. "You won't have to do it for a long time," she told me. "I promise."

"I ain't ever gonna do it," I said. My clothes were damp with sweat—I could smell that childbearing scent dripping through my skin, perfuming the air around me with the iron-hot smell of blood and spices that have been baked inside a woman's belly.

"It's called midwife's mercy," Mama started to say.

But I was having none of it. "You can't make me," I told her, saying words I never would have dreamed I'd say to my own mama. She was suddenly a stranger to me now, this woman who could hold down a pillow on a baby. I thought of the goose-down filling the cracks around the baby's nose and mouth, the image of the baby's face pressed into the pillow, pressed by my mother's hands.

I went out the back door and purged my belly as hard as I could, trying to make myself clean.

When I was done, I looked around me, seeing a place I'd always known, but was now foreign. The darkness seemed so dense and heavy that I could hardly make out the rim of Denniker's Mountain looming behind the house. I could hear the churning water of Kettle Creek, reminding me that the woman inside was my mother, who carried me in her womb. I covered my ears with my hands and slumped against the steps, waiting until the wind changed and a warm summer rain began to fall.

The house behind me was quiet, as still and dark as the mountain before me. Only then could I go back inside.

When I woke that morning, Mama was gone, leaving only a note saying that she was at Mary Switzer's. The room felt strange, and I thought at first it was her absence. Then I realized that all of the birthing ledgers were gone.

I rummaged through the kitchen cupboards and even picked up the rugs. I checked the fireplace, but there was no ash in the grate. There soon would be, I thought, and headed for Mama's room.

The dark-blue-and-white quilt on the bed was pulled so tight that the cotton fabric looked stretched across a quilting frame. The long pine shelf above was crowded with books, but no ledgers, and no red books of any kind. Behind the corner curtain where she kept her clothes, I found her dresses and underthings, hung on hooks or folded neatly. Her extra pair of shoes stood together on the floor.

Above my head, tied to nails driven into the beams of the ceiling, hung bunches of herbs, and the air was spiced with their scent. Horseweed for cramping. Spreading dogbane, the pods hanging from the stems, good for helping a swollen woman pass water. Some I knew, some I did not. Mama's mortar and pestle sat clean and shiny on a small table, next to an oil lamp.

Then I saw the only place those ledgers could be—the cedar chest, buried, no doubt, among the winter wool quilts. The chest was locked, but the key was sitting right on top. I turned it, lifting the chest just enough to breathe in wood-scent so rich it turned my stomach.

I slammed the chest closed. Wouldn't do any good to burn the books, for I knew I would always remember the names written in them. I would always know that some had come down their mother's tube where my mama's hands were waiting.

I had to leave my mama's house. I was too young then to think of ways to make peace with such terrible knowledge except by running from it. I went into my room, into my own cedar chest, and started packing. I packed my winter things, not knowing when, if ever, I would return. I made my bed, sliding my hands across the yellow-and-green bow-tie quilt Great-granny Denniker had made for me when I was born, and wondered when I would sleep beneath it again.

I realized how few places I had to go. I had family, with whom I'd never been close. I had some school friends. I could go to Pittsburgh or Baltimore or Wheeling as so many others my age had done. But to leave meant more than leaving Kettle Creek, or even Mama. I'd heard talk that Alvin Denniker was home, living on the mountain that bore his family's name. Though folks said otherwise in the year he'd been away, I'd always known that he would come back. And though I'd not laid eyes on him yet, just having him so close was enough to hold me fast.

In the end, I went to Granny's. For most of my life, Mama had been the one catching babies while Granny studied herbs. Herbals were a healing gift, I thought.

Besides, Mama and Granny had never gotten along. By going to stay with Granny, Mama would not only know how upset I was, but she might also feel a little bit of pain, too.

This last thought shames me most.

T W O

Granny Whitely lived in the Homestead, a large frame house on the edges of the town of Philippi. "It's in the town, but not of it," Granny told me one day when I was too small to catch the biblical reference. This made perfect sense though, as I could see the town buildings if I stood in the middle of the road, facing the setting sun. I loved being outside the town, for the land around the Homestead had been my playland— the great thickets of trees, the holly bushes taller than a grown man. Blue spruce trees shaded the back in summer and filled the air with that tangy scent of pine.

I remembered a house filled with people, not surprising as Granny came from a family of more than twelve and Granddad called eight men brother. I can remember seeing Great-granny Denniker sitting in the kitchen, wrapped in scarves and blankets and hats—summer heat or winter cold made no different to her—rocking in her chair sipping red wine from a pewter cup I was told had come from England. Great-granny had long since passed on, but the cup was still there, resting on a shelf in the parlor. As a child I was allowed to polish it.

Still, the Homestead was not a happy place, not for Mama, and so, not for me. My first eight years, I lived in a world loud with the angry voices of Granny and Mama's quarrels. A house filled with bitter sighs and mutterings from my granddad. Mama bore the brunt of his tongue, and I often saw her leave his bedroom, running out the back, headed for the woods. "He's dying" was all she would say when I asked her about it.

The thought that we would leave never occurred to me. Women without men didn't live out on their own. Wasn't until the day Mama and Granny were fussing about my cousin Nettie marrying Benty Wilken that I realized Mama had other ideas.

"At least Benty Wilken will make an honest woman out of her," Granny told Mama. They were sitting on the porch stringing pole-beans, their fingers moving so fast they seemed to whisper like hummingbird wings. I was sitting on the steps, hidden by a trumpet vine.

"Honest woman?" Mama muttered. I could hear the discarded ends of the beans thrown so hard against the ground that they bounced like hail. Chickens fought for the choice bits, squawking and flapping their wings.

"Not everyone cares to be living the way you do," Granny said. I heard Mama's intake of breath and peered through the leaves.

"He'll beat her, like his daddy does Doris," Mama said. "And you know the kind of girl Nettie is—she'd call a man to take out a spider rather than kill it her own self."

"It's unlucky to kill a spider," I said, poking my head around the porch post.

Both Mama and Granny jumped, and then frowned when they saw me there. Mama rose and put down the crockery bowl. "Well, at least my daughter won't have to marry some man just because I choose him."

"Believe me, you might wish you had a choice," Granny

shot back, angry and loud. But Mama had already taken my
hand and was leading me down the road.

"Where are we going?" I asked, my small legs skipping to
keep up.

"Just walking," Mama said.

We walked until I wore great fat blisters on my heels and
had to take off my shoes to continue without pain. We walked
along the Philippi road and then along Kettle Creek and
around the foot of Denniker's Mountain to where the Harry
Meroes lived. Everyone knew they had the best orchard in the
county, and we passed now between trees so old and loaded
with wares that they appeared pressed into the earth. As we
bent under the trees, I could hear birds and small animals
moving through the twisted branches, taking their tithe of
the ripening fruit.

"Stand back a ways," Mama said. She was standing now beneath the biggest and greatest of the trees, one filled with
fruit as gnarled and bumpy as an old woman's hand. I was a
bit taken aback when Mama walked about the trunk twice before grabbing the branch above her head and scooting her feet
up the side of the tree.

I saw a flash of white as her skirts fell away and then her
legs, pale and furry looking. She inched across the branch, and
then, clinging with her arms and legs, pumped her body up
and down until the tree shook and creaked. Apples rained to
the ground in a great green storm. I could hear the soft splat
of flesh opening, and when the wind blew over us the air
smelled like a cider press.

"It's true," Mama said, too winded to say more. Looking up
at her, I could see the line of sweat above her lips, but her color
was better, no longer that angry red. When she saw me, she
smiled. Not a happy smile, for even a child as young as eight
knows that all smiles are not happy ones.

"What's true?" I asked. The world seemed suddenly quiet after Mama's whirlwind.

"The apple never falls far from the tree," she said, with a laugh no more pleasant than the smile had been. She turned her body around and dropped back to earth. "That's what your granny is always telling me."

The floor of the old tree was littered with apples—pale pink ones, pearly green ones. Hard nuggets that hadn't quite yet been born. No apple lay more than a step or two from the tree's farthest branches.

Mama took my hand and led me out of the orchard. "I need to tell you something, but I want you to keep it a secret."

"Even from Granny?" I asked. The thought was exciting and scary.

"This is just our secret. At least for now." She took a deep breath, staring out along the edges of the mountains, out to where the land smooths out and becomes a flood plain, headed west. "We're moving to a new house. Our own house."

"Leave the Homestead?" I asked with a child's fear of change. "Leave Granny?"

"She can visit," Mama told me, not looking pleased. "Elizabeth, think—our own place. Just you and me. Won't that be fun?" When I didn't say anything, she tried to smile. "I have a few things to work out. I have to talk to, well, someone."

"Who?" I wanted to know.

"Someone," she answered, looking worried and unhappy again.

"Will it be a pretty house?" I asked, wanting to bring even the sad smile back.

"Yes," she said. "A very pretty one. This is a good idea, Elizabeth. You'll see."

And because I knew she wanted it to be, because I knew she

wanted me to want it, too, I nodded, and the smile she gave me was truly happy.

"You need to know just one more thing," she said, looking back under the apple trees. "It may be as your granny says, but apples don't only fall. Lots of things could happen. An apple might roll to the ends of the earth." Mama picked up a tiny apple from the ground and threw it as far as she could. We watched it tumble down the mountain a minute before falling into the high grass near a bend of Kettle Creek.

"To the ends of the earth?" I asked, wondering where such a thing might be.

"Well," Mama gave a slight shrug, "down the mountain, anyway."

When I showed up nine years later, back on her doorstep, Granny didn't even looked surprised. She never glanced at the satchel in my hand, or asked what I was doing there. "You can help me with the pickles," she told me by way of a greeting, holding the door open long enough for me to skirt through. I followed her large form back into the house where the kitchen was, the smell reaching me the moment I stepped inside.

She'd been harvesting. There were vegetables spread out everywhere. Beans piled up and over the edges of the sink, tomatoes rotting on the windowsills. Small piles of corn, some husked, some still wearing green jackets, rested on the floor, in the doorway, scattered like chicken feed across the back porch, the edges gnawed by mice. Wilted cabbages stood on the table. Only the shiny green peppers did not show the result of days spent in a kitchen hot and heavy with summer heat.

"You thinking of doing some canning soon?" I asked, although I didn't see any evidence of work—just the spoils of picking. I wondered how much more there was out in the garden.

"I can't say," Granny said, her eyes looking dazed a moment. She sat down into a chair and stared at it all. "I don't remember it being so hard," she said, brushing her thin, unkempt hair away from her sweating face.

Looking at her, I felt a chill sweep through me. She looked old sitting there. As Mama was her eldest girl, I could remember back when Granny had been a fairly young woman, thin and hearty, with hair as bright red as Mama's but without the curl. We all knew that Granny had sugar—she'd had it for years—but it was only lately that it had started eating at her, adding pounds even as it wasted her true flesh.

The pain I'd felt last night seemed to have sharpened my eyes, for I could see that Granny was dying. Just two weeks ago, I'd been right in this kitchen, and while Granny had been slow, there'd been none of this obvious frailty. I wondered what else was going on around me that I still had to face, seeing the world in this clearer, harder light. I felt as though I'd taken ill in winter and woke in summer heat, having missed spring.

"I don't know what to do," Granny said, her voice peevish.

"I'm here now," I said. I rolled up my sleeves and took one of the aprons that hung on hooks behind the back door—aprons that had always been there, like Great-granny's pewter cup. "Looks like you've made a start."

"Yes," Granny said, standing up for a minute before falling back into the chair, where she fell asleep.

All that day I canned, cooking food, boiling jars, sealing them with paper soaked in starch. By evening, Mama came looking for me, finding me still in the kitchen, pots of water boiling over a stove going blue-blazes. She put on an apron and stood there, right next to me, and all that long night and all that next day, we said nothing to each other unless it had to do with putting summer food away for winter.

I stayed with Granny that fall, and into the winter of 1916, when she was taken to her bed. Some days her mind was clouded, other days she was as sharp and cranky as anything. Because of her illness, no one thought twice about my leaving Mama and coming to stay. Aunt Annie and Uncle Russell even went so far as to say nice things about me, and Mama too, which they'd never done before. Cousins young and old were about the place from sunup to sundown, but come nighttime, it was me, Mama's baseborn bastard, tucking Granny into bed and seeing that her feet were warm.

Mama would come down most every day and sit with Granny so I could go to school and finish my high school course. She looked lonely, and she was losing weight. I worried about her, no matter what had passed between us. But I still could not go home. I could not talk about birthing babies.

Granny wasn't so patient with me, though. "You were born to be a midwife," she said. "And it will do you good, being away from your mama a little while, learning what I can teach you, least as long as I'm on this earth."

"You're doing great," I said. I always said this. "Doc Woodley was real pleased."

This didn't impress Granny at all. "Doc Woodley do be a fool of a man," she said. "Thinking that them little pills and potions he buys off of strangers are likely to do a body much good. Probably trying to kill me off so he can marry your mama."

"No one's trying to kill you, Granny," I said. On her worst days, angry and childish, she would darken the air with insults and accusations. Some days she wouldn't let anyone but me in her bedroom. Today was a sort of in-between day, which were harder in their own way, since I didn't know how to be. "Besides, Doc's married."

"Never needed a wedding to keep a man from taking up another," Granny answered. "He's always been sweet on her."

"No secret that he cares for her," I agreed, thinking what might have been, if Doc hadn't been married, if Mama hadn't gone with a man I didn't know that resulted in my birth. "I think he really loves her. I know he got those pills for you from Morgantown."

"Couldn't tell me what was in 'em, though," Granny pointed out. "Might be something awful."

"I'm sure the apothecary's good," I started to say.

Granny shook her head. "Get all that scientific nonsense out of your head and let me tell you what you need to know."

Granny was determined that I should learn everything she knew about herbals. When she spoke of them, she was at her best, so I listened at first from politeness, but I soon grew fascinated by what she taught. Guided by her fingers, I touched and smelled and tasted plant after plant, learning how to take the healing powers from the roots and stems and flowers. I learned which were good for holding a baby fast and which would hurry it along. Some herbs eased breasts heavy with milk, others filled those that hung dry.

Each herb had its own story. "The trick with birthroot," Granny said, "is to mix it into a man's food. Taste like rank poison, but makes 'em randier than Noah coming off the ark." She laughed. "I gave it to Jeddah Teller once, when he crawled home with his tail between his legs after the Spanish War. He found himself a woman right quick, he did, and never left this place again."

In summer, birthroot was a pretty plant—three great green leaves with purple flowers poking through—but its roots were nothing much to see. I made a note of it, and of all the

other roots that were good for making a man happy. These
were things I wanted to know.

"You know an herb that will make a man fall in love with
you?" I asked. For I'd seen Alvin Denniker that day, coming
out of Switzer's store. He'd smiled and winked at me as he un-
tied his horse, and offered me a ride home. "How's your granny
doing?" he had asked as we rode, me leaning against him,
breathing in his smell.

"All right," I answered, thrilled that he must know I was
staying with Granny.

"Mountain's a lot quieter with you gone." I could feel the
heat of his back against my chest. He missed me, I thought,
and could hardly stand to sit still, even with him.

When we reached the Homestead he climbed down first
and offered me his hand, as if I'd never climbed down from a
horse before.

"Thank you," I said, but the words stuck in my throat. I
tried to think of something to say—anything—that might
keep him there with me.

"My pleasure" was all he said and was gone.

His pleasure indeed. I was thinking entirely about my own.

"An herb that charms a man, now that's a useful herb," I
said to Granny, a little too heatedly, no doubt, because she
laughed.

"I'm not God, nor a witch neither." Then she leaned closer
and whispered, "Who you have your eye on?"

I just shrugged. I rummaged through the herbals, still half
convinced I was going to find one that would make me bloom
before Alvin's eyes.

"Ain't that MacFarland boy, is it? Your mama says he's
gone on you, even if his folks always did think they were better than the rest of us." She clucked her tongue. "I'll just tell
you, those men are all weak as dishrags."

"Isn't Horace," I said. "I don't like weak men."

"Trust you to know it," she said. "For all your mama has raised you in a world of women, you'll run off with the first man to walk past your door." Her eyes widened. "You've gone and taken a shine to Alvin Denniker, haven't you now?"

"And you say you aren't a witch," I teased.

Granny looked at me a little sadly. "You know what they say about those Denniker men, that they love only one woman. And I heard tell that your fine Alvin has taken him a pretty wife."

I looked Granny straight in the eye. "No concern of mine. Everyone around here knows she's foreign. He can't know nothing about her."

"Sometimes, honey, the ones you know the least are the ones you can love the most. Knowing a person too well can be a heavy burden." Her voice was gentle, not sounding like the warning it was.

"I don't want to talk about this no more," I said, and Granny hushed, kissing me on the top of my head.

By spring, Granny had all but wasted away her great girth. I'd taken to sleeping with her, for fear she'd slip away from us without warning. Folks started visiting more often now, knowing we were talking about weeks, perhaps days.

She was her own self, right up until the end. She was telling my cousin Nettie the best way to treat a boil, and letting Uncle Russell know that she'd always loved him best of all, no matter that he only came to see her on Sunday afternoons.

Often we'd lie there in the dark, the two of us alone, and she'd tell me stories about when she was young. How poor they'd been, living up on Hudson's Ridge, and how proud she'd been to come to the Homestead as a bride. "I used to

climb them stairs a dozen times a day, I was so taken with them,"
she said. "No Barlow had ever lived in a house with stairs."

I understood then how right Mama had been, about a little
privacy making a woman talk. And I knew also that the night
was a time you'd tell the person next to you most anything,
whispering and laughing to keep the dark at bay.

"You plan on telling me, ever, why you left home?" she
asked me once.

"Ain't important," I said, wrapping a quilt around her. "You
needed someone here and I could come." I rarely thought about
Mrs. Whipple's baby now, living with Granny's death as I was.

She reached out her hand and patted my arm. "I did need
you, child. A blessing, having you." For a long moment, we
just sat there. "But it's time you went home. Almost time,
anyways."

"Mama told me about the red book," I blurted out, hardly
listening to her at all. "I don't know how you could hold those
babies in your hands and do that to them. How can you claim
to care for women and babies, knowing what you do."

"Your mama cares for more babies and women than anyone
I've known," Granny said, her voice sharp and clear, sounding,
in that moment, like her old self.

"It ain't right," I said, repeating those words I'd said to
Mama last summer.

"No, it ain't," Granny agreed, "but it ain't always wrong,
neither." She struggled to sit up in bed. "That's why you need
to know the herbs—use them to knock a baby loose." She
took a deep breath, and I knew she was in pain. "Better that
way. Easier on the eyes and on the soul. But sometimes things
don't right themselves no matter what you do."

"What herbs?" I didn't like sitting here and thinking about
Granny, about Mama, about my whole long line of women-
folk shaking babies from this world. But I knew the talking
soothed her.

"Pennyroyal," Granny said. "Tansy. Nothing like some tansy tea to ease a woman."

"I don't want to be a midwife." The anger burst from me. I'd spent this whole year being sorrowful, but you dig deep enough into such feeling and there's anger at the core.

"I know, honey. But you don't change who you are just by wishing."

"Don't have to wish," I said. "I can just pick myself up and leave here, go anywhere I want. Nothing keeping me here but birthing babies and killing those that aren't wanted. Some life that is."

Granny sighed. Her eyes were clear again, and I knew the pain had passed. "Least you have a life to live, and that's more than some." She closed her eyes. "Now go and make your old granny a cup of star-grass tea. Isn't any woman, midwife or no, that makes a cup of tea as tasty as yours."

I lay there not moving, suddenly not wanting to serve her. "I don't have to stay here," I said again.

"Be glad you have a home," Granny retorted, her own temper starting to show. "Now don't deny a dying woman's request. No matter what you do in your life, you'll have plenty to confess to our Maker in the end, so you needn't be adding this."

I got up then, still angry, but I went. She drank her tea as sweet as could be, and settled down to sleep, as though we'd talked about nothing more than the weather.

Wasn't long before she took a final turn. Trees had barely turned green before I was bringing teas that she couldn't swallow. There were no more talks in the night, or any other time. Days were filled with aunts and uncles, talking about the end times and the passing of days.

"Only God could save her now," Aunt Annie muttered at the foot of the bed.

When Mama heard her, her eyes turned hard. "Hush," she whispered, fierce and loud.

"You hush yourself," Aunt Annie said. "Wouldn't hurt you any to say a prayer."

"She doesn't need my prayers," Mama said, her voice low.

"Of course not," Aunt Annie said, not hiding the bitterness they'd always carried between them. "Would take more than Mama's death to make a believer out of you."

"Girls," Uncle Russell scolded, as though they were children. Mama stood then, her hands gripping her elbows. When she left the room, he shook his head and sighed.

I glared at them both, then followed Mama out to the porch where she stood, taking great gasps of air. For a moment we stood together, watching the stars coming out. I wished then that I knew just what to say. That I could take away the stricken, lost look she had worn all this long year. So I offered the only thing I had.

"I'd like to come home," I said.

Mama turned and faced me, her hands sliding down her arms so swiftly I could hear the swish of cloth against skin. She nodded and kissed my head as Granny had so often done.

Then she went back inside.

THREE

Lauren Denniker was born during a full moon week, else I might never have played a part in it. She was born during Harvest Moon—that big huge ball of light that seems to pull babies out of their warm swells like bean plants bursting forth from the earth. Birthings are likely to go faster too, which can be a blessing.

A midwife is never busier than during Harvest Moon, and that October of 1916 seemed busier than ever. Mama could hardly find time to stand still, and was often up late reading or mixing herbs. I watched her writing things down, trying to remember. Once or twice I thought about offering her the knowledge Granny had taught me, but even the healing gift of herbals seemed too close to the life my mama lived. A life I didn't want.

Mama was pure worn out. I can still see her now—the dark purple rims about her eyes, the skin as thin as onion peel. Her curly hair frizzed about her face, making her look thinner than she already was. After a long night, she would come in so tired her hands would shake, but they'd be steady as a rock when she was called again. I kept waiting for her to ask for my help, to demand it, but she never did. Instead she did what she needed to do without me.

Not that I was idle—I took over the garden, and the washing, including the birthing cloths. Each week I boiled the sheets and rags, creating clouds of steam that smelled of blood and sweat. All these things were then ironed dry, without the benefit of starch, as that would keep them from sopping up the mess that came from a woman's body. Good clean laundry can make the difference when a birthing gets hard.

On the night of Lauren's birth, Mama was long gone when the knock came. Having labored all day over a hot kettle and iron, I was not of a mind to answer it, preferring to doze by the fire. Not until the door itself started shaking did I realize that the person outside aimed to come in, no matter what.

When I opened the door, Alvin Denniker stood there.

Seeing him—his yellow hair blowing around his face and his wide green eyes looking right into mine—I felt, in that instant, fully, intensely happy.

The Denniker clan had lived on the mountain that bore their name since the time of the Revolution. Once Kettle Valley had been full of them, and nearly everyone around here could claim a tie to the family. My own great-granny had been born Ada Denniker, so that made Alvin kin to me, though a very distant one. You could tell just by looking at him who he was and where he came from. The gold hair, the beak-like nose and fleshy chin, the skin pink as cranberries poking through a fog.

Denniker men were known for many things, but mostly they were famous around these parts for being wildcats. Hellions. Granny, for all our connection to them, had turned her face from her kin as long as I knew her. "Live like Indians up yonder, 'cepting Indians are better tamed," she would tell me. "Doing things to women that the Bible says just aren't right." I didn't know what such things were but my body seemed to, as it twinged whenever I saw Alvin.

When we moved from the Homestead to the house at Kettle Creek, I took comfort that Alvin, at least, was still in his proper place, as the Denniker family had always been. Not that I saw much of him—the young man he was then had no reason to pay attention to a little girl like me. I had no reason to think he knew of me at all, until I woke one night and realized that I was alone.

I knew that Mama had gone to make a call—she'd told me where she would be going—and I was pleased she thought me old enough to leave alone. At the Homestead, there had always been someone about, and I fell asleep pretending I was running the whole house.

But when I woke, sometime later, I called for Mama and she wasn't there. My room was so different from the one at the Homestead—the trees tapping on the window weren't friendly, but dark and finger-like. I reached to light the candle by my bed, but it fell and rolled, the hollow sound going on as though forever.

I huddled there, recalling every ghost story I'd ever been told, stories of peddlers buried in root cellars and babies beneath the hearthstone, all calling out to be found.

Soon I was so spooked I leapt out of bed, sure a haunt was just behind me. I ran into the living room, the light of the banked fire washing the walls in red. The sap hadn't yet dried from the fresh-cut wood, and the house looked as though it were melting. I pictured the fire climbing the walls and roaring up to the roof. Just then, a wood knot exploded in the grate, showering sparks across the hearthstone. Who knew what might be buried beneath it?

I rushed outside and started running, mindless as a rabbit. I ran and ran, stumbling over brush and wetting my bare feet

in Kettle Creek. I could feel stones rip my skin but I kept going until I'd climbed up nearly the whole mountain and there
wasn't anywhere else to run. I was breathing so hard and so
loud I never heard the footsteps behind me.

He must have been hunting possum or coon, but all I knew
was that there was a light shining in my eyes, and a big
shadow behind it. Scared as I was, I opened my mouth and
screamed.

"Hush," he said, putting the lantern down and picking me
up as though I were an infant. No one had picked me up in a
long time. "You're all right."

I kicked and fought for all I was worth. Granny had told
stories about girls being taken by fairies in the woods, vanish-
ing without a trace. But Alvin held me tight, and when I finally tired out, I felt his great hands holding my head against
his chest, making his voice rumble in my ear. "It's OK,
Elizabeth. You're gonna be all right."

This surprised me. "You know who I am?"

"Of course." He smiled, the lantern making his face shadowed and thin. Then he winked. "I'm Alvin," he said, as if I
didn't know.

"So what's got into you?" he asked.

"I thought the house was burning down," I told him.

His eyes went wide and I felt his arm stiffen. "Is it?" he
asked, the voice sharp.

"No," I confessed.

Instead of telling me I was talking like a fool, he led me
over to a boulder where we sat down. "You ever been in the
woods at night?" Alvin asked, tucking me against him with
one great arm. I could feel the roughness of his skin, the soft-
ness of his shirt, and I leaned against him.

"Did you know that when the first men came to these
mountains there were buffalo? And elk with horns so wide
you could sit inside of them."

I liked the idea of riding inside such horns, safe and high. Back at the Homestead, when I was small, my uncles had carried me on their shoulders. Elk horns would be even better.

An owl swooped over our heads, but with Alvin, I wasn't scared at all, for a mere owl wasn't a great animal like a buffalo—or a bear. "Were there bears?" I asked him.

"Thousands of them," he said, his voice sad. "Gone now. Every single one."

"Where did they go?"

"West." He sighed, and I could smell the tobacco on his breath. "But at one time, a man could come on this mountain and live without ever leaving it. You could build your house here and be your own man."

I could do that. Together Alvin and I could build a little house with a thick door to shut out the buffalo and bears. I would make Alvin coffee—Mama said I made fine coffee— and so thinking, I fell asleep as only a child sleeps, so soundly that I woke back in my own bed, unsure about what was real and what had been born out of fear and dreams.

After that night, Denniker's Mountain became my home and I loved Alvin for giving this to me. Over the next many years I would climb to visit him, only to grow shy upon seeing him, and would instead hide behind trees and rocks. I realize now, if I didn't know it then, that he knew about me all along, for no matter how far he rambled with me as his shadow, we always seemed to end up along Kettle Creek, where I could wait in the raspberry briars until he'd gone. Some days he stripped the bark off a birch tree, rolling it into a cone-shaped cup. He would drink, then leave the cup behind, and I would pick it up, to keep inside my treasure box. I've kept some of them still. The bark is dry and splintered now, but the tiny cups still hold their shape.

The morning after the night I'd run through the woods, I told Mama, "I'm going to marry Alvin." She smiled, and put

a bowl of oatmeal before me. "I want to live on Denniker's
Mountain."

"You do live on Denniker's Mountain," she answered, sitting down across from me. She'd only just come home, and
her eyes were pink and heavy rimmed.

"I want to live at the top," I answered.

And that made her laugh.

But she, more than anyone, knew how serious I was. She held
me when I cried, at sixteen, because Alvin was leaving to join
his brother Union somewhere. I wanted to go with him, but she
wouldn't let me. And when he did return a year later, she did
not tell me to forget about him, for all he had a wife.

I was the one who belonged up on Denniker's Mountain.

The night Alvin stood at my door I was stung. He had come
for Mama and her skills and not for me.

"She's with Betsy Teller," I said. "Over on Folly's Ridge."

"Take me all night to get over there, and Ivy's already been
childing for hours now," he muttered. I could see him ready-
ing himself to go. "I thought you did birthings, too," he said,
heading for the door.

"I used to," I told him.

He stopped. "Then come with me."

Alvin was standing there, waiting for me as I had always
dreamed he would. Asking me for something that I could
give, though it was not what I'd been prepared to offer. For so
long now I had longed for a chance to show him I was woman
enough for him. I could not deny him anything. Even this.

The path up Denniker's Mountain wasn't even half a mile as
the crow flies, but the foot trail wound around the mountain
covering nearly twice that, making our steps slow and steady.

The bundles we carried were heavy, as I took every blessed birthing means I could imagine.

He walked before me, carrying the lantern. Old cross-cut stumps would loom in the sudden light like great bears. The mountain had changed since the night we sat together. Most of the great towering trees had been clear-cut, and scrub pine filled its place. I could hear small animals moving in the night, a few birds, the last of the cricket calls.

We stopped and rested against the old iron fence at the old Methodist church with its night-blackened steeple tucked against the mountain. I could see the graveyard between the bars all the way to the far hillside where old-time folks had carved out small caves to bury their dead. The ground rippled as though the wind had blown waves of earth that had frozen still.

In the silver light of the Harvest Moon the marking stones seemed to glow, and I thought for the first time of what would happen if something should go wrong tonight. Alvin was the last in our parts to bear the name Denniker, excepting those whose bones rested beneath our feet. All that whole family come down to one foreign-born woman giving birth on this cold night.

As much as I hated the notion of Alvin's Ivy lying up there bearing his child, I knew that if she somehow came to rest here, buried beneath her own stone, under my watch, then Alvin would be lost to me forever.

We crossed the last ridge and started walking down into the cove where Alvin's house set, squatting small and gray like a mushroom. Built originally as a pioneer cabin, I knew it wasn't more than three rooms wide, with a lean-to kitchen on the back, but it loomed large before me. More than a year had passed since I'd helped Sarah Meroe give birth, and here I was, about to aid a woman who was a stranger to me, her family story unknown.

I looked past the house to the rim of the mountain. I could see the lights of Philippi off in the distance, and the sky above my head was a great blue bowl filled with the shine of stars and moon. Down the mountain, living in the valley, we never had a sky so large as this.

"Elizabeth," Alvin called to me from the house. He had run the last few steps.

Once inside, I crossed through the main room into the sleeping quarters. I was glad to see that Ivy was resting out of Alvin's sight. Men in the birthing room make a woman scared, for the man is usually so frightened that he's jumping out of his own skin. Men can't be looking where they have gone into many a time and find someone else there without raising some sort of fuss.

"I need more light," I hollered to Alvin—the first of many orders I would give him that night. Ivy's white face peered through the darkness like a ghost, and I could hear her hair move against the pillow. I wished that I knew something about this woman, other than she was Alvin's wife, brought over the mountains when he came back from living in the South.

"How are you doing?" I asked her. I couldn't recall a thing Mama or Granny had taught me, or so it seemed until I reached out and actually touched Ivy's belly, letting my hands remember what my mind would not. I traced the baby's shape with the tips of my fingers. The head had dropped already, and had settled in right.

When Alvin handed me the lantern, I could see the bed, foul and wet, the blood seeping through the sheet. "I need sheets," I told Ivy, trying not to think of her as Alvin's wife, but as a woman with a baby inside of her pushing to get out.

She looked at the door, and I wondered if she understood.

Folks said she didn't speak English, yet Mama told me she could understand fine. I waited to hear some of the foreign tongue, but she made no sound, even when a pain rolled over her. She scrunched up her face, still not crying out. "Where are the sheets?" I demanded.

When she didn't answer I went out into the main room and rummaged around until I found them in a chest. "Your woman's not helping me," I yelled at Alvin. I knew this was not the way to handle a birthing. Mama would not be pleased and I was surprised by just how much I wanted her to be proud of me.

I went and changed Ivy's bed, for a clean bed is best, as midwives have always known. Ivy still said nothing to me, glaring with eyes that were piercing blue, but then the pain gripped her and she reached back to the spindle spools of the bedstead and pulled so hard that the wood cracked like gunshot. Alvin came racing in the room.

"What's going on?" he asked. He stood watching as I went to Ivy and took her hands in mine. Wood slivers were embedded in her skin, her wrists bleeding from scratches.

"You should have come earlier," I scolded, angry that he had put me in this position. Angry that I should have cause to think less of him in any way. "I'll need more sheets," I told him, and he left the room. I cleaned and bandaged Ivy's hands and tied bits of cloth around the jagged edges of the spokes to keep her safe.

"Can't be long now," I said, touching her belly again and feeling it grow firm and then soften against my hand. Alvin's baby was right there, resting just beneath our flesh. "You're gonna be fine," I told her, hoping I sounded like Mama.

She smiled then—a fragile happiness that made her seem suddenly less strange. But that smile faded as the pains gripped her, and took her again and again, all through that long night. Wasn't long before the floor was damp with birthing fluid and I wondered how much more there could be inside of her. "Get me some water," I called out to Alvin. Fear of a dry birth ate its way through my belly. My herbals were useless. I had given her blueberry root and hardhack. I'd forced bitter summer cohosh straight down her throat. Now there was nothing to do but wait.

"You push, Ivy," I said. I said this so often that I was soon hoarse with it. I was tired myself, my hair stuck to my head with sweat. We were both fighting now to get this baby out, and whatever jealousy I'd carried was lost in the heat of the battle. I knew her in the way a woman knows a woman and will never know a man.

She reached again for the bedpost. Before I could stop her, she'd latched on and the blood ran fresh into her hands.

I was the one that called out.

Alvin stood there and when I saw he carried no water something inside of me snapped. Last thing I needed was a worthless man in my birthing room. "Where is my water?" It felt good to yell at him—to bring some sound into that room.

He didn't even look at me.

"Get it," I told him, giving him a shove, my hand leaving a bloody print on his shirt. I could hear him walk through the main room and into the kitchen, and I hoped he was man enough to know how to boil water.

Ivy lay there so exhausted that I could hardly see her breathe. She'd kicked her soaking shirt above her waist and her white belly quivered like an egg. I reached into her again and felt the baby's head press against my palm.

"Hurry the water," I called to Alvin. Ivy had stopped moving, and I knelt before her, ready to reach inside as though I could pull the baby free.

Then without warning, Ivy lunged up, almost sitting before falling back into the sodden bedding. The baby shot from her and landed in my lap.

A little girl, with Denniker yellow hair drenched against her skin. Blue skin. I blew my breath into her lungs and slapped her on her bottom, on her feet, on her cheeks. I remembered Hannah Switzer's baby looked like this, back when I was training with Mama, and I knew it was too late.

Ivy's belly heaved one last time pushing out the afterbirth. I cut the cord and handed her the baby, tears running down my face. "I'm sorry," I said, knowing I had failed her. Knowing that I had failed Alvin. Failed Mama, and Granny, too. Who was to say I hadn't overlooked something? If only I had gone with Mama all these nights, I might have been prepared.

Alvin was standing in the doorway. I thrust the afterbirth at him. "Bury it," I told him. I started cleaning up Ivy's body with the water he had brought.

"I can't," he whispered, his eyes stricken.

"Bury it in the yard," I repeated, and he took one more look at his wife talking to a dead baby in some foreign language and was desperate enough to make himself useful.

I was alone with Ivy when I heard the cry. Then a laugh. I looked up, expecting to see Ivy Denniker gone clean out of her mind for birthing so much for so little, but she was smiling. Smiling at the baby who moved her head to find her mother's breast.

As the little one fed, she began to unfold, like a flower at first spring. Her color was pink and warm. When I approached her, she opened her eyes, and I saw that deep blue.

Ivy grabbed my hand and pressed it to her lips. "Thank you," she whispered, and she was crying now instead of laughing. My own eyelids burned, but I felt wrung dry, as though I was the one who had given birth and not just the one who had tidied up after.

I left Alvin sitting on a clean bed with his stranger wife. He couldn't seem to stop touching her, pulling her against him, and she would let him and then move away. Ivy only had eyes for her baby. I wished hard for a moment that I was the one sitting there, showing Alvin with my own baby how much I loved him.

He looked up at me once. "Lauren Elizabeth," he said. "We're naming her after my ma and you." And I knew I had to leave this room or else I would fall to the floor, unable to ever pick myself up again.

Mama was coming up the mountain path as I was coming down. When she saw the birthing bag in my hands she began to run. She grabbed my arms and I could see, in the early streaks of dawn, the dark shadows around her eyes. "Did it go well?" she asked me first thing.

I started to cry. I talked about Alvin and how he'd come for me, and the whole story of Ivy giving birth up on that mountain. Of the baby being born dead and coming back to life again, with no help from me at all. I talked and talked and talked, making up for the silence that had stood between us all this past year. She listened, her arm wrapped around my shoulders, guiding me down that long trail, past the church, past the clearings, down to the familiar sound of Kettle Creek.

"I've seen it happen," she told me. "Miracle babies, we call them."

"Didn't seem like a miracle," I muttered. I could see the windows of our house just across the creek bed.

"It is," Mama said. "And to have a miracle baby as a name baby is a great honor."

"Doesn't matter," I said.

Mama stopped and turned me, her hands on my arms again. "It does matter," she said. "Babies like that are saved for a reason. You watch and see."

"Is that midwife's mercy, too?" I asked. But there was no bitterness in my voice. I wasn't angry with her any longer. We were at the creek's edge now, and I watched the waters pouring past us, bound for the Tygart, headed for the open sea.

"It is a mercy," Mama said, waiting until I had hopped from stone to stone. "You should be thankful."

From the far bank, I watched Mama make her way across the creek. I saw her almost stumble, but catch herself just in time and straighten. When she wobbled on the last stone, I reached out my hand and took both of hers. Even when she was safe upon the other side, I kept holding them, letting the firm flesh settle around my own. My mother's hands, I thought. My hands, too.

"I am thankful," I said. Because I was.

FOUR

After a baby was born Mama always made a point of taking the family a gift. A knitted shawl, a blanket, a pretty dress if the baby was one of many and money was tight. "All babies need to be welcomed," she said. Taking a gift was also a way of checking up on things without being obvious about it.

I wasn't the fancy stitcher that Mama was, but I did passably. I could knit well enough and made baby booties and buntings by the dozens in the fluffy yellow wool Mama bought by the pound. But that wasn't good enough for my miracle baby. For Alvin's daughter. For Lauren I went to Philippi to buy the finest wool I could find in a shade that matched those deep blue eyes.

Was after the New Year, in 1917, when I'd finished the gift and was ready to return to the top of the mountain. Now that I was delivering babies again along with Mama there hadn't been much time for visiting. Not that I knew what I would say to Ivy when I saw her, for though I found it hard to hate her when we'd walked together through the valley of the shadow of death, I still was not yet ready to be her friend.

Ivy made most folks around here uncomfortable. Alvin

seemed bewitched by her, and folks wondered that he never walked down into the valley anymore, never played his fiddle at gatherings, never took her about like a man should when he's got himself a pretty girl like that.

In the year since she'd come to Kettle Valley I'd heard all sort of things about her. That she was from Europe, that she was part of a lost Indian tribe, part of the lost tribe of Israel. Didn't seem real likely, given that most of the Indians in these parts had either up and taken for the West or hidden themselves along the highest ridges they could find. Some folks claimed that the people up on Hudson's Ridge were mixed-bloods—white, Indian, and Negro all. I knew about them because Granny had come from there, but Ivy didn't look nor talk anything like them. Everyone knew she had no kin nearby, excepting Alvin, and now her baby.

So when Mama and I headed up Denniker's Mountain for a visit when Lauren was about ten weeks old, we didn't expect to find anything or anyone unusual, just each person in her right and proper place.

We heard the music before we'd reached the top. Mingling with the sound of January wind, the fiddle tunes quickened our steps, pushed us onward.

Ivy opened the door at our knock. She had been laughing, and long dark hair was pulling loose from the braid she wore. Dressed in wine-colored poplin, with cutwork lace at the throat, she looked so lovely standing there that I felt drab and shabby even in my good brown dress and dark green shawl. I wished I'd dressed better. Wished I had something fancy to make my hair glossy and bright instead of the color of pine bark and straight as pitch needles.

Ivy hugged me close, as though welcoming a friend. "Come in," she said, taking my hand. I shoved the present at her, feeling a little nervous. Didn't she know I loved her husband? But then, why should she be jealous, she who stood there beautiful, wearing her joy like sunlight.

"Come on in," Alvin called out. He was standing by a roaring fire with his fiddle in his hands. As his fingers plucked the strings, music tiptoed over the stillness of the room. "Got someone you'll want to see."

"Why, Union Denniker!" Mama said, staring at the man standing by Alvin.

He looked like a Denniker, that was for sure. Looked an awful lot like Alvin, with the same sharp nose, same heavy chin, but older, nearer forty than thirty, with lines about his mouth and eyes. But he was Denniker blood through and through, his thick hair so neatly combed you could tell it'd been done just recent.

"How do, Meribeth," he said, walking to us. He took Mama's hand and smiled at her, but Mama was having none of that and reached up and kissed him. "Been too long."

"What, about ten years, fifteen?" she asked. I felt her hand on my arm. "This is Elizabeth," she said. "My daughter."

"Lauren's godmother," Ivy said, almost in my ear. She'd come back holding two glasses of wine.

The man turned then and smiled at me, and all the lines of his face fell into place. I realized this was a courting man, and I caught myself smiling back before I could think. Union I knew only from stories. He'd been gone since I was a very little girl, having left Denniker's Mountain when a local woman had thrown him over.

"How are you doing?" Mama asked, turning to Ivy again. I felt shamed. Mama was first and last a midwife, not letting thoughts of men she had no claim on pry into her thoughts.

Ivy nodded her head. "Get Lauren," she called over to Alvin, and I could hear the pride run through her voice like a chord of music. The room was filled with happy people. Ivy touched my shoulder again, but I shied away.

Alvin brought the baby over and I had my first good look at her in many weeks, since the heavy snows of December had covered the Tygart Valley. Her eyes were still blue, her hair still like her daddy's, yet truth be told, she was as homely a baby as I've ever seen.

"Go to Elizabeth," Alvin said to her, and passed the baby to me. I didn't want to take her—for I knew better than anyone that this baby was holding Alvin to Ivy and therefore not to me. But when I held her and gave her my finger to hold, I couldn't help but remember the way she'd seemed to come back from the dead the night of her birth. A miracle baby, Mama had called her. She had been saved for a reason, destined for great things. My name baby. And I would be there, watching her grow to see what her life would become. I promised her this. I would think of her not only as Ivy's, but part mine, too.

"Music," Ivy called out, picking up the fiddle and handing it back to Alvin.

"My turn," Mama said, taking Lauren from me. "Go tell Union that you're looking for a dance. He always was one for dancing."

But he was already dancing with Ivy. I watched him spin her around the room, her skirts swishing across the floor. Alvin played faster, louder, and when Ivy stepped back, breathing hard, Union turned and swept me into his arms, taking me by surprise.

The music seemed to be all around me. My feet moved from one note to the next, charmed as though I wore enchanted slippers. I felt light as air dancing there with Union, and for a moment I felt the sense of homecoming that those around me never questioned.

Then Alvin handed over the fiddle to Union and danced with Ivy. When I watched the way he looked at her, how they moved together, the sadness came over me again. I'd never had a man look at me like that, never known a man's touch, and I felt a great longing in my chest, a rushing beneath my skirts.

When the dancing was over, we filled our glasses again and Ivy cut great pieces of pie. Union came over by the table and sat next to me. "What are you thinking about, here by your lonesome?"

"Nothing," I answered.

"Mighty serious girl you are," he said, smiling. His breath smelled of blackberry wine and freshly baked bread.

"I'm in love," I told him. I couldn't believe I was telling him this—telling Alvin's own flesh-and-blood brother—yet it felt right that I should be sitting here, saying these words.

Union nodded. "I can tell. Women that are in love have a glow to them. You can see it here . . ." he touched my forehead, "and here . . ." he touched my eyes, "and here." He put his finger on my bottom lip, a place where no man in all my eighteen years had ever touched.

"He don't love me, though. He loves someone else."

Union bent his head near mine. "That's the wonderful thing about women. It don't take being loved in return to give them the glow. Men spend their whole lives looking for that glow. They find it in a woman and try to take it from her but she won't give it up to them. It's her secret pleasure, that feeling of being in love. And when the man realizes that it's gone, he only feels lonelier than before."

His voice was so like Alvin's that I caught my breath. When I shut my eyes, just enough to blur the lines about his face, I could pretend I was sitting there with Alvin, feeling his fingers touch me. My face began to burn from the inside out. Soon, I thought, I would be scorched clean through.

I opened my eyes wide. "Mama tells me you live out west," I said.

If Union noticed the abrupt change in conversation, he paid no attention. In the lamplight his green-gray eyes sparkled like the stones of Kettle Creek after a rain.

I looked around Alvin's cabin, wondering what he saw. Everything was in one room, the beds and table and chairs huddled together to create the warmth and companionship folks need during winter's cold. Mama was in the kitchen, and I could hear her washing up. Alvin and Ivy stood in the doorway of the kitchen, turned away from us. His arm was around her, and he whispered to her, his mouth so close I could see her hair shimmer with his breath. I felt a wash of loneliness that even another man—even one as close to Alvin as Union— couldn't take away.

"Meribeth is still as beautiful a woman as she was when I left."

"Mama is beautiful," I said, pulling my eyes away from Alvin and Ivy. "I've wished many a time that I took after her."

"Who do you take after?" Union asked, and I realized he didn't mean to hurt me but the question did.

"I don't know," I told him. "I suppose my daddy, whoever he was."

"You don't know?"

I shrugged and looked away. "When I was a child—hardly more than a baby—I heard my granddad say to Mama, 'Too bad she don't look like you.'

"Mama got real stiff—I was standing right next to her, holding her hand—and she told him, 'Elizabeth has skin like swan's down.' Then Granny goes, 'All babies got soft skin. But we all know it isn't her skin you want to be touching.'

"Mama only held my hand tighter and I remember her saying, 'Elizabeth is her own person.' She was looking at Granny then, with these angry, unblinking eyes. Then Granny looked a little shamed and said, 'I guess she is.' "

While I was talking, Union had put his left arm around me, holding me against him. I was trembling. I'd never told anyone about that memory. Never even told Mama I remembered.

"It's true, you know," Union said.

"What?" I had pressed one of my hands against my mouth, and Union reached up and held it in his. With his free hand he drew his fingers across my cheek, making a line from my mouth to my ear. "Your skin. Swan's down."

For a moment I wondered that I didn't burst into tears, for I certainly felt like crying. "What's it like, out west?" I asked him, trying to distract myself. I freed my hand and gripped my shaking knees. "Is it true there are no mountains? No trees? I can't imagine a world without trees."

Union looked at a point just above my head. "Where I live there are plenty of trees and you can see the mountains way off in the distance on a clear day. Big ones, that only make a man feel small against their largeness."

"I can't picture that," I said. "These hills are all I know. Sometimes I think I'd like to get away. Feel some different ground beneath my feet." Union's eyes lit up. "Like everyone already knows all about me, or thinks they do. But they don't. They don't know anything about me at all." The words I'd always felt but never given voice to poured from my mouth like a water spill in heavy rains. I couldn't keep them back. And some part of me had never even known I'd felt this way at all.

"I like it out west," Union said. "It's a place where a man can be, if he wants to."

"I want to," I told him.

When he kissed me, I reached my hands into his thick hair and held on to his ears. Beneath my fingers the heavy folds of skin felt like wild carrots, picked in spring when they are tender enough to eat straight from the ground. In my own head there was a roar like a summer whirlwind and I wondered if he had covered my ears with his great hands.

Then Lauren broke into a loud cry and I jumped back from Union so sudden that I nearly fell to the floor.

Ivy left Alvin's side and went to the trundle bed by the fire. She settled herself down and loosened her blouse so Lauren could nurse. I could see the shadow of her flesh and the movement of Lauren's head against her. Alvin looked on, his face raw with emotion, and I felt angry anew that he should look that way at her and not at me. I wondered if Alvin had seen when Union kissed me. I wondered if they would talk about it later, as I knew women would. I wondered now what Alvin would think of me. I realized how little I knew of the ways of men.

Mama came in from the kitchen, wiping her hands on a towel. "We best be going," she said, and I could tell by her voice that she had seen me. Her mouth was set in a twist that meant she was displeased. But with her I felt no shame. Instead I stared at her like she'd stared down Granny all those years ago.

"I'm ready," I told her, standing up.

"I'll see you ladies home," Union said, and he was there, right beside me.

The three of us walked down the mountain, following the path that had been crossed by hundreds of Denniker feet long before that night. Feet that linked the three of us together with blood and flesh more powerful than any kiss or even a night's coupling. We said nothing, that whole way down, the wind in our faces, freezing them into stubborn masks.

At our door Union took Mama's hand a moment and tipped his head. "My pleasure, ma'am." He gave her a wink. A courting man indeed. How many women had he kissed, wandering out west? No doubt he'd be kissing again in another week, the taste of me grown stale.

Mama's eyes softened a minute as she looked at him. "Peace be with you," she said, and it struck me as an odd thing to say. This day had been many things, but peaceful wasn't one of them.

"Good night, Elizabeth," Union said, standing there. In the cold winter starlight he looked like himself, not like Alvin at all.

"Good-bye," I said. For there was nothing else to say after all.

When he was gone and the door closed behind us, I waited for Mama to say something. I watched her unwrap her shawl and hang it on its peg, watched her bend and brush the snow from the hem of her skirt.

"So he told you he's going away again?" she finally said. I was still decked out in my winter coverings and she reached out and helped me free of them. I didn't say anything.

Mama held my scarf, running it through her hands. "Would you," she paused and turned around, reaching for the wall by feel, "would you want to go with him?"

"Go with Union?" I shook my head. "You know Union isn't who I care for," I said, and felt bold as brass, saying these words right after I'd been kissing him.

Mama sighed. "Your granny always said that the Denniker men love only one woman, but I think poor Union has too much of his great-grandfather Reese in him."

"Who did Union love?" I asked. But I was thinking—perhaps Alvin bore some of old Reese Denniker's restlessness, too. Maybe enough to see beyond the one woman he was with. I did not come down from Reese's line, but from his brother Harold's. Great-great-grandfather Harold was married to his woman for more than sixty years.

"He should have married Katie Barnes, but her daddy didn't feel Union was good enough for her." Mama rubbed her stockinged foot. "So instead of one unhappy old man we have one young one and a woman who married a man she didn't love. She bore his babies right into an early grave."

I thought of Alvin on his mountaintop with Ivy. The way he watched her. The cold wind that had kept my head clear on our trip down the mountain was muffled behind the thick walls of our house. The warmth of home was soothing.

Denniker men love only one woman. This wasn't quite true, I realized, though not on account of Union's kiss, or Katie Barnes. Wasn't just the men-folk who loved their women—I was part Denniker, too.

FIVE

Mama always said that the life of a midwife was like living in the needle's eye. She would hold up our needles one by one when she said this, checking for signs of rust or wear before piercing them through a piece of red felt she kept closed with twine. She also had strong silk thread, so thin it looked like human hair twirled on spool, stored in her medical bag.

The Bible tells us that it is easier for a camel to pass through the eye of a needle than it is for a rich man to enter heaven. The Bible also tells us thou shall not kill. I thought about passing through the eye of a needle, of making myself small and crossing through. I wondered what would be on the other side of that door framed in shiny silver metal. I wondered what the eye of the needle saw when it was looking at me.

When Ivy Denniker took to sewing, she did work like no one else I'd ever known. She and I became friends, although folks around here wouldn't believe this if I told them. Knowing what they know about my life, they would think me telling stories. But what I'm telling is the truth—my truth, at least. For no one ever had reason to see us together. No one heard our laughter up on Denniker's Mountain. No one saw the world we created for our own selves up there, all by our lonesome, just Ivy, Lauren, and me. Ivy was the first woman friend I ever had. First person other than Mama who knew I'd grown up.

By 1917 Alvin was working downstate more often than not, one of the many who left to haul coal out of the mountains as fast as men could find it. There was a war going on in Europe, a war that seemed ready to swallow every bit of land we could scrape up—the coal sent out in long trains, made into steel, and sent across the sea. I thought of him working in the mines, how closed in they must make him feel.

Ivy herself came down to ask if I would come and stay with her. "I don't like to be alone," she said. "It's too quiet." But over the next many weeks I was to learn how silent her world was. Ours was a closeness born of doing, not of speeches or idle chatter. Ivy was the most silent woman I've ever known.

The reason I agreed to visit was a selfish one. I wanted to know something. Something I'd learned about her that summer, before Alvin had gone south.

We were working in the garden—or Mama was—right at the moment that Alvin stopped by. I was coming from the house, having gone to fetch Mama some rose-hip salve to ward off the sun.

"Do you want to come in?" I heard Mama say. Then I saw Alvin standing with her, his great mane of hair tossing about as he shook his head. He had spread his feet apart, almost planting them before her the way a child does when he knows his mother is going to make him mind.

"I'll say my piece here," Alvin said.

I've noticed that when women have something to say they want to talk where there is a wall behind them, someplace safe. But when men come around they won't have nothing to do with the house.

"You sure Elizabeth ain't about?" I heard Alvin ask. "I don't want this spreading around."

I dropped to my knees and scampered in the garden and under a bean tent. The green leaves twinkled with sunlight when the breeze came up. I had to tuck my knees up under me, but I had a clear view while staying hidden, and that was all that mattered.

"Elizabeth doesn't tattle," Mama said, and I felt very proud when I heard her say this.

"Don't mean that," Alvin said, and I was glad to hear that, too. "I just didn't know if you'd want her listening to talk like this."

Mama laughed. "My girl helped your Ivy give birth, so I don't imagine there is a great deal you can tell us that would upset her."

Alvin looked down at the earth, then back at Mama. "She's still so young," he said, and I could hear the misery in his voice, but the words stung. I felt like rushing out in the open and showing him the woman that I was.

"She's nineteen, not much younger than your Ivy." Mama crossed her arms. I knew she was growing impatient, as she often did with men, waiting for them to spill out words that formed and stuttered from awkward tongues.

"Ivy's why I've come," Alvin said. "She ain't herself these days." He wasn't looking at Mama now, but staring off towards the creek. "I was wondering if you had something, you know, something medicinal-like. Something that would make her happier."

"Happier?" Mama looked up into Alvin's face and let out a sigh. She glanced over towards the row of bean tents. I knew then that I'd been found out, but she said nothing.

"I don't understand," she said after a minute. She brushed

her hands against her skirt, as if they were covered in dust. "What do you want from me?"

"Maybe happy ain't the right word." Alvin pushed his boot toe into the ground. His face was bright red and for the first time I was looking at Alvin Denniker humbled. And to think it was Ivy, his want to make her happy, that had brought this out. A cold feeling moved from my belly into my chest, and I could hardly breathe from it.

Alvin stood there for the longest time, until Mama bent down and began yanking weeds again, throwing them on top of his boot. My own feet turned numb beneath my skirts and I felt that time was passing so slow that I could watch the beans ripen on the vines.

"She don't want to be with me," Alvin finally said. "She don't like being my wife." His face had puckered like the edges of an old apple core.

"So she won't have sexual relations with you," Mama said, and I gasped at her boldness. I couldn't begin to think of asking a man—asking Alvin—something like that. But Mama wasn't to be distracted. "She had a hard time before you were married."

The dirt covered boot stopped moving. "What you be knowing of that?" Alvin asked, his voice careful, like a man asking the price for goods but already knowing it will be too high.

"I talked to her, when she was getting Lauren," Mama said, her voice giving nothing away.

"So you know." I could tell just by looking that Alvin Denniker was shamed clear through, as though something dark from inside his body had been brought out and exposed to light.

"Yes," said Mama.

Not wanting to be found, I knew I had to stay here, crowded and curious until Mama went inside and came back out with a paper poke. Until Alvin gathered it in his great man hands like a pearl of great price, and headed back up the mountain.

Mama wasn't real happy about my decision to stay with Ivy. She knew that I welcomed any chance to be with Lauren, but living with a woman when I loved her husband wasn't right, and we both knew it. But I had to go and learn the secret of this woman Alvin loved so much, even as she denied him. When I came out of my room with my things, Mama was standing there, her thin body curved against the table, her jaw moving about, so I knew she was upset.

"I packed you some things to take with you," she said. That's when I saw the box on the table, loaded down with jams and jellies. There were two jars of pickles in there, too, fancy pickles, the kind that take more than a week to prepare just right. My pickles. In the middle of the box was a jar of rose-hip salve, just like the jar I had been bringing to Mama two weeks ago when Alvin came.

"What's this?" I asked, holding it up.

"Ivy has such lovely hands," Mama said. "She'll ruin them if she isn't careful."

I didn't want to be thinking about Ivy's small, lovely hands. "I don't have to take anything." I realized that the gifts were a peace offering, something to make Mama feel better, when she felt so strongly that my going was wrong. "Ivy's the one that invited me. I would think you'd like me having a friend," I told her, the sharpness of my tongue cutting the air.

"You aren't going up there to be friends with Ivy," Mama said, her own temper getting the better of her. Then she sighed and pressed her fingers over her eyes. "I've been up all night with Leslie Teller," she said. "I don't want to fight with you."

"I'm not fighting," I told her, tasting the falseness of my lie. "But this is who I am. I'm a Denniker, Mama."

I saw her eyes flash and knew I'd wounded her. "You're a Whitely!" she said, raising her voice.

We both stood there, our words between us, pulled taut like a piece of thread. I waited for her to say my daddy's name.

"There are other men," she said, in the same gentle voice I'd heard her use for women who had been hurt. "Gil Teller's been calling since you could walk. Or that MacFarland boy. Lots of men are only waiting for a sign that you would welcome them."

"I only want one," I said.

Suddenly Mama looked weary. She had always been so thin, and I could see the bones in her hands. I put down my bag and walked over to the stove and stirred the coals. "Let me make you a cup of ginger tea."

"That would be nice," she said. I let the tea steep before I handed her the pot, a cup, a spoon. About her eyes, I saw the sheen of tears. But it was too late—I'd made up my mind to go. At nineteen, doing what I wanted was more important to me than doing right. So I left her there, sitting all alone.

As soon as I had crossed Kettle Creek, I pitched that jar of salve into the woods. I didn't need Ivy waving her hands under Alvin's nose when he returned. If I'd known that I'd be visiting I would have prepared one of Granny's special receipts—salve of goat innards, lupines, and lemon juice. Did the job of rose hip but stank so bad he wouldn't stand near her.

On my way up the mountain I stopped at the Methodist church and rested by Old Caesar's grave. Caesar was the founder of the whole Denniker clan, settled on this mountain after fighting in the Revolution. Some say he was Swiss, others say Dutch, but he had a mane of golden hair and was short and sturdy as a fence post. His monument stands more than three feet high, jutting out of the graveyard with four smaller stones around it, for each of Caesar's wives.

When the first wife died, Caesar buried her in the graveyard—it was just a graveyard then, not even a log church house to speak of—with a nice stone marker shipped all the way from Maryland where she was supposed to have come from. Back then there weren't quarries around here and most folks were marked with a field rock or piece of wood. That wasn't good enough for Old Caesar. Had to have a slab of marble to show how fond he was of her. Maybe he thought it would remind her of home. Carved "Beloved Wife and Mother" deep into the rock, although her name has since weathered smooth.

Story comes down that Caesar cried like a baby when they lowered the casket into the ground. Waited a good four weeks before taking a woman up again, which is saying something when you got three squalling babies at home. Seems his first wife came from people that ran to twins.

When Caesar's second wife died, leaving him with two more babies and the first three not yet old enough to wipe their noses, he buried her a good ways away from the first. It was said that he did it on account of he wanted to make sure there was plenty of room for him in the middle. But I've heard that his second wife was so sick to death of hearing about the first that she came back after death and told him to make sure she was buried a ways away from the other.

Old Caesar got back at her, though. The living always do. That second wife has only a tiny marker, just a rock really. Don't even know if it marks her head or her feet.

So here Caesar is with five babies only part grown. No one was surprised when he fetched himself another wife. Brought her over the mountain this time, from back in the lowland counties of Virginia.

Caesar's third wife—her name was Fannie—was supposed to be a beauty. Red-haired she was, like Mama and Granny. I do know she and Caesar were married a good long time, and she bore him a passel of boys along with raising his other kids. I expect she was simply plain wore out when she died. When he went to bury her it had been over forty years since he'd married his first wife. He didn't hardly think it fair to bury his third wife of so many years way out beyond his second, especially as now he could hardly recall her face. So Caesar up and unburies the first, moving her over a few feet so she would be stretched out above his head whenever he took it in his own mind to die. After all those years together, it only seemed fitting that he should lie beside Fannie.

I'm told he cried at her funeral, too. The third wife's got a stone big enough for both she and the second if you want to know the truth. Is on account of that marker that we know her name was Fannie.

He took up his last wife, Verna Dell Tucker, for the same reason King David did—nights were too cold to be facing an empty bed. His fourth wife was a sight younger than he was but he managed to have two babies by her, after his first woman's children were having babies of their own. They were two girls and there was talk about them looking a lot like the Meroe clan, but I doubt that this was true.

For even after he died, though Verna Dell was still a young woman, she remained true to him. Never married another, although she could have had her pick seeing as how Caesar had left her a fair piece of his land. Verna Dell kept the family homeplace up and welcomed all his children and grandchildren home every year at midsummer. What a sight that must have been—all those Dennikers crawling over that mountain like ants on a sugar tit. At one time there were more than fifteen Denniker families living on the mountain.

Mama told me that Verna Dell's youngest daughter, who

was getting on in years even when Mama was growing up, said that her mama was happy to have been with Caesar Denniker even if it was at the outside instead of the outset.

When Verna Dell died she rested at Caesar's feet, marking off his spot in a perfect square—less'n you believe that wife number two is buried too far up or too far down. I like to think that he's right in the middle of all his wives. Equals in the end, so to speak. Nothing fancy about Verna Dell's marker, though it's respectable enough. Used to be a grave house over them but that's gone now, too.

From the very beginning this story has been told to me. This was the first history I'd ever learned, and what with being baseborn, I know it better than my own, seeing as how half of mine is lacking. This then was my history, coming down through Great-granny. As much mine as Alvin's, for all he bore the name.

When I reached the Denniker cabin, I helloed the house, hoping I didn't sound as nervous as I felt. Ivy came out, shading her eyes from the sun. In the bright light her skin looked hard and cracked and her hair almost gray. Then a cloud passed over and her face was as smooth as a polished wood, her hair black as night again.

"You came," she said, as though she'd had her doubts. She took my arm. "Come in, please."

After the sunlight, the inside of the house was dim, the windows small and square. I couldn't tell you how many women have made this their home. All of Caesar's wives, and several generations in between. Yet the place was very much a man-kind of place—half house and half pioneer cabin. There weren't none of the fancy little touches I was used to, living as I had down in the valley surrounded by women. No sunflowers in the yard, no protective marigolds ringing the garden, which was plain foolish, as well as just plain.

"Some water? Wine? Food?" Ivy was bustling about, and seemed disappointed when I shook my head. "Lauren's there." When she gestured with her head I realized she was hurt that I wasn't as excited as she.

But I was—just nervous, too. I reached down and picked up Lauren from the rug, pressing her cheeks to mine, hiding behind her. Lauren smelled like cinnamon and her sticky fingers tasted like apple butter when I kissed them. I had made that jelly last fall, even before she was born, and brought it up when Alvin told me that Lauren had taken to it and would eat no other jam but mine.

Ivy bade me to sit and I rested in the willow chair next to the window so as to catch the breeze. She took the rocker and picked up a pillow she was sewing, just the way Mama did, and this made me feel at home. The needle flashed over the stiff white cloth, the silk threads dazzling in their color. She stitched birds and flowers and animals that I'd seen only in picture books, and none so bright or so shining as those that burst into being on Ivy's linen. She was always stitching this way, but what she did with the things was one of my greatest wonders. There was none of them to be seen in the house. There were no pillows on the faded yellow-and-gray quilt folded on the cedar chest in the corner. There were no scarves hanging over the fireplace. Lauren sat between us, on a braided rug so worn it frayed in the center ring, stacking spools and rolling about as any small child. There was nothing strange about Lauren. Not then.

"Your garden coming along all right?" I asked. I wished I had brought something to do. Just watching Ivy sew made my fingers itch.

"Ver-rry good," Ivy answered, nodding as she spoke. I

watched the late afternoon sun move over her head, making the strands of her hair shine and sparkle blue and purple, like the threads running through the silver needle in her hand.

"You need any help? With gathering or canning or what-not?" I asked. Now that I was here sitting and looking at her, I didn't know what to say. I wondered what I'd been thinking, down in the valley. That by just coming here I would some-how learn not only why she turned from him, but what made him want her still.

"I am doing all right, thank you," she said, nodding again. The words seemed to spin on their soft foreign sounds like the spools rolling across the wooden floor. One spool rolled be-neath my foot and I caught it and handed it to Lauren. I no-ticed that Lauren had hands as square and solid as Alvin's.

All that afternoon we sat there. I was to learn that this is the way Ivy always sat, how quiet her life was. From time to time she would look at me, her face wrinkled about the brow, her head tipped to the side, as though she thought I had said something and was thinking about how to answer it.

By evening I was feeling like a fool. The more she kept look-ing at me, the more I struggled to find my voice. Finally I started talking about Caesar, about the history of the Denniker line. I told Ivy about the third wife, the woman who came from nowhere, and this made her smile. I realized then that Ivy was this woman in some way.

Once I started talking, it was like I couldn't stop. I told her about Granny, and Mama, and the babies we'd caught. About the time Bruce Meroe was so excited about his baby girl after six boys that he'd broken his leg, tripping over a stump while running to tell his brother. I often told stories like this late into the night, lying next to Ivy in the bed where she had lain with Alvin. The bed where Lauren had been made between them. Where she had turned away from his company.

Over those weeks, I explained the world where she and her

daughter had come to live. Ivy was the listeningest person I've ever known. Mama had been right, months ago, when she said that Ivy understood more than she let on, though you might not think so, as quiet as she was. I did learn some things about her, things that she told me. Once, when we'd gone walking on the mountain just before sunset, she put her hand to her chest. "Fina," she said.

"What?" I asked.

"Fina," she said again, pointing to herself. "My name."

"Your name isn't Ivy?" I felt unbalanced, as though the earth had shifted beneath my feet.

"Fina," she said for the third time, this time with such conviction that I repeated it and she smiled.

"Why does Alvin call you Ivy?" I asked her. She looked at me and shrugged. "That's not right," I said. I didn't like the idea of men going around, giving women names. Taking away the words their mothers had whispered over their heads at birth. "You should give him a name, too."

Ivy laughed. "I do," and she smiled and looked around as though he might be standing there, lurking in the shadows. "*La nariz.*"

"Lanee?" I shaped my mouth to the slippery word.

"*La nariz,*" Ivy said again. Then she pointed to her face. "It means nose."

"Oh, my." For my love might blind me to many of his faults, but even I couldn't help seeing that beaky nose. And then I started laughing and she was laughing and little Lauren heard us, and she was laughing, too.

Ivy told me other things. About her childhood, about the house she had lived in, which she told me was very grand, back in Cuba, before the Spanish War. She told me about the nurse she'd had as a child, who'd been very strict, and about her mother, who prayed to Jesus' mother Mary, many times a day. I could picture Ivy as a pretty child in a white dress, playing hide-and-seek in fields of sugarcane. How she would crack the stalks open and suck out the sweet. She said these things in stiff sentences, rocking with Lauren sitting on her lap, kissing her daughter's head as often as she spoke.

I came to know that she didn't love Alvin, for all she spoke kindly of him. Other things meant far more to her than he did—when she spoke of Lauren, or her home or past, I could see the flame behind her eyes and hear the passion in her voice. I was the one who spoke of him, often without thinking. Ivy would smile and make me feel that it was all right.

During that whole summer, we fell into a routine. Ivy went to bed late and woke early, but enjoyed an afternoon nap. I took to wandering the mountain carrying Lauren, showing her the land that would be hers someday. We tasted raspberries together, staining our mouths bright red. I ran her tiny fingers over the letters carved in the graveyard stones, reading the names as Mama had read the names in the ledgers to me. We would go down and visit with Mama, taking her gifts of herbs we had gathered on our treks.

At night, Ivy and I took turns putting Lauren to bed. Then we would sit up, she with her sewing, me with my yarn. I watched her sew late into the night and then pull out the bright strands, for silk thread was so dear then. On those nights I took to calling her by her given name and I could tell this pleased her.

I taught her useful things that every woman in the mountains needed to know, surprised to learn that Alvin had never shown her in the two years she had lived with him. Perhaps he didn't know these things himself, for household skills were passed down from mother to daughter, one generation following the next. How to make soup beans. How to clarify lye soap. How to scrub the wooden floor with a round motion so the wood looked as though waves had washed across it. We planted piney-bushes next to the door and blue flags under the windows.

Ivy taught me many things, too. Things no one in Kettle Valley could have shown me. I can make pastries so full of air that the sun shines through them. She pinned my hair to give it curl. One afternoon she pierced my ears, telling me the earrings were a gift. For those many weeks I enjoyed the sparkle of gold, the twin circles making the light dance against my skin. But I knew that folks down the mountain would object to such a heathen thing so I let the ears close again after I came back to Kettle Valley.

There's a small scar on the left lobe—sometimes I let myself touch it and remember.

S I X

Mama always said that after harvest comes a second planting. What with the December wind blowing down in full force, men and women stay indoors and make do with what they have. Mountains swirl in snow just cold enough to have some might behind it, like a young man coming into his own strength. Come that next September on, babies fall out of the women in time with the falling of autumn leaves. Makes a double burden for the women, having to bear wintertime love babies in the midst of harvest work.

There are fewer babies born in the early winter, maybe on account that folks are thankful to be outdoors in early spring. Of course, for a midwife, this is good. I'll be the first to say that there wasn't anything worse than being warm and snug beneath the feather quilts only to be wakened in the dark by the knock of a man desperate for help.

In 1918, though, we never were called out into such a night, for there wasn't much winter at all, just one long gray span that had no claim to any month or season. Such strange weather made the old biddies start quoting from the book of

Revelation, murmuring about the end of times. Granny had talked that way. "Need to purge the old year of its sins," she would tell us. "No snow means a dry spring, and a dry spring means a land that breeds disease." As a child I had feared this talk. I had known plenty who had died from diphtheria, typhoid, whooping cough.

"That's poppycock," Mama said, when I would try to ask her about it. "Granny always did have to bring God into everything." But in 1918, Granny's words became truth.

Mostly we were all caught up about the war. Every day brought news from the outside about the fighting, about those who were being sent over and those who were taken away, as though God had called them home. So much talk of spilled blood that I wouldn't have been surprised to hear that the sun and moon had turned red, as the Bible taught us. I admit I began listening to the whispers.

Mama had no patience with such talk, from me or anyone else. "We're winning" was her answer when someone like Nelson Meroe would start talking about a blood sacrifice, to atone for the sins we all shared. Nelson was always one for seeing the darker side of things. Word was that his wife wouldn't let him own a dog, else he'd kill it and try to offer it up like an Old Testament priest.

All that year, feelings ran high, especially among those that had lost someone. Twenty-two men from Kettle Valley had gone overseas to fight, and although we had rung the Methodist church bell on Armistice Day and laughed and cried and cheered, less than a dozen of those boys were coming home.

Henry Teller was one who wasn't so lucky. I'm told he ran straight into German machine gun fire, armed only with a stick and a bit of wood lodged between his teeth to keep him from screaming. I'd always liked Henry, and he'd been nice enough to me during our school days. Wasn't so fond of Ben Switzer, truth be told, but no one should have to die of dysentery—although to hear his family tell the tale you'd think he'd gone over the top and personally saved the world.

Another one who didn't make it was Horace MacFarland. I can't hardly recall what he looked like now, but I remember his smile being shy and skittish on account of his being ashamed of a crooked tooth. He had the kindest smile I'd ever seen on a man, and it was on account of that smile—of that kindness—that I agreed to let him be my sweetheart in the days before he left to go overseas.

Horace was the oldest son of old John MacFarland, who lived on the other side of Battle Hill, across the covered bridge from Philippi. The MacFarlands had done pretty well for themselves, and Horace stood to get a nice piece of land when he reached his majority. Course the army considers you a man when you reach eighteen, even if the law don't recognize you for three years after. Not that the land mattered to me, but the farm meant something fierce to him and I liked seeing that in a man who was otherwise so gentle.

I had fun being courted, both being with Horace and coming home to tell Mama all about my adventures. When I visited with Ivy now, her laugh came easily, as I told her stories. If either of them noticed that I never talked about Alvin now, they didn't comment on it. I hadn't forgotten him, not at all, but Horace had so little time before he was sent over that giving him everything I could struck me as only fair.

Seems like the whole world was spinning faster just then. We did something every day. Bonfires or baseball games. A church picnic or a dance. When a man is going off to war, last thing he wants to do is have a chance to think.

I still have the fancy buttons Horace bought me. He would have showered me with gifts, though I didn't want to be beholden. I was already giving him everything I could, and gifts would have required more. Still, the buttons were too beautiful to pass up. They're in my button box looking like wheat among the chaff. I have no use for them, as they're old-fashioned now, being carved of bone, but I still like to open the box and see them.

When he gave me the buttons, I thought maybe I could do this. That I could love Horace, in a quiet, wintry-night sort of way. We could marry and sit together, warming ourselves with cups of tea. He wanted to see something of the world, and I thought that might be fun. Mama had a book of maps from when the railroads were going up, and I would stare down at the strange names—Tuscaloosa, Alabama, Charlottesville, Virginia—wondering what was in all those towns. In the end, only Horace got to leave.

When he got on the train, headed for the sea, I was sorry to see him go. I cried then, because all the other girls around me were crying and I thought he would feel badly if I didn't. He deserved a girl to be waiting there, to kiss him good-bye, and I'm glad I did these things, although I felt a little shamed at the time, knowing I was seeing him off without the love he wanted from me. At the last minute he grabbed my handkerchief and took it with him, just like we were people in a picture show. I don't know what happened to my handkerchief, and I've often wondered if it made it as far as France— if he had it when he died.

His sister Alice came and told me, when they got the telegram. She brought it with her, no doubt didn't think I'd take her at her word. Alice was the least'un in the family and was rotten long before she was ripe. They spoiled her something awful, and that day of all days, she came up to my house dressed in her Sunday best as though making a social call.

"This just came today," she said, handing me the paper, which

I remember much clearer in my mind now than Horace's face. The telegram was a yellow square, too bright and cheerful colored to be carrying such sad news.

Alice was always a dramatic one, but I was a little taken aback when she reached over the transom and hugged me. I wasn't used to being hugged by anyone other than Mama, and sometimes Ivy. Horace wasn't a hugger, although he did all right when it came to touching other things.

"Mother knew you'd want to know," she said. Fat tears filled her eyes like a sap blister on a sugar maple. "If you feel like crying," Alice said in a hiccoughing sort of voice, "you just go right ahead." She sounded pitiful enough, but I'd never liked Alice and wasn't about to cry in front of her. After a minute of her blubbering, she stared at me through glassy eyes. "I didn't think you'd have any feelings," Alice said, and I knew it was the grief talking, but still, it made me mad. I was sorry to lose Horace, who had been so good to me, and when she held out her hand for the telegram I kept hold of it and instead slammed the door in her face.

I knew Mama was behind me. In my mind's eye I could see her standing there.

"When your daddy went away, I felt as though my whole world had closed in around me," Mama said.

She sounded like she talked about my daddy all the time. But in all my twenty years, with all the moments I'd begged her with my heart, she'd given me only silence. A child who has no stories will invent pictures in her head, and this is what I did—my favorite was that of a cowboy, like the ones I saw in the newspapers and serials Granny kept around her house. My cowboy daddy had a horse that was black with white socks.

"His name was Nathan Riley, and he was from old Virginia," Mama said. I stared into the ancient wood of the door in front of me because I knew that with Mama's words the cowboy and his horse would fade away. Both he and Horace would dissolve into the mist of memory.

"We first met when I was seventeen, when everything about a girl's world is new and exciting. He was a drummer, with a cart filled with wares. Everything you could imagine, from cooking pots to castor oil. I loved the idea of a little store on wheels, and he was happy to let me explore while your Granny and he bartered. After a year or two, they struck a deal that he could have a night's lodging for sharpening the shears and knives, making sure we had plenty of needles and thread. When he learned I liked books, he would bring one to me every trip. I couldn't pay, of course, but he told me that seeing me so happy was enough. I knew it wasn't, but I wanted the books and I took them."

Mama was standing right behind me now. I could feel her breath in my hair. I could smell the scent that was Mama's— part sweet like the flow of a woman before the baby comes and part tart, like green apples in early fall.

"I paid him with kisses—hidden ones. He had a wife, and two children besides, and I had this idea that we both had old women who made us keep our love a secret." Slowly, Mama's arms crossed over my shoulders and caught against my chest. She pulled me against her and I collapsed, the force of my fall knocking us both to the floor, one on top of the other. I could feel the cushion of her breasts beneath my head. I could feel the fall of her chest when she took a breath. Her voice sounded as though it came from inside my own head.

"Why did you do it?" I asked, thinking of all the whispers and sighs from women in town. Women who invited us into their homes when they needed us but wouldn't greet Mama on the street.

Mama tightened her arms around me and rested her chin on the top of my head. "I had been birthing with your granny since I was fifteen, and like you, I didn't see what Granny didn't want me to see." Her voice shook a little. "I suppose that Gertie Switzer's baby was to me what Old Lady Whipple's was to you. Only I was there when your granny did it. Came home and watched my mother sign her name in the little red book.

"That night I couldn't sleep. I could hear Nathan in the next room tossing and turning, and knew without knowing that he was awake and listening to me move in my own bed. I got up and took myself into his room. He was a good man—for all his kissing, I'm not sure he would have done what he did if I hadn't dropped my nightgown to the floor and settled my body against his. Then he took me and loved me until I could hear the birds singing for daylight. It hurt a little, but I had expected that and I wanted it to hurt. And somewhere in my mind, I meant for you to happen. It's certain I knew enough to stop a baby, but I didn't."

I thought about that lovemaking between Mama and the man I knew now as Nathan. I thought of their coupling—a night born out of the death of a baby. A night that resulted in my being.

I knew well what Mama must have been feeling. Perhaps Granny had felt this way, too, the first time she'd seen a baby killed. Perhaps Great-granny, too, and all the women reaching back through our line who have held out their hands to help a woman.

When Luella Porter's bastard baby came just before Horace left for France, I took the red book from the cedar chest where it had stayed since that night in 1915. I wrote her name in the book, the father's name, and that she'd borne a boy. There was no letter D, as the baby was perfect. Another name in a long list of names that spiraled down the page like maple seeds in early spring.

I went alone to Luella's birthing, as Mama was over at Mary Meroe's. Mary was known for having britches babies, and I wasn't skilled enough yet to turn them in the womb. Luella's baby didn't require skill, although her ma told me first thing that the baby was coming too soon, which made me worry. Turns out she was giving birth to a whopping ten-pound little boy.

Luella's ma and me looked down on that baby and knew that Luella's husband of only a few months would never accept that baby as his own—especially once the tongues of the women of Philippi got to talking. I understood why Luella had asked for me, and not Doc Woodley.

I realized why Luella had cried, "I didn't mean it," the whole time she was laboring.

When the babe came down her tube and into my hands, I saw the twisted cord about his throat. "Was a wonder he didn't choke hisself," I said without thinking to Luella's ma. At that moment, I took this as a sign. This was a lucky baby.

But Luella's ma's mouth tightened until the color was gone. I saw in her eyes the fear of a woman who had paid for bread by the slap of men's hands and hoped for better for her daughter.

"She can't be having this baby now," the mother whispered in my ear.

"Babies come when ready," I said, as if she didn't know. I washed my hands in the pail of hot water at my feet and unwrapped the cord. Luella gave a final push and the baby, red and perfect, settled itself in the bloody sheet stretched across my knees.

"Give it to me," the woman above me hissed. I looked up into her eyes. I could see the firelight reflected in them, the flames swirling like a dance. "I'll take care of it." Her hand stretched out like the claws of a hawk, about to swoop down on a whisper of wind too soft to give warning to the prey below.

I looked over at Luella. Her lower body rocked and pumped, shedding the afterbirth. The bed she lay in was new and store-boughten. Against the bright colors of the blankets, too fine for a birthing room really, the black iron bedstead shone. The house Luella lived in was new, too, built on a corner lot right in the middle of Philippi. A fine house—there were pictures on the walls and a chair right in the bedroom, should you feel the need to sit. A brown horsehair chair, finer than anything that had graced even Granny's parlor at the Homestead. Richard Porter was a rich and able man who had showered gifts upon his new bride.

Luella herself came from nothing. Her mother was from up on Hudson's Ridge, a trashy sort who was known for pleasing men for money. Luella was a baby born without a father—a wood-colt like myself.

"He won't ever need to know," Luella's ma said. She reached into my lap for the baby, who had opened his eyes.

The baby in my lap began to squirm and breathe. The pink color was rising in his cheeks. I could see his hungry mouth open and close, reaching out into the air for sustenance.

I knew that she meant to kill him. I hated her for forcing me to do myself what should never have needed doing—for having to choose between a clean death and a brutal one.

Luella looked up at me and began a wailing that almost made me stop, but her ma hushed her, stroking her hair and crooning as though Luella were the little one in my lap.

I pressed the new pillows bought by a man who was not the baby's father into the child's face. The little boy never cried, but I did. I pressed down until he was still, then with shaking hands I cut the cord that even yet coursed hot blood into his silent belly.

When I had cleaned the body and wrapped him in the finest blanket I could find, I let Luella's ma go out and tell Richard Porter that the child he believed to be his son was dead. When I came out, Mr. Porter never questioned me, never asked to see it, but then men rarely do, when they know it's dead. I kept waiting for him to ask about Luella, to rise up in righteous anger and accuse me, but he just sat there, in his fine house, and mourned his loss until I'd heard so much crying I couldn't take it anymore.

"Give her anything with sage in it," I told Luella's ma as I packed up my things. "Sooner we dry her milk, the more comfortable she'll be." I shook the blankets and made them smooth over Luella's spent form.

"I'm sorry," Luella whispered, turning her head from me. I knew she could never look at me again without remembering.

"Go with God," Luella's ma said. She looked me in the eye.

As I walked through Philippi that late night, I found myself thinking about Mama, about Granny, and about the God that had been fought about between them. I understood now why Mama had cast those beliefs off, for I too wondered about a God that watched such things happen and did not interfere. Yet a world without Granny's God seemed a dark and frightening place.

I thought of someone who wanted me, no matter if God did or not. At the courthouse, instead of heading for the road that led for home, I turned and walked until I'd crossed the covered bridge, walked until I'd reached the MacFarland farm. At Horace's window, I tapped, and he came out. I told him that I wanted him, for I knew what he would answer.

"Did my daddy ever come back?" I asked Mama, my voice sounding hollow against her.

"Once," Mama said, and I could feel her body stiffen beneath my own. "He knew about you. When I asked him for money to buy this house, he sent it."

"Why didn't you ever marry? Someone else?"

Mama laughed, and her body relaxed. "After I had the house, I didn't need to marry," she said, her voice light, but I knew the thoughts she spoke were heavy ones. I wondered if she had loved my father, for the child in me wanted this to be so. Yet I was torn, since my own actions had been rather wanton, and I wanted Mama to understand.

"I never loved Horace," I told Mama, as we sat there together on the floor still facing the closed door.

"It doesn't matter," she said. But I knew it did. I knew that I should never have let him lie with me unless I loved him. I thought about the way Horace had known me that night and the way I'd moved beneath him like a log caught in the tide of a flooding river. How'd I'd seen Alvin's face over me, how I'd pretended that it was he taking his fill.

"He thought we were going to get married," I said. "That was the only reason he agreed."

Mama chuckled in my ear. "I doubt that was the only reason," she said. She hugged me. "You're a right pretty girl, Elizabeth."

I felt the blush creep up my neck. The heat from Mama's body mingled with my own and for a moment it was hard to know where Mama let off and where I began. The arms around me could have belonged to either of us, the blood pumping through our bodies coursing through both our veins. Mama and me, together. This is how we once were, I thought, my ear listening to the gurgle of her belly. And how, in part, we would always be.

SEVEN

Kettle Valley paid for the mild winter of 1918 throughout the next year. Our soldiers were coming home, though they weren't the boys we had sent off. I would peer into their faces, wondering what Horace MacFarland might have looked like, had he returned to me.

Jebediah Teller came home with no lungs. His mama put him to bed the moment he passed through the door and he didn't get out of it until he died fifteen years later. Folks said he never smiled, for all he'd been such a prankster before the war. He made a nice corpse, I'll say that much, his face as silky as a sheet of satin.

Derry Hander came home suffering from other things, but it didn't take a war to catch them and you won't hear me speak poorly of the dead. Especially anyone who died the way he did, stark raving mad trying to open his blind eyes to find the sun.

Others came home finding the people they had left were the ones who had changed. Daniel Boone Meroe walked all the way from Washington, D.C., only to find his girl, Mavis Benton, married to Howard Woodley, Doc Woodley's boy. Course those Bentons always did live high off the hog, and there was no doubt in anyone's mind that Howard could provide for a family and then some. I'd always thought highly of Daniel Boone, and if his mama hadn't been a Denniker from my own line, I might have thought about going after him myself. He was Denniker enough, though. If he ever married, I've never heard tell of it.

There was change in the air, though I hadn't breathed it in yet. I actually thought that things had gone back to the way they had always been. With Horace gone, thoughts of being with Alvin became all-consuming. Mines were booming all around us, and there was no reason for Alvin to be away from home now. Many nights I would watch for him to come home, and we would climb the mountain together. "I needed to tell Ivy something," I said, and this wasn't untrue, for I couldn't imagine my life without all of them in it.

When Lauren rolled over and grinned, Ivy and I clapped together. I saw Lauren drink from a cup for the first time. Many afternoons I borrowed Lauren to take to Mama's so Ivy could nap. I helped her to put up her winter canning. We pieced a quilt for Lauren's bed.

Alvin loved his daughter almost as much as he loved his wife. "I can't tell you how it pained me that year," he said once on one of those nights as we walked, "being away from here. Being away from them." We came to a rough patch and he offered me his hand. Greedily I reached for it.

"We missed you, too," I said.

He stopped a moment, just inside the treeline. He touched me with his fingertips, all five gently on my arm. "Made things easier, knowing you were here," he told me.

My arm burned. I stood there, looking up at him, knowing I would finally dare to reach out and kiss him.

Just then Ivy burst out of the house. She ran headlong for

us, her dark skirts and hair flapping behind her in the wind. I couldn't have been more shamed, and I stepped back.

She grabbed my arm. She never said a word, as was her wont. She pulled me to the house, my feet stumbling as we ran. She pushed me inside the door and waved her hands in a grand gesture of presenting. She finally spoke. "Look!"

Lauren sat on the floor, her eyes wide and blinking.

"Oh, no!" Ivy said, putting her hands to her face. She began to laugh. She went over to her daughter and tried to stand her up, but Lauren was as unsteady as a rag doll. Soon they had both made a game of it, and the squeal of Lauren's giggles filled the room.

"She stood," Ivy insisted. "She did."

Then I came over, lifted the little girl, hardly more than a baby. I picked her up under the arms and set her on her feet. For a long moment she stood there, then she began to sway back and forth until she pitched forward.

Ivy and I moved to catch her, banging heads in the process. We were all three jumbled there, laughing when we saw Alvin standing in the doorway. He smiled at us—all of us.

1919 was also the year the Blicker twins were born—those strange little babies who from their birth seemed to make our fears of change become flesh. Hazel Blicker and Mama had been good playmates in their youth, grown up across the road from each other, and Mama loved Hazel something awful. Whenever we had much to spare she could be found making gifts for her—mostly baby items, for with Hazel, there was always a baby. One on her lap, another at her breast.

Mama wouldn't allow me to visit the Blicker cabin—said it was too nasty for a little girl. One of the things she and Granny agreed upon. When she returned, Mama would drink a glass of whiskey, swallowing like a man.

"Why do you bother with her?" I had asked her once. We were making little clothes for the latest baby. We were alone, so I was probably about ten.

Mama snapped off the white thread with her teeth and held the tiny shirt up in the air—a beautiful shirt, with tucks and embroidery all about the hems. I thought of that bright white cloth in that dirty cabin. "I stood up with her when she married Caleb," Mama said. "And I shouldn't have." She reached for a piece of flannel so soft it felt like feathers.

"Why not?"

"She was over the moon about him, but I knew he'd been seeing Lis Barlow all the while he was courting her. I tried to tell her that he wasn't a good man, but I didn't tell her about Lis, and I can't forgive myself for that."

"But she loved him, didn't she?" I asked.

"That isn't enough." Her needle flashed in the candlelight.

"What more?"

"Hazel would have done anything for him, and he only wanted one thing."

"But at least he married her. He didn't marry any of those other women."

"You aren't the first person to tell me that, and you aren't the one who will convince me."

Mama and I were in the garden when Hazel's time came. I remember that it was springtime because we were planting in the signs of the moon. For all Mama's talk of science, she still planted with the signs. Corn planted when the oak trees' leaves were the size of a squirrel's ear. She started watching the moon from March on, waiting to see the barest crescent of light—that's the best time for planting anything that needs rooting in the earth like carrots, potatoes, turnips. Tomatoes, squash, pumpkins, those are planted when the moon is fat and full, like the fruits you are trying to tempt from the earth.

Beans don't care when they're planted, so long as you cover them with deep earth and leave them be.

We were on our knees, pressing the furrows closed, hurrying to finish before dark, when I heard Caleb's whistle. "How do, Meribeth," he called out to Mama, grinning as though he'd won a prize. "Guess you know why I come," he said with a wink. "Not that you aren't a woman worth seeing anytime," he said, wiggling his eyebrows as he looked her over. Mama's cheeks were bright red, but he kept talking. "Let me help you get your things," he said, in his great rumbly voice. As he came close, I noticed Mama pulling back, holding her arm out so I was kept behind her.

"Don't bother," she said. "Come, Elizabeth," and I knew she didn't want me out there with him.

I took my time, anxious to see Caleb close up. His light brown hair was bushy about his face and when I sniffed the air about him there was no hint of whiskey. Instead I caught a whiff of soap and leather and gunpowder. He smelled like Alvin.

Inside, Mama gathered up sheets and blankets, knowing that she would find none when she arrived. She handed me the pile of blankets, diapers, the new shirt, and all the other little items she had made. "I'll need you," she said. "Hazel's as wide as a church door, so she's carrying a big one."

We walked behind Caleb, heading for the Ridge a few miles distant. We passed the tidy farms that stretched along Kettle Creek and soon began the steep climb up the mountain. The woods were denser here, having never been cut, and the evening air seemed to thicken as we stepped. Beneath our feet, I could just make out the faint lines of the fox trace we were following, Mama putting her foot in the shadow where Caleb's had been, me walking into Mama's.

Under the trees, it was nearly pitch, the light from the frail moon glimmering through the tops of the mostly leafless branches. Halfway there, I couldn't see more than a few feet on either side and I stuck close to Mama, to Caleb, and the lantern light. Yet I knew that all around me were the shacks and cabins that the people of Hudson's Ridge called home— tumbledown structures with just enough tar paper strapped across the top to keep the smell in. I knew these people were watching us with dark eyes passed down to them by their Indian and Negro ancestors. These bloodlines mixed with white men like Caleb who came to this mountain ridge to hide from the valley. Hudson's was full of people like that—people who had nowhere else to go.

We were almost at the house when a great sigh of wind brushed over our heads. Mama paused and listened, bending her head into the breeze. When the breeze came again, carrying the keening sound with it, Mama picked up her skirts and began to run.

Caleb and I tripped over each other, trying to follow. We righted ourselves, pretending that we hadn't touched, and stumbled up the path into the house. I felt dizzy, partly from the fall, partly on account of the cabin, which was built as crooked as the hind leg of a dog. The door hung all askew, and the floors ran downhill, making it hard to know where to put my feet. When you looked up, the cat-and-clay chimney looked about ready to fall in on us.

Mama was by the bed, holding Hazel's hand and listening to her belly.

"It's all right," she was saying. "I'm here now."

I knew that Mama was talking out of the other side of her mouth, for Hazel looked about as awful as a woman can look. She tossed from side to side, half out of the narrow bed. Her nightgown, as chalk gray as her face, was sweat-soaked to her shoulders and breasts, pulled up over a heaping mound of flesh that hung over her privates. When she moved, I watched the belly swing like the white roll of an old man's gut. Her hair was so thin I could see the scalp in the dim light.

"Help, Elizabeth," Mama snapped at me. I ran across the tipsy floor and took one of Hazel's flailing hands. "Caleb," Mama called out, "I'm gonna need whatever whiskey you got on hand." When Caleb didn't move she looked so angry that I thought she might strike him. "Hurry up about it."

"Yes, ma'am," he answered, but he just stood there, looking at the three of us.

Hazel let out a cry that grew and grew and grew until I could feel it piercing through my skin. Caleb put his hands over his ears, then ran out of the cabin.

Mama and I worked all night. At one time the baby—we didn't know it was twins then—stuck out a hand wrapped in the bright red birthing cord like a ribbon bracelet. Before Mama could loosen the cord, the hand was gone again, pulled back through the great gaping hole between Hazel's legs.

There was cutting, the cruel metal of the scalpel slicing into flesh. There was blood. Rivers of it running down from the bed, soaking through the mattress and dripping into puddles on the floor. Still the baby could not come through. Mama tried rubbing and stretching the skin about the opening but there weren't no way two girls stuck together were coming through without cutting Hazel wide open. Finally, when the first baby burst out, dragging her sister behind her, Mama cut the cord and tossed the twins to me. She never looked up, her whole mind taken with the task of pressing the gushing wound with cotton bags filled with herbs. She packed the canal with parsley. The smell of blood, that hot iron smell like a skillet left on a roaring stove, hung in the air. Mama opened her bag and began threading her needle.

"Let me see them." Hazel held out her arms for the babies, but I held off, seeing what she could not. The backs of their hands were stuck together, like a new pair of gloves. Two hands, ten fingers, two palms turning live-pink from birthing-blue, and nothing but flesh between them. I cleaned them up best I could and wrapped them together in a blanket, before handing them to her.

"Where's Caleb?" Hazel asked.

"Hush," Mama said, her face creased into a frown. I could see her hands moving, but they were so covered in blood that they blended against the red folds of skin between Hazel's legs. "Be still now." She was trying to piece Hazel back together like a crazy quilt.

"I want Caleb," Hazel said again, her voice rising.

Mama looked at me. "I'll find him." I was happy enough to take a breath of fresh air.

Caleb was by the barn, passed out cold, the whiskey smell hovering about him like a mist. I picked up the empty bottle next to him and stuck my finger in it, then licked the last drops from my salty skin. Then I walked back into the house.

"Caleb's drunk," I told Mama. She looked up at me and a mean smile flittered across her mouth. She bent back over Hazel's body and I watched her hands, moving one on top of the other, sometimes together, sometimes apart. The needle was slippery with blood, and Mama had to struggle to pull it through the flesh. I marveled at her hands, at my own, that were free and whole.

The Blicker twins might have been a sign, which is what they say along Hudson's Ridge. For not long after their birth the horrors of influenza came down upon us, as though blown across the earth by a deadly wind.

At first, we had no reason to think Hazel wasn't ailing from being plain worn out, but then her children started taking sick, too. Mama and I arrived late one evening to see her stretched out on the dirt floor of the cabin, halfway between her bedstead and the water pail. The pail was dry as smoked wood, so I went to fetch water from the rain barrel while Mama got Hazel back into bed and covered her with a sheet.

"We need to open the windows," Mama said. "And don't drink any water that we don't boil first."

We bathed the boys' heads, giving them drinks when they could take it. The oldest girls coughed, but seemed to be pulling through. I can still hear their breath wheezing like a bottle-fly caught in a window frame. The smallest children, including the twins, were still beneath their bedclothes.

I figured they were all sleeping until Mama lifted back the quilt and then flung it forward again. "They're dead?" I asked.

Just then Caleb rose up from where he was lying beside Hazel, his hair wild and his eyes glowing like coal fire. For the first time I smelled that stench of influenza, the bitter scent from the bottom of the bowels. He crawled out of bed and pulled himself over to where we were standing.

"By God," Caleb whispered. "They've been murdered."

"Get back to bed," Mama told him. But her voice had no power. He brushed her aside and threw himself out the door. I could feel the cool night air being sucked into the house.

"I will not forgive this," Caleb hollered. His voice was loud and strong, even if it did come from that now wasted, bony frame. "I curse you for what you have taken from me."

At first I thought he was talking to Mama and me, but I realized then that he was talking to God. I held my breath, watching him shake his fist and then fall to the ground.

"Oh, for Pete's sake," I heard Mama mutter.

Somehow Mama and I got Caleb back inside the cabin and cleaned him up and poured some willow bark tea into him. I know we saved his life that night. We kept at it, until the death left his face and he slept next to his sons. By then, though, it would be too late for Hazel.

Mama walked home with me, white as a sheet. "Caleb shouldn't have done that," she said, her voice low and quiet.

"Done what?" I asked.

"Curse God," she said. She looked up at the sky, which was filled with summer stars.

"I thought you didn't believe in God," I said, more shaken by the experience than I cared to admit.

"Well, I don't believe in cursing," Mama said. And that was the most Granny-like thing I ever heard her say.

By summer, the land was hot and dry, overrun with death. The Tygart River ran green with rot. Kettle Creek was hardly more than a trickle and Mama would often pour well water into damp pools where the minnows gasped for breath.

There were few births that year, which was a mercy, for every able body was needed to care for those who weren't well. Not that you can do much about the influenza. Truth be told, we did as much housekeeping that year as we did nursing. My hands were soon raw from scrubbing quilts and hauling them outside to dry in the sun.

Mama became Doc Woodley's second pair of hands, as he was driven to distraction riding from hither to yon, trying to keep the epidemic down. Every week or so he'd come to our door, dropping off supplies to Mama and telling her the latest news. Once he almost fell off his horse—that's how tired he was—and Mama put him to bed for the night in her own room. Normally there would have been talk, but sickness makes people think only of their own selves.

I'd asked Mama about her and Doc once, and she said, "He likes a woman that can answer back." She laughed then, and I saw her eyelids flutter as though she was watching something she remembered. "And everyone knows that I can think for myself."

"What about Mrs. Doc?" I'd asked.

"What about her?" Mama asked in return, and I didn't know what to say to that. Only thing I knew about her was that she lived in a big fancy house in Philippi and crocheted bookmarks in the shape of crosses to put in Bibles. When I was a girl Doc would always bring me one when he stopped by our house. Mama and me would boil them in sugar water to make them stiffen up, but after the fourth or fifth one wasn't much point in keeping such things.

Even now, I'll get asked about Doc and Mama. Asked if they were carrying on back then. I still don't have an answer, assuming I'd feel like giving one. The only time I ever walked in on them unawares I didn't see much. They were sitting at the table with an open book between them, the mortar and pestle in Mama's hands. Doc's gray, old-fashioned whiskers seemed to quiver when I entered, but when he saw me, he broke into a smile that made his thin face seem less severe.

Even Granny never minded it, and she was never one to put up with any shilly-shallying. "He loves your mama," she said once when we were still living down at the Homestead. "I don't care to press it." We were watching them walk up the road to town. Their heads were close, although I could make out a slight band of light between them.

In 1919, Mama nearly worked herself to death. She would move in with the family if too many had taken badly, and I would go back and forth, taking her clean linen and medicines as quickly as Doc could get them to me. She was up at the Teller house, over on Nickelback Creek, where she'd gone after their girl Halley had come down here complaining of stomach pains. She had stomach pains all right—her belly pooching out before her for all she'd wore a wedding ring a month. But we played along and to this day I'm glad, for not two days later she was dead from the influenza, and it isn't like she and Ted were the first to harvest their corn before they'd built their barn.

That line of the Teller clan was always strange. Halley's daddy wore a beard that came down nearly to his knees—thought cutting hair was sinful-like, razors were a curse of Satan, as if he were Sampson in the Bible. His wife June was known for her old-fashioned remedies and her incantations, though most of her mutterings were simply taking bits and pieces from Bible verses and stringing them together until the person was either cured or dead.

By the time Mama found her way home from the Tellers', she was almost out of her mind. "June's gonna kill the whole lot of them," she kept saying over and over. "Delmar's already dead. And there wasn't anything I could do about it." I knew that upset her most. "She's using polecat grease. Shoving it in them with a spoon." Mama's color was high and there were white lines around her mouth and eyes. Her ears looked as shiny as wax and she was waving her hands in front of her like a pair of mating birds. "She's gonna kill 'em," she said again. "That old fool."

Wasn't until I put her to bed and tried to get some willow bark tea down her—she heaved it right back up—that I got that scared feeling in the pit of my stomach. I knew what was happening and how little time I had. I put my fists over my eyes to think, going over in my head everything we'd been doing for sick folks, week after week. "Mama will get well, Mama will get well," I said over and over.

I knew I had to bring her fever down. Already the sheets were clammy with her sweat and I could see the gaunt shadows of her body through the light fabric of her cotton shift. I opened the window and breathed the pungent smell of burning leaves. Some folks thought smoke was a way of killing off the sickness, and the valley was filled with the stench of it.

All that night I sat with her, trying everything that I thought she might take, a little peppermint, a bit of ginger. For all of Granny's praise about my teas, Mama's body scorned them now. By dawn she was no better. Her lips were so cracked that they had no color at all. The cabin reeked of vomit, her bed sour. At midmorning, I tried washing some of the sheets but while I had gone to pin them on the line, Mama rose from her bed and began walking up the mountain. By the time I'd helped her back to the porch, she'd collapsed completely and I had to drag her inside.

The fear that had been in my belly was now in my throat. I could hardly swallow, so big did it seem. I choked down a heaping spoonful of lady-slipper root to calm my spirit but I was running out of time. Mama's fingernails were turning blue—a sign that her lungs were filling with rot, clear and thick as white sugar syrup. I needed Doc Woodley, but that meant a trip to Philippi three miles away.

I decided to take the risk and climb Denniker's Mountain. Ivy would help me, and Alvin could go for Doc. He could take Lauren as far as John Teller's, where I knew she would be safe.

I let Mama sit up a ways, for I was scared to leave her lying flat for fear her lungs would drown in their own mess. When I put my ear to her mouth, straining to hear the death rattle that had filled my ears these past months, I heard only the wheeze of breath, and this gave me some hope.

I crossed Kettle Creek, my feet slipping in the mud where there wasn't enough water in the shallows to cool the hem of my dress. Denniker's Mountain had never loomed so tall above me, the shadow of it dark against the bright noon sky. The laurel hell at the base was the color of lye soap, the twisted branches gray and menacing.

When I reached the ridge, I saw the three of them standing in the doorway as though they were waiting for me. Relief washed through me—that jolt of joy that comes with learning you are not alone. I opened my mouth to call, but just then Alvin pushed Ivy into the cabin. I stopped short when he came back out, carrying a rifle pointed at a spot above my head. He looked like a man who's been scared so badly that he's no longer afraid.

"Don't come any closer," he called.

"It's Mama," I hollered back.

"Stay back," he said. "There ain't no reason for you to bring the plague up here."

Ivy stood behind him, holding Lauren in her arms. She was talking in his ear. I saw him shake his head. She put her arm on his, but he shrugged it off. Lauren began to cry.

"I aim to do whatever it takes to protect my family," Alvin yelled. "Even if it means staying here on my mountain till we've seen this thing through."

"It's Mama," I said again, my legs collapsing in on themselves. I felt like crawling across the ground, taking him by his knees and shaking him until he understood. "She's gonna die." My words sounded weak. The late autumn sun had crested the mountain and seemed to be burning down on me, and I knew we were past the noon hour. Time was passing, passing, and Mama was down there, maybe dead.

I don't know what I started yelling at that point. I raised my voice and let it carry the words to him—I might have told him that I loved him, I don't know. I might have begged. In the end he handed Ivy the rifle and came down to the spot where I was sitting and helped me up.

"I'll fetch Doc Woodley, so long as you come no closer," he said. His eyes glared as though he'd knew me not. For that moment I hated his strength—hated his body as if I'd never loved it—as he was well and Mama dying.

"I won't," I said. I looked back at the house, seeing Ivy still standing there. Lauren put up her hand and waved to me.

"Ivy is my woman," he said as he came nearer. "I love her like my own soul."

"I know," I said. I started crying then. He looked back at Ivy and I heard him sigh. Then he reached out and hugged me and I let my body sag against his. We headed for the barn where he had to lift me on the horse, for I was so weary.

Alvin pushed the horse as hard as he dared, coming down as we were, and it was only minutes before I was back at Mama's side. The room when we entered was so still. No hush of breath at all. "Mama," I called, crying like a child until Alvin took a mirror from Mama's dresser and put it to her lips. Together we watched it fog with mist, and when he pulled that bit of glass away from her, I took it eagerly in both hands.

"I'll hurry," he said, running from the room. I heard the horse gallop down the road. I sat there, watching the sun move across the floor, inch by inch, while I changed the hot cloths for cool ones to place on Mama's forehead and wrists. When I felt that pinching fear I would put the mirror to her mouth and watch until I was calm again.

I left the bedside once, only for a minute. There was a knock at the door, and thinking it might be Doc, I ran to open it. But there was no one, just a box sitting on the stoop, fitted with a roast chicken and a jar of broth. The jar was sealed with wax, the letter D carved deep within it.

"Thanks," I called to Ivy, but all I heard was the rustling of leaves. I knew she was there, though, hidden in the trees.

There were long shadows on the floor when I sat up to find Doc Woodley coming into the room. He loomed over us, pressing against Mama's bed so hard that I could feel the wooden frame tremble. He laid his hand upon her forehead and was taking her pulse before I'd had a chance to do more than look up. He moved with such purpose, yet was so gentle that I realized he wasn't just sweet on Mama, the way Granny and I had always supposed, but that he loved her in the way God had created man to love a woman. Doc wasn't going to let my mama just go and die.

"We've got to get this down her," Doc said. He handed me a waxed paper poke filled with crushed white powder that smelled sour.

"What's this?" I asked. I put my finger into the mixture and tasted the tiniest bit, trying to keep from choking at the sharp taste. I looked at Mama's pursed-up mouth, and wondered if I could open it wide enough to get the horrid stuff in her.

Doc Woodley was listening to Mama's lungs, and wouldn't answer until he took the tips of the stethoscope from his ears. "It's aspirin—a new medicine that they used over in France. Will bring down her fever. We'd beat this influenza if we had more of it."

I looked at the powder, remembering Granny's death-talk about apothecaries making poison. "She won't take much willow bark tea," I said.

"This is better than drinking gallons of tea," Doc Woodley answered.

"This ain't some patent medicine, is it?" I asked. I knew Mama frowned on patents, and I'd seen plenty of folks take them only to suffer a cure worse than the disease.

"No, honey," the doctor said kindly. He took the paper from my hand and mixed the powder into a glass of cold water. Then he dribbled a bit into Mama's mouth.

"Hold her nose closed," Doc said, and I sighed, for he was treating me like the child he no doubt thought I was. I'd been giving breast babies medicine for nearly six years and knew my way.

Mama choked, but swallowed. I got the bucket ready.

"Maisie," Doc Woodley whispered into her ear. His face was lost in her loose hair. "Come on, Maisie. I can't let you go."

I wondered about the name. I'd never heard it before.

"Sweet Maisie," Doc was saying over and over. He had taken her hand in his own and I could see the dark hairs creeping across his fingers like spider veins in a woman's leg. "It's all right now," he said, cooling her head with water.

"If she can take that foul drink, maybe I can get some broth down her," I said to Doc, and he nodded. I went out and heated the soup Ivy had brought, and gnawed a moment on a chicken wing, feeling a rush of hunger so intense that I picked the meat clean to the bone.

When I got back in Mama's room, Doc was using a medicine dropper to dispense the water. The glass with the white powdered mix was half empty. I took a spoon and put a little of the broth between her lips. A taste of soup, a drop of water. Seems like we sat there, Doc Woodley and I, until the sun set, nursing her a teaspoon at a time. If others suffered with the influenza that day, they did so without help from Doc Woodley or me. But we saved Mama's life. Come nightfall, the hot flush had left her cheeks, and she'd coughed up most of the bile. Doc Woodley bent over her chest, listening at first, then resting, his face so peaceful now that I knew he'd gone to sleep. Together they moved, his nearly bald head bobbing with the rise and fall of her breath. I covered him with the quilt off my own bed and smoothed the sheets around Mama's body.

Then I curled myself up on the rag rug by her bed. I could feel the rough wool beneath my cheek, a rug that had been alongside my mama's bed for as long as I could remember.

Doc Woodley woke me at the first crack of light. "She'll be weak yet," he whispered, and indeed, when she stirred she couldn't yet hold a spoon. For that day and the fortnight after, I did little else but sit by her bed, caring for her as if I were the mama and she were my child. I would read to her, when she felt rested, comb her hair, wash her face. Doc Woodley stopped by when he could, but he was busier than ever, as though trying to make up for the people who had died while he had spent his time here.

I thought about the way he had called Mama Maisie and how Alvin had named Ivy. I knew that both men loved these women in the same way, wanting to make a mark, the way a woman names a child. I recalled Doc's face, when he looked down on my mama. Alvin's eyes on Ivy the night of the party after Lauren's birth. The way no man had looked at me, and I confess that in my weariness I felt lonesome clean through.

Foolish thoughts, these were. Selfish, even in the face of death, as only the young can be. For while it's true that there was no man watching over me, Mama was with me still, and I was glad, so glad. And there was Ivy, who cared for me as best she could. If I knew then what was to come, Ivy's shadowed presence would have been enough.

Every day, there would be jars and dishes outside the back door. Fancy foods, too, delicate little bits of batter and fluff that seemed just the thing that Mama was craving on any given day. Soups made of cream, the vegetables cut tiny to slip down an ailing throat. Meat so tasty it gave me strength just to look upon it.

I came to count on that food, watching through the window for Ivy's form in the trees. Once I even opened the door and took the food from her hands. I stood there holding the jars, the fresh bread, as she took my face in her hands and kissed my cheek.

"Mama is safe?" she asked.

I put the food down on the table. "She is." Ivy hugged me.

"You are too thin," she said. "You can't be sick next." She

put her hand on my forehead, as though checking for fever. "Where is she?"

"Come see."

We went into Mama's room, and when Ivy saw Mama there, she closed her eyes and made a motion with her hands that I knew was Catholic—part of Fina, the woman she had been before, and that made me glad.

During those days, Ivy and I never had more than a minute together, for she came in the cracks of time when Alvin went to town for news, or when he was clearing wood for cash-money. Whatever time she could steal from Alvin's watch, Ivy gave to me.

I wasn't surprised to open the door one day to see the porch empty. I had known all along that the food would one day stop coming. At least Alvin had found out after Mama was doing better. Already she was sitting up most of the day, walking about some, eager to be back on her own two feet.

Wasn't until another week had passed before word came to us. And then everything already had taken place and there wasn't anything we could do. For while I had sat at Mama's side, while I had been happy to see the color return to her face, Ivy had taken sick. While I had slept peacefully in my bed, Ivy had died in hers.

EIGHT

Today I doubt that more than a dozen folks who live in these parts remember Ivy, the woman that she was. Few ever saw her, fewer still spoke more than a word or two of greeting to her on the rare trips she made to town. As was so often the case, I came to know her on account of midwifing, but I take pride in knowing that was not the reason she became my friend. It takes more than bringing a baby into life to bind two women together.

Ivy, more than anyone, taught me what it meant to be a woman. Before her, I was only a child, with a child's way of loving. Ivy was the first outside my blood kin to love me by giving of herself, instead of demanding something from me.

That was the first gift she gave to me.

The second was Lauren.

More than a week passed from Ivy's death before she could be properly buried. The long time wasn't unusual then, what with the epidemic in full force. Wasn't a preacher to be found that didn't travel from graveyard to graveyard, saying words

over the dead from dawn to dusk. Every undertaker was working round the clock, for those that could afford such things.
Carpenters built coffins out of packing boxes, out of bits and
pieces of wood so raw and green that the coffins bent and
groaned as they were lowered in the ground.

Folks took to gathering in one house after another, bringing in food, fearing not to, lest they be needing it next. When
it was known Mama was past the crisis the women came,
those whom we had helped with birthings, family women,
women who came in memory of Granny—the women, their
daughters, and even their granddaughters came to visit us, to
feed us, to sit and talk, their voices rustling like scissors cutting cloth.

"No one has seen hide or hair of Alvin in days—nor his little girl neither," Alice MacFarland said. Her words chilled me
as thoroughly as the November rain outside. I had been looking for Lauren and Alvin since I'd learned about Ivy. I'd gone
up the mountain, but the house was empty. I took to spending
part of each day wandering about the mountain, searching
Alvin's haunts—the cave at the foot of the west side, where
Dewey Dalton hid his bootleg whiskey, or the deer-spot where
you could spy upon the whole ridge. "Please be all right," I
would whisper. I couldn't bear the thought of losing all three
of them.

"I was just up there today and the whole place's been de-
serted." Alice looked directly at me, as though accusing me of
taking them from her. Evidently Alice was watching for Alvin,
too.

I wasn't pleased, for Alice was a pretty woman, in that
washed-out, fair-haired sort of way. She had gray eyes like her
brother Horace, and Horace's well-shaped hands.

"Harriet Switzer said he was down on Friday, to talk about
the burying," Aunt Annie told us, as if I wouldn't have known.
I was glad that Ivy had been taken there, for the Switzers were

gentle folk, and the best undertakers in the county. "No way to be burying her until day after tomorry." Aunt Annie waved a hand in front of her nose.

"She'll be ripe enough by then," my cousin chimed in. Even Aunt Annie frowned at that, but Gussie's blunt tongue bothered me less than her mother's did. We all knew she wasn't all there in the head and often said things other people only thought. When we were little girls, she'd called me Elizabeth Bastard, like it was a family name, as Aunt Annie had said I was one of them. Mama cut Annie cold for nearly a year over that.

"I heard Alvin bought her the nicest coffin Switzer's had to offer," Alice said.

"It was pine." Aunt Annie was unimpressed. I knew she was recalling the handsome walnut coffin she'd used to bury her only son in a few years ago.

"But it did have a pink velvet lining. She'll rest comfortably enough in that."

"She isn't going to rest on anything," I said, my words sharp amidst the chatter.

"Well, of course she is." Aunt Annie stopped knitting the long black stocking I knew Gussie would be wearing that winter. I was glad for many reasons not to have been born to Aunt Annie, and itchy black stockings were one of them. "She'll be taken care of."

"She's dead," I said. I didn't want to talk about her this way. I wanted to talk about who she had been in life.

There were steps on the porch, and the door swung open. My uncle Drake stood there, his rifle in his hand, his boots muddy. "Look who Daddy found!" Gussie announced. "Guess she ain't dead after all."

Lauren stood there and I rushed to meet her.

"Poor baby," old Fanny Teller said, and it was true. Lauren's hair was snarled about her face. Her cheeks were streaked with dirt and her mouth was cut on the left corner, making her seem whopper-jawed. She looked as scared and lost as only a motherless child can look.

"She was wandering about John Teller's orchard," Uncle Drake said. I'd always liked Uncle Drake—never understood how he came to marry Aunt Annie. He saw the terror on my face and spoke kindly to me. "She's all right, Elizabeth."

Lauren started to cry then and I hugged her close, whispering to her as I had done since she was a baby. Ivy would have wanted me to have her.

"Ivy made me Lauren's godmother," I said, knowing as I spoke that most would think this a heathen custom—I had myself when I'd been asked. "That makes me her mama now."

Aunt Annie stopped knitting, her mouth open as though to say something. Fanny nodded her head, as though things were now taken care of with her approval. Alice glared at me and I glared back.

"You always did want her daddy," Gussie said. Alice laughed, a mean, harsh rattle of sound. Even Aunt Annie smiled, so I knew they were all thinking this.

I raised my chin, the way I'd seen Mama do a hundred times when I was growing up. "Come, little one," I said to Lauren, picking her up and holding her against me. I carried her into my room and closed the door. I took off Lauren's shoes and settled her against me on the bed, wrapped my body around hers, and gathered the quilt about us both.

The day of Ivy's burial was cold and clear. The trees were bare of leaves, but the ground was covered with them and they blew into the hole in the earth as though trying to soften the edges of the coffin.

Mama stood with me, her first time out since taking sick. Lauren stood between us, ducking her head in my skirts. Most of the women who had been in and out of our home stood with us. Ivy might have been a stranger in Kettle Valley, but she had carried the Denniker name. More, she'd died in the influenza like so many others. She was foreign to us no longer.

We were all watching for Alvin. No one had seen him since he'd gone to choose the coffin.

At the service, I tried to remember Ivy as the woman I had known, but all I could see was the little girl Fina, running through Cuban sugar fields. Fina wasn't here. Fina was still running.

Several men took up the shovels they had hidden away behind the tombstones. I gave Lauren a handful of dirt to toss inside the grave, because I knew folks would be expecting it.

"Oh, precious Jesus, oh, precious Lord," Verna Sue Switzer moaned like she always did at funerals. Went to them just for this purpose, whether or not she knew the one being buried. Several had joined in the wailing when the rifle shot rolled over us like thunder.

I grabbed Lauren, pulling her to the ground. Folks began to scream. Two men ran for the wagons to get their own guns, and poor old Gertie Teller fell to her knees and started begging God's forgiveness for this "surely is the second coming."

Mama just stood there, her eyes shaded by her hand. I followed her gaze and saw a man running along the upper ridge above the church-house, waving his rifle in the air. He shot it again and then threw back his head and began an awful keening sound. Alvin.

"He's gone crazy," I said.

"He's been drinking," Mama answered, kneeling down and covering Lauren's eyes from this image of her father.

"You can't put her in there!" Alvin cried. The men with rifles held them ready. "She ain't in there, and I'll kill the one who says she is!" He fired yet again, the bullet so close I could hear the mosquito whine against my ear. Two of the men made moves to give chase, but their women held them fast.

Even from this distance I could see the stubble-beard against his cheeks and chin. His clothes were filthy and there was blood on his left arm. That blood worried me like nothing else had. Alvin was a fine shot, but a wound that sheds that much blood could throw off any's aim.

None of us knew what to do. Alice MacFarland was in her mother's arms, crying and begging Alvin to stop. "Let me go to him," I heard her say. But Sarah MacFarland wound the heavy wool coat of her daughter through her fingers and held on tight.

Alvin was bawling now, the way a man will do when the whiskey begins to wear off. Alice was still tugging, and I looked over at Mama. I gestured to Lauren, squirming between us. Mama nodded, just the smallest bit.

As I began to climb, I knew that I had crossed some line, made some sort of declaration as boldly as if I'd waved a flag. That I had chosen Alvin was public knowledge now, seen by dozens of eyes. They would tell my story, creating it as they went along, for none of them knew of my love for Ivy, for Lauren. I was going up on that mountain as much for them as for Alvin or myself.

When I'd almost reached the top of the ledge, I realized that Mama and Lauren had followed me, and Lauren now ran to her daddy. He fell to his knees, putting his hands over her eyes and removing them slowly. "Where you been, baby?"

he asked. "When I couldn't find you, I thought I'd lost you, too."

Alvin noticed me then. "She done good to you?" he asked Lauren, who pulled back from his heavy, liquored breath. She grabbed one of my hands in both of hers.

"She's been a good girl," I said, trying to find my birthing voice, a voice Alvin might listen to. "Now you run along to Nana," I told Lauren.

Mama reached out and picked her up. Lauren squirmed a little, but I could hear Mama say as they walked down the hill, "It's all right. Elizabeth's just going to take care of your daddy. She'll come for you soon."

I will, I thought, though when Alvin stood, I wondered just how I'd do this. The eyes of the folks in the graveyard pierced through my dark clothes like a rain of flint-worked stones, but I reached out my hand to Alvin, and when he took it, we began the walk to the cabin.

In the yard, I went over to the well and drug up a bucket. Then I tossed it over his head, dousing him so the drops caught along his ears and his head sparkled in the sun.

"You go in there and get some decent duds on," I told him, using the same tone I'd used down at the graveyard. I gave him a push and he turned and went into the house and closed the door behind him.

I turned my back to the cabin like a gentleman caller with a mail-order bride. I waited longer, and still longer, telling myself that I was staring down the whole valley I knew to be buzzing with news of what I'd done. But up this high, there was only the sound of the wind whistling through the pines. "I'll be good to him," I said back. "I'll do my best to love him the way I ought." When the wind died down I moved to open the cabin door.

He was standing there before the chimney shelf, dressed in nothing but the skin God gave him. I could see the pale bands of flesh along his back and down his thighs. His arms looked dark when seen next to that strange, baby-like skin. The wound on his left wrist was raw and bloody.

When the door clicked shut I saw his body grow taut. I knew enough not to speak.

"I met her down in Louisiana," he said, his voice sharpened by grief. "After my mama died, I didn't know what to do with myself. Thought I'd travel a bit, as Union had done. Went as far as New Orleans before I'd spent all my money and was homesick clear through. I missed the mountain. I missed the creek.

"There were women everywhere, especially for a man who looked like he could offer a good time. But broke as I was, most wouldn't give me the time of day, until I saw her— this dark-haired little woman with blue eyes so deep, eyes that still believed a man could do right by her. For all their foreignness, she had eyes like my mama's, like women I'd known here in the mountains. And I wanted to do good. I did."

I knew that look myself—saw women staring up at husbands as their birthing bodies heaved, thinking that a man ought to be strong enough to take the pain from her.

"She hadn't been a harlot long, as I'd seen enough of them to tell. She was clean yet, smelled sweet. I thrilled to think I might save her from other men who would make her old and broken like the women who hung about the streets, offering their bodies in exchange for cheap drink." Alvin's shoulders slumped, and I took a step forward. "Knowing I could save her is what made me into a man that night, not the bedding of her, although I did that plenty, taking from her what I blamed other men of wanting. I did save her." His voice broke and I stepped so close to him that I could see the damp hairs on the back of his neck. "I did."

This was not the Ivy I had known—the woman who walked

with me to the top of Denniker's Mountain, swinging her baby on her hip through a field with timothy grass three feet high.

"When an old man, call himself her daddy but I knew he weren't, came the next morning, I offered him everything I owned. I argued with him, with her sitting right there in the bed, her nightgown down around her shoulders, her hair mussed about her face. At last he agreed to flip me for her. For the labor I could give him. Five years of my life against the girl."

I could imagine the coin in the man's wrinkled palm. I could almost see the sunlight sparkle off the coin as it spun in the air.

"When I won, the old man threatened me. Told me they would steal her back and put her in a convent where I'd never find her. I told him that she was mine, that I won her fair and square. We left that day for home, for this mountain where I could hide her away from everyone."

I was leaning against Alvin's back now. My hands were on his shoulders and my head rested in the curve of his neck.

He turned then and held me in his arms. I would like to say that I offered him comfort, as we moved over to the bed, and perhaps I did. I would like to think that I offered him something, for all that I took, quenching the thirst I'd had for him, his body, all these many years. As I listened to him call out her name, "Ivy, Ivy," in great gasps of breath, I gathered him up into myself, and held him there, until it was done.

Two days passed from the time that I went to the cabin with Alvin until I went down the mountain, wondering after Lauren. The days had been endless, like in the biblical story of Joshua, where the sun stood still and the moon stayed, stopping all of time—so those days seemed.

I cared for Alvin, preparing food when he slept. After that first coupling there hadn't been any since, only our shared grief. This was something that could at least bring us together. Everything we did was filled with Ivy—when I went into that barren little pantry, I was undone by recalling that she had always brought her best to us, helping make Mama well and strong. During those two days, I'd hardly slept. On the morning of the second day I dozed a bit, only to wake up and find that Alvin was gone.

He'd hung my dark dress on a nail, my shoes on the floor beneath it. There was a fire in the grate. I took all this as a sign that he knew I was here to stay.

I hungered, suddenly, for my own things—a clean dress, my treasure box, the goose-down pillow I'd slept on since I was a child. All around me were Alvin's things, and a few of Ivy's. The great bedstead that generations of Dennikers had lived and died and pleasured each other in, Ivy's apron on the kitchen wall, her hairpins piled on the bedroom shelf. Seeing them hurt and comforted me at the same time. I needed my own bits and pieces around me. Even as I walked down the mountain, I thought about what to bring back.

Mama was reading to Lauren when I found them. Lauren had her head on Mama's lap but she jumped up quickly when she heard my footfall. Mama stood too, looking me over. Did I look different to them? I felt as though so much had changed these past few days, what with finally being with Alvin. Surely I must be marked outside as well as in.

"How's Alvin?" she asked. She poured me some coffee and sat at the table.

"Was gone when I woke up," I said, taking the coffee. I did not sit down. My fingers ached from being still even to hold the cup and drink, so anxious was I to pack and head back up the mountain.

"He all right?" Mama asked. She pulled Lauren on her lap and handed the little girl a set of spoons to play with.

"He ain't drinking," I said, and I heard the pride in my voice.

"Did you make him take the temperance pledge?" Mama teased, and I felt a rush of heat to my face.

"I just came for my things," I said. At my abrupt words, the playfulness vanished from Mama's face. Once before I had gone away from Mama, moved into Granny's house. But this was different, for I wasn't coming back. "I'm all right, Mama. I was right to go. We'll be a family. Lauren can come home."

I could see the lines in Mama's face, and knew she was upset. But she said nothing then, and finally nodded.

We were all a bit more cheerful as we spread out my things in Alvin's house. I'd brought the quilt from my bed, the only quilt I can claim to have pieced all my own self, and the red and blue squares brightened the whole room. The tin where I kept my sewing needles and spools of thread shone from its new place on the dresser.

"What about the mirror?" I asked Mama. As was the old-timey custom, someone had draped the mirror in black cloth.

Mama shrugged. "It wasn't her tradition," she said, for she didn't believe in such superstitions. I knew some would say by removing the cloth I was trapping Ivy's spirit in the house.

"I'll just leave it be," I said. "It will come down in a few weeks anyhow."

I worked hard all afternoon, scrubbing floors, making up beds, and dusting cupboards. Lauren never left my side, opening doors as I shut them, patting the rugs and bedding after I'd smoothed them.

Together we found the linen Ivy had sewn, worn thin from so much stitching and pulling out. She'd been doing letters, like a sampler, and her initials were at the bottom. F.G.D. I didn't know what the G stood for. The edges were done in green chains of ivy. I missed her then, as I had not since the funeral. Missed the woman who had embroidered the bright colors in a room awash with gray. "Your mother made this for you," I said to Lauren, though I knew she didn't understand. Granny would have offered visions of Ivy watching us from heaven. Mama would have praised the life Ivy had led. I couldn't bring myself to say anything other than "I miss her too," and hold Lauren tight against me. Finally I put the white square of cloth away.

Was nearly evening when I went into the kitchen. The pantry shelves held jars of pickles and jams. Mama had pulled up the last of the potatoes from Ivy's small garden, and they spilled over their barrel. Two loaves of bread, both pressed in the middle by Mama's hands, baked in the oven. The butter crock was full, as was a jar with cookies.

"You talk to Aunt Annie?" I asked, hoping Mama would rest a moment. She was doing too much, too soon.

"You know I don't bother with idle talk," she said.

I laughed. "I'm sure there's plenty of it."

"You survive talk," Mama said, her voice firm and her chin out. But there was a shadow in her eyes yet. I knew she would always remember when she had nodded to me in the graveyard, that in her own mind she had been the one to give me leave.

"I always told you I would be with Alvin," I said, trying to put some pride in my voice. "And I'm here. This is my mountain now."

Mama smiled at this. She reached into the nearly empty basket and put two brass candlesticks on either side of the chimney board over the fireplace. Long ago, when Old Caesar had built this house, he had carved his initials into the hard wood, and Mama traced these now with her fingers before she turned back to me. She opened her mouth to say something, but Lauren pushed her way between us, holding up two candles in her hands, her chubby little-girl arms looking as pure and white as the wax itself.

"Thank you," Mama told her, and a look of tenderness stole across her face—a look she had given me when I was small. Lauren might have lost her mother, but it seemed that she had gained mine.

The sky was still light when I convinced Mama to go. I offered to walk with her, but she refused.

"I know the way," Mama said. She reached up and touched my cheek, her hand bony from the waste of sickness. "You are a good daughter, Elizabeth," she said. This was my blessing then, from my mother who believed in science over God, but who had always believed in me. I bent my head beneath it, hearing the words in my ears long after she was gone.

Alvin did not come home until Lauren and I had eaten and the little girl was tucked in bed. He knew that I was here, would have seen the candles coloring the windows golden. He stepped into the house like a stranger, like a traveler who is stopping for the night.

"I'll get you some supper." I watched him take in all the changes—the blue-and-white tablecloth, the shining windows, the afghan covering the worn horsehair chair.

"Smells good," he said, his voice polite. He hung his hat on a peg and took off his boots before crossing the room.

I went into the kitchen and scooped up some sauerkraut and a bit of sausage onto his plate, poured water into a cup. I wanted so much to do this right.

Alvin was sitting at the table. "It looks nice." He ran a

hand through his hair, making it stick up on ends, the way it always had. I found it easy to love him in that moment.

"Best eat while it's hot," I told him, and handed him the plate. I sat down next to him, wishing I'd made myself a plate, too. Seemed more friendly if we could eat together.

"You been busy?" I asked. I wasn't prying, just wishing we could talk.

He looked up, eyes wary. "Been about," he said.

"I'm not trying to keep check on you."

Alvin closed his eyes a minute, took a deep breath. "I know you aren't. You're a good woman, Elizabeth." He started to eat.

Somehow this sounded different from Mama saying I was a good daughter. I was willing to bet that he had never told Ivy that she was a good woman. Beautiful. Lovely. Loved. Good seemed hollow in comparison.

"Is there anything about I can be doing? Make things easier on you?" If only he would talk, I thought, things would be all right.

Alvin pushed the plate away from him. "I appreciate you coming here, taking care of me. I know I needed it." I started to speak, but he shook his head. "And I know how much you love Lauren, and how much she cares for you. Don't think I don't."

I could have pushed him then, demanded terms, definitions, rights. But I didn't. There was a relief in just being there, knowing we were home. That Lauren was safe, asleep in her own bed. No matter what came between us, she would always be there for us.

"I got chores to finish," he said, and was gone. I picked up the dishes and went into the kitchen. Here I was, where I'd always wanted to be, and I'd never felt more alone. I banked the stove fire and blew out the lamps.

Alvin had still not come back inside when I got into bed. It was long after midnight when I heard his steps, felt the bed creak beneath his weight. We lay there most of the night, as far apart as two hawks circling in the sky. Just before dawn, I awoke from a dreamless sleep to feel him there, around my body, my body about his. He called her name. But only once.

NINE

Mama always said that a person's needs are just some wants wrapped in plain paper. "You can't tell the difference, most days," she told me once, trying, as always, to make a point. I must have been six, and we were still at the Homestead, sitting out on the porch. "A woman that looks plain on the outside can be beautiful inside."

I can still hear Granny's laughter. She laughed so hard that she had to place her hand over her mouth, to keep her teeth from falling out.

"What's so funny?" Mama asked. Her skin was tinted pink, but only around the edges of her face, so I knew she wasn't too upset. Her mouth was twitching too.

"Women on the inside," Granny said, wiping her eyes with the back of her hand. "They're all bright red where it counts."

Mama had sighed, as though Granny were her child, and a naughty one at that. She looked over at me, to see if I knew why Granny was laughing. Course I didn't, not then.

"What I meant, Elizabeth," Mama said, "is that when a man wants a woman, she might be plain paper, but he won't see her that way. She'll be prettier to him because he wants her."

I still couldn't understand. "Granny's best silk dress is pretty," I said. "But it came in brown paper from Switzer's store."

My turn to blush red, when both Mama and Granny busted out laughing.

Within a few months of living with Alvin, I knew that he never saw anything beyond the brown paper wrapping. He needed me, this is true, but he didn't want me in the way a man wants a woman. Alvin was kind to me, as he had always been. He liked having someone in his kitchen, at his table, in his bed, where, as Granny had promised, I would be red enough where it mattered. Together we worked the land, raised Lauren. Alvin made cash-money mining, going most days down in the coal towns. My birthing money helped keep us free and clear of debt during those early years of the 1920s where folks seemed to be buying fancy play-pretties on credit as fast as the stores could give it.

The first year was hard enough. I think we both kept expecting Ivy to open the door and we could all go back to what we'd been. Folks down in the valley muttered about me when I came to town, but I held my head up just as I'd seen Mama do. As Mama had promised, I learned to live with talk.

The second year was harder than the first, because there was no way of pretending even to ourselves that things were working out the way we'd hoped. Wasn't helped by Alvin taking to drink after mining, though he was not alone. Bill Meroe was crushed one shift, the stony roots of an ancient tree falling on him in the dark. A drink, or two, or three made working with the knowledge that the world could come crashing down on you at any moment easier to bear.

There were times he was out of hand, times when he was charming. More than once the drink made him forget that I wasn't Ivy, and he was happy to know me as a woman. When he wasn't too tired, we would wander about Denniker's Mountain, Lauren on his shoulders, following the old pioneer trails. We tracked deer and I learned to whistle birdcalls almost as well as he.

There were dark nights, too, when the mines made him feel closed in and coming home to a woman he didn't love only fueled the anger he carried with him. Times like that made the happier days seem far away.

We never married, for all I made his house my home. I planted a huge garden and took pride seeing my dresses hanging on the line next to Alvin's workclothes and Lauren's little things. I whitewashed the kitchen and hung curtains in all the windows. I braided rags for the sides of the beds.

The third year, we'd come to understand each other. We knew what the other could offer and what we could accept. If he never forgave me for not being Ivy, at least he stopped blaming me for being myself. I learned to live with the uncertainty of wondering which Alvin would be coming home. I knew too well the terror every miner's woman feels when she hears the whistle scream between shifts. We sent our men off every morning, never knowing if the land would offer them back to us at night. Living with this knowledge made it easier to be satisfied when we tumbled together in our bed out of the sheer animal need to seek its own kind.

And of course I had Lauren—for no one, not even Alvin, thought of me as other than Lauren's mama. "You mind your mama now," Alvin would say to Lauren, as he gathered his mining gear—the heavy helmet, the dinner bucket, the pick and shovel. I dressed her in fancy clothes, and I knit her sweaters of the finest wool. She grew up healthy enough, and from a very early age took to reading, not even the tiny letters in the Bible keeping her from her task. But I knew something wasn't right.

Lauren couldn't speak.

The first year, I talked all the time, trying to get her to respond. She listened well enough, obeyed me without question, yet didn't answer me with words. Soon I wondered if I hadn't talked too much, when Ivy had been so silent. Mama told me that Lauren would grow out of it, but even she became concerned. I know she asked Doc Woodley about it, because he came up one day to visit, bringing his black bag with him. "Since I'm here," he said, his voice too cheerful, "I might as well take a look."

As I visited women for their birthings, I began to talk to them, seeking their advice as they sought my knowledge and my hands. "Queerness is in her blood," one woman told me. "You don't know what her mama put into her," said another. Their words hurt me, as their gossiping about Alvin and me had not. Soon I quit asking altogether.

As I had learned to accept Alvin's distance, I learned to accept Lauren's silence. I too became quiet, as still in speech as Ivy had been. Sometimes I would hear Lauren humming, a little tuneless sound, but mostly the only sounds we heard until Alvin came home were those of the mountain itself.

Until November 1922.

Our well had gone bad, and on a mountain, water means the difference between good soil and land that is as tight as a rich man's fist. The difference between staying put and going off. We noticed it the day we'd been butchering—we needed a drink to rest us from the heat and smell. Alvin dropped the bucket down among the leafy green ferns that kept their color no matter what the time of year. When he pulled the bucket up, he took the dipper and drank deep.

He spewed the water out. "Laws, that's awful." His hand fumbled around his mouth as though trying to remove the taste.

"Let me try," I said. "I just drew water off this morning and it was fine." Adam might have blamed Eve, but I doubt that he believed her when she told him he was buck-naked and she was too. Had to take a bite of the apple and see for his own self.

When I drank, I couldn't hold the water on my tongue any longer than he, so foul did it taste. "Try another batch." He emptied the bucket and filled it again. Alvin smelled the fresh water and shook his head.

"You smell that?" Alvin asked, peering over my shoulder.

"Don't know as I smell anything." Better to tell stories than to admit the stench.

Alvin swore and I frowned. "Lauren will hear you," I said. She was playing by the kitchen stoop with the quilting blocks Alvin had carved and painted for me. She was six now, but still enjoyed turning the squares and triangles and half-moon pieces in patterns I'd never seen in any quilt. I thought of Ivy's fancy sewing, of the silk threads that made pictures on the white linen cloth.

I turned back to the well. "You gonna try and clean it?" I asked. All that darkness down there frightened me. Wouldn't take much for the mountain to swallow a grown man whole.

"I might." Alvin was still bent over the rim. Neither of us said what we were both thinking. Without a well, there is no way to farm a mountain. "Wonder what happened?" He just kept staring down, his hands at his sides. We both smelled of hog fat and there were spots of blood on his clothes and on the backs of his arms.

"Might be us," I said, raising my arm to my face and pretending it smelled worse than it did. "Not like we're any too clean."

He looked up at me, and his eyes flickered a bit in the sun. Then he nodded. "Might just go away."

But it didn't. After more than a week of hauling drinking water up from Mama's I knew we had to do something. I spent my days worrying, about the well, about the farm. Worried that Alvin wouldn't know what to do. All night long, Alvin snoring beside me, I would lie there fretting about that well. Nothing could keep me from worrying over it. Not even Alvin's promises that we would just up and dig a new one.

Before you dig a well, you need to determine where the water lies, and finding water on a mountain is a perplexing thing. Down in the valley, this is easier, what with the many rivers and creeks spread across the land like a young girl's hair set out to dry. On a mountain, it's different. With all the water running downhill to find its proper place, knowing just where the spring is closest to the surface is powerful knowledge. Wisdom that neither Alvin nor I possessed.

So when he told me he'd called on Herman Teller, I was much relieved, for I knew that if anyone could find water on this mountain, he could. Old Herman was about the best diviner that ever was.

Herman came from a long line of diviners. His family hadn't married anyone but a descendant of Massie Teller or Micah Meroe for more than five generations. Marrying that close to home brings out the best and worst in the blood, but no one denies that double cousins are tighter weaved than a laurel thicket. Herman was probably one of the few in Kettle Valley that couldn't claim kin to Alvin or me.

I also knew that Herman was stone deaf and mute. I'd heard stories as how the deafness had come about from Granny, who had known Herman as a grown man when she was just a girl. "He's always been deaf," she had told me when we ran into him once. "And silent on account of it."

Tales differed, depending on who was telling them. Some folks said Herman's daddy had let a gun off too near the side of his son's head. But that didn't explain why both ears had shut down cold. Granny knew there had been sickness in Herman's ears when he was a toddler, and his mama did everything she could before calling the doctor. Had poured chamber lye into his ears, still warm from her own body. Chamber lye do be a nice way of saying piss, and if it didn't cause the deafness, I doubt it did much good.

But deaf and dumb, Herman had a gift.

The day Herman came to divine a new well the air was warm and spring-like, although it was nearly Christmas by the calendar. Not typical weather at all. Some of the trees about the house had begun to form dark red buds, which I knew would hurt them come March.

Herman just showed up at the door. He was a big man, or, better, a long one. He couldn't have been more than a foot wide when he stood crosswise to the wind. He stretched above you like a porch post without causing more than a blink of a shadow.

"How do," I said, out of habit, forgetting he couldn't hear me. He saw my mouth move and nodded in return. He had his forked stick in his left hand—everyone knows that left-handers make the best diviners. That stick, folks said, had come all the way from Europe, but seeing as how it is plain hickory which is plenty enough around here, I had my doubts. Not that I cared where it came from, so long as it worked.

Lauren came up to my side then, which surprised me. She wasn't much for strangers, and seeing that long skinny form of Herman's should have put her off. But when he smiled at her, showing his dark, toothless gums, she broke into a grin herself.

He stretched out his hand and gathered Lauren's in it. He tipped her palm up and traced the lines inside. Her hand looked so white and small in his old, spotted one that her skin glowed pale blue, like August sky.

Course right then, I didn't know what I was seeing. Just that minute I was looking at an old man shake hands with a little girl.

The rest of the afternoon, I watched Herman walk along

the mountain. As I grated pumpkin for pie, I could see his shadow weaving with the branches of trees that ran along the edges of the land. I stirred the mixture, adding molasses and ginger while watching his long-legged gait as he stepped around the meadows where the farm buildings stood. While I rolled piecrust, he wandered around the fruit trees and through the cranberry thickets, going from the top of the mountain and then down the small ridge, where we grazed the cow and kept the mule when it was warm enough. In all that time I never saw the dousing rod swerve in his hand, the stick as straight in its course as a plow in flat, dry land.

At sunset, he knocked. I'd finished the pies and had supper ready. When I opened the door, I could see by his face that he had found nothing.

"Well," I said. "Eat."

I knew Herman was embarrassed, so I didn't say any more. I called Lauren to the table and she pulled the block of wood she used for a stool next to him and sat down.

"Well, if we can't dig a new one, we'll just have to clean the one we've got." I was trying to keep cheerful, on her account. Scared me, thinking about leaving the farm. I knew that without this place it was likely that we would be thrown apart. Alvin would have every right to take his daughter away—to the cities where there was work, or to Union, out in the western plains. No place for me but back in Mama's house where I would suffer the tongues of women telling my sorry story all over again.

I could see her in my mind's eye, the woman Alvin would find. She had dark hair and a silver tongue. She would be Lauren's mama, and Lauren would find a voice for her.

This last thought was so hurtful that I felt like crying, right there at the table, and would have, too, except for the company sitting at it. "That cow's gonna drop her calf any day now," I said. If I could keep talking, I wouldn't have to think about the way things stood. Didn't matter that I was chatting to two people who wouldn't answer. Herman never even looked up from his plate. That man ate like a hired hand. I'd fixed plenty—green beans and celery from my own garden. Pork from our pigs. All this food I'd grown around us. Come next harvest there would be nothing but dry land. I pushed my own plate away, uneaten.

Herman scraped the last of the pie from his plate with his finger and then stood up. He nodded to me and then reached for his hat and the divining stick he'd placed in the corner by the door. In a blink, Lauren was up, too, plucking his sleeve and pointing to the rod. He took her hands in his and slowly ran his fingers over her palm. Then he handed her the stick.

She skipped out of the house, waving the stick before her. Herman and I followed her into the dusk where the early stars and a near-full moon threw cast-iron shadows onto the land. We watched as Lauren began to move about the farm in the dim light.

"What's going on?"

Alvin's voice in all that silence was so sudden that I jumped.

"She's pretending to be Herman," I told him. I tried to keep my voice light, glad she was walking towards us now. She was such a little thing and the mountain seemed so large in the darkness. I could hear animals prowling in the trees just below the house.

"He find anything?" Alvin asked.

"No." I thought I saw a flash of blue about her, but it might have been a cloud freeing the light of the moon. The stick wobbled in her hands beside the dirty well.

"There's water here," she said, tiptoeing on her small bare feet and peering down into the depths.

At first, so amazed by her voice, I paid no heed to her words. I ran over to her and put my arms around her, hugging her as close as I could. "Lauren," I said, laughing. "You can talk!"

"The water, Mama," she said. Her voice rose as clear and delicate as the sound of Kettle Creek.

"Honey, it don't matter none about the water," I told her, for I no longer cared about the well. Lauren could speak. She had called me Mama.

She slipped from my grasp and ran over to Alvin. "Daddy," she said. "Daddy, drink." Her voice was low for a child—more musical than any's I had ever heard.

"Listen to my baby!" Alvin said, picking her up and tossing her into the air. Normally she loved this, but she shimmied down and planted herself in front of him.

"Drink!" she ordered him.

Alvin looked at me and I shrugged, unsure. Lauren had gone for the bucket and was holding it before him. "Please, Daddy," she said, her voice cracking a little, as though she was about to cry. "Drink." We waited as he dropped the bucket down and brought it up again. I could hear the water splashing around, echoing off the stones. He drank right from his hand, his face grimacing in expectation. But then the water reached his tongue and he cupped his hand and drank more.

"It's clean."

"I don't believe it." I pushed him out of the way and scooped up my own share. The water was cold and clear and so sweet that I wanted nothing more than to drink and drink of that water until I'd had my fill.

Herman's gnarled old hand reached into the bucket as well. When he had drunk, his face broke into a grin so broad that his eyes disappeared. He nodded.

"Here," Lauren said, holding the stick up, behind Herman's back. "Thank you."

"He can't hear you," I reminded her.

She looked searchingly into his face, then motioned with her hands for Herman to bend down. When he did, she reached her hands into the bucket and touched each of his ears.

"Stop that now," I scolded.

At that minute a flock of wild turkeys came running across the meadow. You could see their shadowed forms, huddled together, their necks jerking back and forth. Their calls filled the air with sound.

Herman went still. Then, slowly, he seemed to unfold, lifting his head, straightening his body until he stood tall. He turned until he could see the turkeys with his own eyes, just as he had heard them with his own ears.

For all I was watching it happen, I couldn't make my mind believe what my eyes had seen. The big tom turkey let out his great roar, and Herman reached and touched his ears, still wet from the well water.

When the turkeys had passed, he grabbed Lauren to him and kissed her hard on both cheeks. Her eyes went wide, for Lauren wasn't used to anyone kissing her much but Alvin and me. She was holding the stick again, clutched so tightly I could see the muscles of her hand.

When he put her down, she came and hid behind my skirts. Her whole body trembled and when I tried to get her to speak again, she shook her head. When Alvin saw this he ran after Herman, who on his long legs was heading swiftly down the mountain, his head moving left then right to take everything in.

"Wait," Alvin called out, and Herman turned around. Then he put up his hand and Alvin stopped. "Where are you going?" Alvin yelled.

Herman still said nothing, but put a finger to his lips. Then he pointed to Lauren and touched his lips again, as though sealing them.

"He won't tell," I said, as though Alvin couldn't understand. Already Herman was halfway down the mountain, disappearing into the trees.

I turned from him, desperate now to comfort Lauren. "Are you all right, honey?" I asked her. I ran my hands over her, from the top of her head to the tips of her toes. She felt solid and warm.

"Yes, Mama." Her eyelids were drooping and she leaned against me.

"We'd better get you to bed," I told her, comforted, strangely, by the ordinary everydayness of the words.

"Can I sleep with my stick?" she asked, and I said that she might. Seemed a foolish thing to deny a child when so much was going on around her. She was wilting when we reached her room and didn't even bother to undress. Alvin came in, bringing a bowl of heated water, and she let me wash her face and hands. I tucked her in and Alvin kissed her after me, as though this were any other night. Doing things the way we had always done seemed the most important thing in the world to me.

When she was settled, I still couldn't stand the thought of leaving her. "What is it, Mama?" she asked, her voice sleepy.

Let her sleep, I told myself, fussing with the quilt. "What happened out there?" I finally asked.

"The well was bad," Lauren said.

"Not about the well, about Herman."

"He wanted to hear," Lauren said, the words fading. "So I helped him."

"But how did you know?" I pressed on.

This time she said nothing and I could hear the rush of her breath. Only by putting my knuckles into my mouth and biting down could I stop myself from asking again, louder this time. Keep myself from reaching out and shaking her awake, demanding that this little child tell me what I saw.

·   ·   ·

I came out into the great room where Alvin was sitting at the table. He'd built a fire in the stove and the air was hot and dry. "She asleep?" When I nodded, he leaned forward. "She say anything?"

I shook my head and went into the kitchen, pouring coffee for myself and fixing him a plate of food. Felt good to have something in my hands, and I took plenty of time to do it.

Back at the table, Alvin pushed beans on his plate and crumbled the piecrust with his fork. I held my hands around the cup, so tired that I could hardly lift it to my mouth.

"What are we—" I started to say, but Alvin cut me off.

"Not yet, Elizabeth."

Despite the fire and the coffee, my hands couldn't seem to warm. I began to gather up the dishes and heat water for their wash. I filled the big kettle on the back of the stove. I kept seeing Lauren in her bed, so small and all alone. "I'm going to check on her," I said.

Alvin rose and followed me. Lauren's skin glowed in the candlelight, her golden hair damp against her face. Her mouth was open a little, and she had made a fist with one hand tucked under her chin. She looked like any little six-year-old girl I'd ever seen.

I reached out and as gently as I could, touched Alvin's arm. "Did Ivy have any," I hesitated, "gifts?" It was the first time I had said her name to him.

The muscles beneath his shirt tightened. "You'd know as much as I would," he said. I brushed the hair back from Lauren's eyes, pulled the covers up to her chin. I was reaching for the candle when Alvin gripped my hand.

"This ever happen before?"

"No."

"You swear?"

I tried to free my hand. "I've never lied to you."

"Maybe this is some fluke—something that won't happen again."

Part of me knew what he was getting at—the fear I sensed in him I felt as well. But part of me was still in the wonder of that moment, when Herman had been made whole. "We saw it happen, Alvin."

"Who knows what we saw?" He let go of my hand only to grasp me by the shoulders, facing me to him. "You want folks calling her some sort of freak? A faith healer? Her a Denniker?" He let me go then, and I fell onto the bed. Lauren stirred but didn't wake.

"Hush." Lauren's face was flushed red, though her brow was cool. I wanted to pick her up and hold her to me, as if she were a baby again.

Alvin began to pace back and forth, throwing shadows against the wall. "Don't you know what could happen? You've been to revivals—it's like the circus has come to town and our daughter is the main draw!"

"Alvin, please." Lauren was tossing now, and I knew she would wake. I didn't want her to see her father this way. I didn't want her to see the fear in me.

As we left the room, I faced the fact that Alvin was a fearful man. I recalled the many times I'd been shown this—the afternoon when he told Mama of Ivy's indifference to him. Him shooting at me during the influenza, and keeping Ivy up here alone. The way he hadn't been man enough to see his wife properly buried in the earth. No matter how much he loved her, I could not rely upon him to do right by his daughter, and this was not a pleasant feeling on top of all the other things swirling through my mind.

"Don't say anything to nobody," Alvin said, and behind the harsh words I could hear him begging. "Ain't your right. She's my daughter. All I got left."

Only the knowledge that Lauren was in the next room kept me from throwing something at him. Couldn't he see that I loved her, too?

"You want people coming here? You want people traipsing in and out of your house? Touching her?"

"Be still!" I said, wishing I knew what to say, what to think, what to do. In the light of the fire, he looked like the wild man I'd once imagined him to be, and something stirred within me, some hopeful, desperate little flame of what had once been a roaring fire. More than anything, I wanted him to put his arms around me, to hold me against him. To offer me even a moment of comfort which I could turn around and give back to him tenfold. If only he would do that, I thought, I would believe that we were strong enough to keep our daughter safe.

His footsteps were loud across the floor as he stomped out, leaving the door open. From down on the mountain, I could hear the Methodist church bell ringing, meaning that Mama was calling for me to help her with a birthing. But for the first time, I didn't go—thinking of Lauren in her bed, Alvin turning from me. She'll come looking for me, I thought. She'll know when I don't come that something's amiss.

I went in again and checked on Lauren, who felt too warm now, so I loosened the blankets around her chin. Then I went back into the kitchen, steamy with boiling water, and began to clean. I started with the dishes and then scrubbed the shelves and the floor until I'd used every drop of hot water. Anything to keep away memories of Herman, visions of Lauren, thoughts of Mama going forth into the night.

Alvin came back, smelling like barn dust and cigarette smoke. He stood in the doorway of the kitchen a moment, before heading for the room we shared.

Not until the kitchen was clean did I go in to him—not

until I'd worked myself into a sweat did I slip beside him in our bed. I tried to speak but he kissed me so hard I could taste the salt of blood.

"Be still," he muttered between kissing me. "For God's sake, just be still."

The Bible tells us that two will become one flesh, cleaving unto one another. We cleaved that night but never became more than two separate people singing together, each in his own key.

When Alvin at last slept, I got up and went to check on Lauren. She was fevered now, and I moistened a cloth and wiped her face. I held her up so she would take a little water, which she swallowed well enough, but her body stayed limp.

When I'd made her comfortable, I went back into the big room, cool now that the fire had burned itself out. I stoked the flames and threw on another log, picking up my knitting.

Mama will be here soon, I told myself as I worked. She'll know what to do.

TEN

When Mama didn't come the next day, or the next, I knew she must have had terrible trouble at the birthing. I tried to think who the woman might have been, but I was so caught up with my own fears that I had little time to spare on another's concerns.

Lauren's slight fever had broken by morning, but she continued to sleep on. She didn't seem ill, just tired, but Alvin and me worried nearly to pieces and we wouldn't leave her side.

Only once did I mention this might be on account of Herman, but Alvin wouldn't hear of it. "Summer complaint," he insisted. "She has it every year."

When she woke on the afternoon of the second day, Alvin and I pretended that nothing was wrong, that nothing had happened. I know Alvin was proud when she called him Daddy, and with her words, I felt truly like her mama. Together, he and I took pleasure in her voice.

Alvin went out of his way to be charming, as I fixed Lauren the custard she had asked for. He told us funny stories, including Lauren's favorite where he'd been chased by a bull as a young boy. Lauren always laughed when he got to the part where the bull's horn caught his pant leg as he dove over the fence, sending him tumbling.

That night at dinner, we were more like our old selves—the people we had been before Herman's visit. "Play your fiddle, Daddy," Lauren asked, and his eyes lit in delight. Together she and I sang as Alvin played her favorite, "Barbry Allen." He played "In the Pines" for me. I liked singing a song to Lauren that had been sung to me by Mama and to her by Granny going back as long as any of us could remember. The words in these songs are gruesome enough—ghosts of women loving unfaithful men, and hardly a body survives through the last verse—but we laughed as we sang them, paying less attention to the melancholy of the tune than our pleasure in the familiar.

Mama came in on us then, just as Alvin was tuning up to play "False Knight in the Road." Seeing her in the doorway, the weariness of the past few days came back to me in a rush.

"What's wrong?" she asked, her eyes going from one of us to the next. When she saw Lauren pale and bundled, she went over to her and knelt down. "Are you all right, sweetling?" She took Lauren's wrist in one of her hands, checking to make sure the heartbeat was strong and sure.

"I'm better now, Nana."

Mama's eyes went wide. "Listen to you," she said.

"Mama says I've been asleep days, but I'm fine now. I ate custard."

"Good girl." Mama reached over and kissed her head, but she was watching me as she did so.

"Do you remember Herman?" I asked Lauren.

She nodded. "He came to find a new well."

Alvin clenched and unclenched his hands so hard his knuckles popped.

"Do you remember the night he was here? How you played with the stick?"

"I didn't mean to break it," Lauren said, sheepish. We'd found it in her bed that morning, broken into pieces. I didn't care about the stick.

"Do you remember touching Herman's ears? With the water?"

Lauren nodded again, but her lower lip trembled. "His ears were broken."

"And you fixed them."

"That's enough," Alvin said.

"How did you fix his ears, Lauren?" I asked.

"I don't know."

"Try," I pressed.

"I don't know?" as if she hoped this was the right answer.

"When you touched Herman's ears, you fixed them. How did you do that?"

Lauren said nothing. I asked her again. Would have asked over and over if Alvin hadn't stood up. "Don't matter none," he said, stepping between us.

Mama had been watching all of this, saying nothing. She looked worried, and I could tell that she was wrung out from the birthing. "Did it go well?" I asked, mouthing the words to her but not wanting Lauren to hear, as I knew what the answer was likely to be.

Mama shook her head, and then rubbed her eyes.

"You been sick, too?" Lauren asked, studying her.

"No, honey, but someone else was."

"Did they get better? Like me?"

Another woman might have lied. I would have. Mama only shook her head, and I knew then she'd lost the woman. The worst kind of hurt a midwife can bear. I wondered who it was, but this was not the time to ask.

"Time for you to go to bed," I said then, standing.

"But, Mama . . ."

"No buts," Alvin said, in that too-hearty voice a man uses around a child. "Come with me. I'll tell you a story."

Lauren sighed like a martyr but went. Mama watched them go to Lauren's room, her eyebrows so high I couldn't help but say, "You look like that, your face might freeze."

"Don't be silly."

"I have coffee on, 'less you'd prefer tea."

"Anything with some bite in it? I'd rather not drink coffee."

"I have some sarsaparilla root I picked last week." And she nodded, looking a little cheered.

When I came out of the kitchen, Mama was sitting at the table. She had taken her hair out of the knot and braided it so it ran down her back. I put a plate of cornbread in front of her, and pushed the butter and jam over. "When's the last time you ate?" I asked her.

Mama sipped the tea, then practically fell upon the food. "I don't know," she mumbled, licking the jam from her fingertip. "It's all been a blur."

"Who did you lose?" I asked, keeping my voice low. I could hear Alvin telling the story of when the circus train had come through Philippi. Lauren was begging now to go to the circus, and hearing her made me smile.

"Janie Settle. You know she was Hazel Blicker's eldest girl? I was there when she was born." Mama finished the last of the cornbread and drained her cup of tea, though I knew it was still scalding hot. I poured her some more, glad to see some color back in her face.

"What happened?"

Mama shook her head. "Afterbirth came out in pieces. Baby'd been in there too long, but nothing I gave her seemed to bring it out." She sighed and rubbed her eyes again. "You know, there are moments where I think I'm cursed, when it comes to that family." I rolled my eyes and waved this away. "So what's happening with Lauren?" she asked. "She been sick this whole time?"

Alvin came out then, closing the door to Lauren's room.

"You want some coffee?"

"You sit, I'll get it." He came back into the room with the pot, pouring a little into my cup. "You tell her yet?"

I was surprised. "I didn't know you wanted me to tell."

He shrugged. "I figured you would anyway."

"Tell me what?" Mama asked.

I blushed a little at his words. I wondered what he thought Mama and I talked about, if he thought we talked mostly about him. Well, we had, sometimes, but not as often as he seemed to think. I realized, too, that I didn't often sit and talk to him and Mama at the same table—one or the other, yes, but almost never all of us together.

"Tell me what?" Mama repeated.

So I told her. She knew about the well, so I started with Herman coming and how Lauren had made the water clean. Then I told her about Lauren touching Herman's ears, and how he'd heard the turkey call. "It was wonderful, watching him hear. I'd never thought about a miracle like that—how it felt to be right there, in it, so to speak. It was scary, too. I mean, I'd always known Herman one way, and then he was another."

Mama had sat back in her chair and didn't move until I'd finished my story. "Is that all?"

"All?" I sat there, stunned. I don't know what reaction I might have been expecting, but this wasn't it. "Isn't that enough?"

Mama frowned. "Was this before or after Lauren got sick?"

"Before," Alvin spoke up before I could. "I'm thinking,

though Elizabeth don't agree, that the sickness might have been part of it. Like the miracle took something out of her body. Made her weak."

Mama looked at him as though he'd lost his mind. Then she crossed her arms and shook her head back and forth.

"What?" I asked, my voice sharp.

"Listen to the two of you. Just listen to what you're saying." She spoke to us as if we were simpletons.

"We're telling you what happened." I was angry now. "You weren't there. You don't know."

"Let's see what you've told me." Mama held out her hand, fingers spread, and began to count off. "You have a well that went bad then ran fresh, even though you don't know what set it off in the first place. You have a man who is known in these parts for being queer as a broody-hen, who doesn't hear, doesn't speak, and yet when he raises his head and smiles, you get all silly about it."

I couldn't fathom that Mama didn't believe me. She was acting towards me as she did the girls who came to her, prattling on like ninnies.

"You have a little girl, who probably drank some of the water when it was off, and took a turn in her stomach. Now she's doing better. Where is the miracle in all this?"

"What about her talking?" Alvin demanded. "The way she talks in complete sentences."

"Alvin." Mama said his name as though he were too foolish to know which way the sun rose. "Such things aren't unusual— I know of several other late talkers, complete sentences and all. Look, Lauren lost Ivy at the time most little girls are learning to speak. Not surprising at all that she held back a little, until she felt ready. We all knew she'd speak in her own time."

I hadn't been sure of any such thing. "What about the

night she was born? You remember what you called her then? You said she was a miracle baby."

Mama's mouth fell open a little. "I didn't mean it literally. Surely, honey, you didn't think I meant this?"

"That's what I told Elizabeth, here." Alvin was happy now, as he hadn't been since that night. This is what he wants to hear, I thought. What he'd been waiting for me to say all along, only I couldn't, because I was there and I know what I saw.

"When's the last time either of you had a good night's sleep?" Mama was all business now.

I shook my head. "This isn't about sleep."

"Elizabeth's been up since Lauren was fevered," Alvin offered. Even he looked at me with some concern. "She never left her side."

"Of course she wouldn't."

I wasn't sure how I should feel—here was Mama and Alvin both caring for me but not listening to a word I said. "You just won't believe in miracles," I finally burst out. "They aren't scientific enough for you."

"You're wrong," Mama said softly. "I do believe in miracles. I see them happen every time a baby's born."

"You know that ain't what I mean."

"Come here," she said then, rising. "Both of you." Alvin jumped up, as though she had pulled him on a string, but I sat stubbornly in the chair. She went over to Lauren's door and opened it. "Come and look. Tell me if she isn't a miracle, just her own self."

And of course at that I had to go, because what mother can't look down at her child and not wonder about her very being?

But I didn't change my mind. I was there, as I had been at her birth. I knew. Lauren was a miracle baby. She was destined for great things. That I didn't know what those things were—

that I feared for her in a way I had never feared for another child—didn't change that fact in any way.

I kept these thoughts to myself. Alvin never talked about that night. And Lauren, though she sometimes played with the sticks, wouldn't speak of it. For a long time after that, I was the one Mama watched, as though I'd been ill instead of Lauren.

There were no more miracles. Herman Teller died peacefully in his sleep, not two weeks after his healing. When I asked his sister if he'd said anything, she acted, as was understandable, as if I'd taken leave of my senses.

Days turned into weeks and then months and then years. Coal was booming, and shantytowns filled the Tygart River Valley. Families who had lived in the mountains for generations were coming down into the towns, taken by the idea of ready cash and a board-and-batten home. People flocked to where there were picture shows, bowling alleys, and fancy clothes sitting in the company store windows, waiting to be bought with the fancy written scrip that coal operators said was as good as money. I've walked many mountain ridges where small settlements once flourished—cabins, a store, perhaps a church. Now, other than a clump of blue iris blooming where a doorway once stood, there is nothing left.

The folks coming from the ridges of West Virginia were outnumbered by the tide of outlanders coming from overseas. Made keeping track of family histories a tricky business. The black ledgers in Mama's house were soon filled with names I'd never known before—Franz, Katinka, Golda. Mama and I would work for petty cash or goods. A coal doctor's birthing might dock ten or twenty dollars from the miner's earnings—which rarely amounted to enough to pay their debts in full.

Alvin and I remained on Denniker's Mountain. Watching Lauren trip off to school, cleaning her skinned knees, celebrating as she lost her baby teeth—soon these day-to-day events filled my thoughts. The visions of carnivals and revival tents began to fade instead of catching me by the throat. We celebrated her birthdays, one after the other. Alvin would play his fiddle and we would sing until we'd grow giddy beneath the light of the Harvest moon.

ELEVEN

In early June of 1929 I delivered Jacob Teller. He was a big healthy baby, taking after his daddy's people. The delivery was long, and I was tired, so I stopped at Mama's for a cup of coffee on my way home.

"You plan to be making any calls tonight?" I asked, sitting down with her a moment.

"Pearl Conley is due soon, but I doubt she'll hurry along."

"You mind if I send Lauren down to spend the night?"

"Not at all," Mama said. "Everything all right?"

"Fine. I'll just sign the birthing books, then." I tried to keep from rubbing my eyes. I'd washed up after the birth, but I was looking forward to a good scrub.

"You sit," Mama said. "I'll get the books."

I took the ink-pen, made a neat line, and wrote the names down, how much tea Marie had drunk and what kind. Never crossed my mind that after Jacob's name, I would never write another.

•   •   •

Alvin was crossing Kettle Creek just as I came upon it. He looked tired and cross, but he smiled when he saw me and I felt a flicker of what I'd used to feel when I was young and would watch for him in these same woods. I thought of the little cups of bark he'd made me, which were now under our bed. "Lauren packed a dinner bucket that weighs more than my gear," he said.

I felt light with happiness. "You coming back tonight?"

He squinted in the bright morning sun. "You need me to?"

"I'd just like to know." I tried not to sound defensive. "There are just some things we need to work out."

"Like what?"

"Nothing big. Just some things." I didn't want to tell him my news here in the open. I wanted us to be alone, in our own house.

I knew he was curious now. "I'll be home." Surely when he had heard what I had to say, he would see we had been given a chance to start over.

I was getting a baby.

For the past three months, I had kept this knowledge to myself. I had wanted to be sure. I kept track of the monthlies, my hopes rising as each moon passed without them. I noted with joy the tiredness, the achings in my bosom, the fiery heat coming from my belly, then racing through my arms and legs and face. In the ten years I'd been with Alvin, there'd never been even a ghost of a baby before. I'd been fearful of even bringing the subject up, superstitious that if I did I would forever keep one from coming.

Mama would brush such thoughts aside, I knew. Nor would she appreciate the things I'd tried. The herbals she would understand, but never the great heaping spoonfuls of

Argo Starch, which Granny claimed helped a baby to stick inside of you. Thirty years old was late to be coming to motherhood for the first time, but come I had. I was a woman, with a woman's body. I was made to be having babies, not just delivering them.

As I felt the baby grow inside of me so did my craving to talk. For years I had listened to other women, and now I was the one who had something to say. I wanted to proclaim it from the mountain—to run down the streets of Philippi shouting my good news.

I couldn't wait to tell Mama. I couldn't believe she hadn't guessed. But the news belonged to Alvin first.

The mountain was quiet when I reached the house. The kitchen was a mess—the peach pie I'd made before I left for the Teller house had a large wedge cut from it. Cooked egg clung to the edges of the skillet. But there was coffee on the stove, fresh and hot. I was just about to call for Lauren when I heard her step.

"Hi, Mama." She was holding a basket of eggs and smelled like the barn. "You look tired." She frowned. "Did it go well?" The familiar question assured me that Lauren was truly my daughter, as I had been Mama's and Mama had been Granny's. Even my own baby couldn't mean more to me than Ivy's girl.

"A big boy." I settled back into the rocking chair by the stove. "But you're right, I am tired." The rhythm soothed me. "I stopped at Mama's on the way up. Told her if it was all right with you, that you could spend the night."

Lauren's face broke into the crooked grin I knew so well. "I can stay with Nana?" she asked. "I'll take her some eggs." Lauren took half from the basket and put them into the blue crockery bowl she was partial to these days.

I loved her so much, this child. Her thoughtfulness, her inner strength, which I'd come to rely on in these past years. She seemed to sense when I needed her, which was more often than I cared to admit. I could hardly bear to let her go.

All that late morning and afternoon I rested in our bed, waiting for Alvin. I spread out across the sheets and sank deep into the feathery pillows. Through the down I listened to the sounds of the morning—birdcall, wind, the gentle movements of our stock, our pigs, our chickens. I wondered what my baby was hearing. Was growing in my body like being wrapped in feathers?

Near suppertime I rose and fixed potatoes and onions in a bit of bacon grease. I breathed in the smoke, proud of my belly for holding fast. I longed for fresh foods, for things not fried, canned, or salted. Soon there would be ripe tomatoes, cucumbers, and squash.

Dusk had fallen in the valley when Alvin came home. He was caked in coal soot, streaky with black sweat, and he held his hand uneasily against his body. "I hurt my finger," he said, cussing. He shook it before me, and drops of blood speckled the wood floor. "Right at quitting time, so I figured you'd do better than some coal doctor."

The finger was split wide by a blast, packed with dust, and crusted with small round rocks. Twice normal size, all hot and purple-colored. I could smell the coal sulfur, and a hint of iron from the blood. I poured hot water into a bucket and started cleaning the wound. Lye burned the tender skin, and I needed all my strength to keep Alvin from pulling away.

"This is god-awful looking," I told him. He squawked a bit when the hot needle pierced his flesh.

"Seen worse," he said, man-like. He tried not to watch what I was doing, but his eyes kept straying to my lap all the same. I wondered what he would think, when he knew what was resting beneath my skin. "Gunter Teller had his whole hand blown off last fall."

"Gunter hasn't the sense God gave a squirrel," I told him. Gunter had once come courting me, but he had awful hands. Not that I put any stock in that tale about a man's hands being the size of a man's parts, but Gunter's hands were as small and pointed as an oak leaf.

"You sure you know what you're doing?" Alvin asked, wiggling his hand against my belly. I knew the baby couldn't feel it, but I did and the heat started again. "This ain't like your normal piece of work."

I bent my head to hide my smile. I wondered if he had ever looked at a woman's private parts before plunging in. After a hard birthing the pieces of skin are so loose that they flap in the wind like a flag on Election Day. This was easy work by contrast.

"Lauren about?"

"Down at Mama's tonight." I reached for my scissors.

"Just as well, her not seeing this."

"You hungry?" I stood up and raked the coals under the stove lid and began turning over the juicy pieces of potato. The scent of onions filled the room.

"I can't eat," Alvin complained, still clutching his wounded hand. Made me think of him holding a baby. I knew that this was the time.

"I'm getting a baby," I told him. If my words had been solid they would have bounced against the log walls that had seen so many Denniker births.

Alvin just stared.

"Did you hear me?" Perhaps it would be a son—the beginning of a new generation here on Denniker's Mountain.

"Get shed of it," he said roughly.

"What?"

"Thought maybe you had enough of babies, birthing them all, and that was all right with me."

Crazy talk, I told myself. "Alvin." I was practically begging. "Alvin, this is our baby. I wanted this baby so badly that I couldn't tell you. I prayed for this baby."

His face was ugly. "I ain't raising no bastard on my mountain."

Shocked, I could hardly speak. "This is no bastard. . . ."

"You see a ring on your finger? You're carrying a bastard, same as your mama did you."

I placed my hand over my belly. "You can think what you like," I told him, hoping I sounded braver than I felt. My mouth had gone dry, but I made myself stare him down.

Alvin's eyes narrowed. "You want to make a baby?" he said, more a growl than a voice. He grabbed my arm and pulled me into the bedroom. I could feel the cloth of my dress rip when we fell onto the bed.

"Stop!" I yelled, but he pulled harder until the dress shredded.

"Be still." His hand pushed up under my petticoat, beneath my torn skirt, reaching for my warmth. I lay there still, as he fumbled one-handed with the buttons on his pants until they fell into a dusty, stinking heap. My legs were soon covered with coal soot, and I could feel the ooze of his smashed finger seeping through the bandage, where his hand gripped my arm.

But he'd barely begun before he stopped. When I reached my fingers down on him he was as limp and moist as the baby must be inside my belly.

"God damn it," he muttered into my shoulder.

"Hush," I said. He was Lauren's father, after all. Father of my baby, too. With such bounty I could give him a little comfort. I arched my body against his gently, working his until he began to stir. I sensed his fear and then his relief when we were done.

The next morning, I slipped out before first light and headed down to Mama's. When Alvin woke, he would head down to the mine and we would have until nightfall before words needed to be said.

Mama was up, heating the great irons on the stove she had brought outside. Lauren was working in the garden. I stopped to watch her as she stripped the plants of pests and dropped them one by one into a cloth bag filled with marjoram and chamomile.

"Your hair looks pretty," I called. She reached up to touch the heavy curls that fell around her shoulders, her face flushing with pleasure. I was glad that Mama had taken the time with Lauren's normally stick-straight hair, and I made a note to do so myself. She was growing up.

"How do," Mama said, lifting the great iron and running it over a skirt spread out on the table. She had sprinkled the damp clothes with vanilla oil, and I recalled my childhood dresses smelling just that way.

"I've got something to tell you."

"Hope it's good news." She put the iron back on the stove. "Can never hear too much of that."

"I'm getting a baby," I said, and the pride in my voice rang out so strong I could almost taste it.

"What?" Mama rushed over and hugged me hard. "How far along are you? Shame on me for not seeing it! I suppose shoe-makers' wives go barefoot, and midwives' daughters go unno-ticed." She stood in front of me, her eyes moving up and down my body in a way I had only seen her do to other women.

"I'm four months, best I can tell. No monthlies since spring."

"Have you felt the quickening yet?" Mama asked. She was

leading me to the house. The hot irons on the stove, the basket of laundry all forgotten in her excitement.

"Not yet," I told her. "Makes me think it's closer to three and a half months, maybe. There's some fluttering, but nothing I can tell for sure."

Mama nodded, and I could almost see her mind working behind her bright red hair. She was beautiful still. She would be a woman any grandchild would be proud to know. As much as I wanted a son for Alvin, I thought of what a daughter might mean, not only to me, but also Mama. I could see her now, with Mama's hair. She had my chin and long fingers. Granny's mouth, round as a button. A girl that looked like all of us together, but was still her own self.

"The placenta may be sitting against the front, which is what happened with me. You may not feel the quickening for some time, this being your first." Mama was talking firm now. I sat in a chair on the front porch, like any other woman come to Mama for advice.

"Feels a little funny." I was surprised by how shy I felt. "Sitting here and talking about this with you."

"Any cramping?" she asked. She must have known that I would have answered these questions for myself, but I didn't resent the process. There was something wonderful in being the person who was asked instead of the one doing the asking.

"None."

"Sickness? Stomach trouble?"

"No," I said, shaking my head.

"Let me get you a cup of parsley tea."

I made a face, but one Mama had expected. Isn't a woman alive that claims to like the taste of parsley tea, or if she does, then she's so gone from her own mind that she needs more than tea to calm her nerves. I was so delighted to make that face, to sit here with my mama on her porch, telling the story of my baby.

"So, you gonna let me hear him?"

"Of course," Mama said. She jumped up and went into the house. When she had been training with Doc Woodley, he gave her a stethoscope. It was Mama's most prized possession, and by putting it to a woman's stomach, she could generally hear the rushing beat of the baby's heart, which sounded for all the world like a train going by. More than one woman had refused to believe there was a baby inside of her until Mama had placed the black-tipped metal spokes in their ears and let them hear for their own selves.

She came out carrying the stethoscope and a bottle of alcohol. She wiped the silver disk until it shone and then placed it on my belly. I felt her fingers, warm and dry on my bare skin. They moved in a calm, knowing fashion, first left, then right, then up, then down.

I watched her face for the moment of joy when she'd found my baby. Instead, she frowned.

The stethoscope fell from her hands and she began prodding me, closing her eyes and letting her fingers tell her what she needed to know. Her hand moved to my breast, pinching the nipple, then patting it with my shirtwaist to check for dampness, for milk.

I was dry. Lots of women are dry yet, I told myself. But I felt a deep drumming of fear. "What is it?"

"Tell me again what you're feeling," Mama ordered.

I told her of the changes, the heat, the sudden rushes of emotion. The great waves of weariness, the thickening of my body. My menses had never been strong, and perhaps that's why I hadn't realized when it gradually lessened before it stopped altogether.

"I'm only thirty." I choked on the words.

"Your aunt Elmira was thirty-two." This was all Mama needed to say. Aunt Elmira was known for one thing—her body aging before its time. Her husband had left her, finding instead a woman that would bear him children.

"But I'm only thirty," I repeated, filled now only with despair.

For the next few days, I stayed down with Mama. I slept in my own bed. Mama brought out one of Granny's prettiest quilts, a pink one embroidered with all the signs of the zodiac. I had forgotten how beautifully Granny could embroider, and when I felt tears coming I would instead follow the tiny stitches until my eyes were dry.

Mama had walked Lauren home, telling her that I wasn't feeling well. Lauren didn't want to go—I could hear her fussing—and not until I told her myself I would be all right did she agree. I don't know what Mama said when she saw Alvin, but I knew that she would never go telling on a woman to a man, and certainly not on her own daughter.

I insisted that Mama go out on calls, for there were still babies coming, even if mine never would. I rested in the moments of quiet, where only the splash of the creek and the settling of the house could be heard. Since I was a girl of Lauren's age, I had marked the passage of time with my own body. Now I needed to learn a new way.

While she was gone, I would prowl through the house. I ran my finger over the name Rachel Barlow Denniker, carved on the cedar chest in Mama's room. Rachel was my great-great-grandmother. Daughter by marriage to Caesar himself. I pulled the black ledgers out of the chest and read them, as I had when I was a little girl.

There were no names of barren women.

I read through Mama's Bible, the one where my own birth had been recorded, and searched through the family tree, looking for women like me. After I went through all the names at the front, I began in Genesis, going through the scriptures page by page. Most women had heeded God's commandment to go forth and multiply, taming the earth with their sons. Some had paid a great price for it—Hagar, who was cast out, and Sarah, who did the casting. Tamar, who claimed her child in righteousness and was made clean.

I found a few barren women, though most were never named. I danced with Miriam, joyous as she shook her tambourine. I cheered the sweet triumph of the daughters of Zelophehad, of the family of Joseph, who were said to speak rightly before Moses himself.

For all the talk of women bearing children in pain, I now believe that the real curse God handed Eve as she left the garden was the change of life. The change is something a woman can fight against with all her might only to grow older from the battle. Only way to beat the change is by dying, and that isn't much of a plan.

"You know I went through the change early," Mama said to me one day. "I wasn't yet forty-five."

I did know this. I did. But there is a marked difference between a woman of forty-five and a woman of barely thirty. And there were lots of folks like Mrs. Fester Teller, over across the Tygart, who brought her last babies into the world as she bounced her grandbabies on her knee.

"The change is aptly named," I said to Mama one evening, when we were sitting together on the porch. The air was filled with late spring sound—as though every bird and animal and insect was finding its mate, forging its own place in the rolling sphere of life and death. "One day you're one woman, and then you wake up and you're another. Now I'm the end of my line."

Mama reached out her hand and gripped mine hard. I realized that it meant the end to her line, too. I was failing her as much as I was myself.

. . .

Lauren visited every day, her face puckered with worry. She would bring me things from home—clean stockings, my sewing basket, my knitting.

"Let's go sit outside," I told her one afternoon. We went out to the steps of the back stoop, where we could watch the birds splash about Kettle Creek.

"Do you remember the time Herman came to dig the well?"

Lauren stared at a ruffled grouse as it scuttled off into the brush. Two chickadees flew in. A woodpecker.

"I need to know."

She shook her head. "I don't want to talk about it."

"Lauren, please." For that moment I had forgotten I was the mother and she just a child. "Please help me with this."

Her mouth trembled. "Nana won't even tell me what was ailing you," she said.

"You're a smart girl. You've heard Nana and I talking enough to know that I'll never have a baby. You healed Herman. Why not me?"

"If Nana was ill, or needed something, wouldn't you do whatever it took to make it happen?"

"Of course . . ."

"Then why do you think I wouldn't do the same for you?" Tears spilled from her eyes.

I was shamed. "No, no, no." I put my arms around her. "I was wrong to ask. I'm sorry. Forgive me."

Lauren's tense body slowly eased against mine. "It's not wrong to ask. I just don't know how to answer. I don't know what happened that night—I don't know. . . ."

"Hush." I rocked her back and forth.

"Please come home, Mama."

I wiped away her tears with my thumb, smudging her cheek. "I will," I promised. "Tomorrow. First thing."

•   •   •

Alone again in Mama's house, I opened my medical bag. There were the spools of thread, the blue flannel packet of needles, the birthing clothes I'd spent so much of my life ironing. The bottles of herbals clinked as I moved my hand around them. I put my face in the bag and breathed deep. My whole life seemed scented by these things.

I closed the bag and set it on the table, then waited for Mama to come home.

Mama was humming when she came in, holding a clump of tiger lilies which grew thick along the banks of the Philippi road. When she saw the bag, I could tell that she thought someone had come for us. "Who is it?" she asked.

I wished that I could find the words that would ease us both through this, but if such a speech existed, I never found it. "I'm not midwifing any more. I can't do it—holding those babies in my hands when I know I'll never hold my own."

Mama said nothing.

"It's on account of the red book."

"The red book?"

"The babies we've killed. Me and you, and Granny and Great-granny, and who knows who else." I could see those babies, all tiny hands and mouths. "When I was staying with Granny, before she died, she told me that it wasn't right to kill them, but it wasn't wrong neither. But I believe we are wrong. We're all wrong."

"The women need us," Mama started to say.

"Maybe I don't care enough. Or maybe I can't care at all anymore. I never really wanted to be a midwife, but I did it because I had to. Maybe this is God's way of punishing me for doing what I knew was wrong."

"Elizabeth." Mama reached out and held me tight. "You're being silly, honey. God doesn't work like that."

"You don't know," I told her. "How could you when you don't even believe in God?"

"I understand."

But I knew that she couldn't. I knew also that I'd now failed her in every way—taken from her a daughter same as I'd taken her hopes for a grandchild. My going through the change had aged her, too. I loved her so fiercely then, even in my own hurt. I tried to claw my way through my pain—to reach her and ease her suffering—but the journey was too great and I was too weak.

"I'm sorry, Mama."

"Hush now."

Early the next morning, I climbed the mountain for home. I wondered if Alvin had thought about me at all in the days that I'd been gone. Without the baby, there would never be more between us than there was right now, and I knew just how little that was.

I was surprised to find him awake, as it was barely daybreak, but he was sitting there at the table, sharpening the kitchen knives and farm tools with a whetstone. Winter work this was, to keep a body busy while waiting for spring.

He looked up at me, and I saw him search my face, my body. "There won't be any baby," I told him.

He nodded. "That's all right, then."

I was so angry I felt like sweeping the table clear. He thought I'd been gone to knock the baby loose, half formed though it might have been. This is what men thought that midwives did.

As much as I had once loved this man, I would have loved his baby more. That Alvin thought my love for him greater than my want for a child was strange knowledge, but like a spring tonic, I swallowed it and was made stronger.

Seeing my fury, Alvin rose quickly and put his hands on my shoulders. "Are you all right?" he asked. I could see the bloody seam on his hand where I had stitched it closed.

"How is it?" I asked.

"It's fine now."

"So I guess we're both fine now."

Alvin dropped his hands, knowing things were wrong, but not sure what to do. "I'm glad you're home," he said finally.

"Well, you need a woman about." The house was a mess and smelled stale.

"I'll tell you one thing. I may have come here on my own free will, but I don't have to stay."

He stood a minute, then looked away.

"Now I best be waking Lauren," I said. "I promised her I'd be home before she woke and I want her to know I'm here."

TWELVE

The winter of 1930 was cold and snowy. The pinch of hunger we would all come to know had started to take root. Coal camps shut down as quickly as they had risen up. Folks who had fled the mountains for the cities began to trickle back, family by family. Anyone who had a few planted acres and a barn with a cow or pig was doing better than most.

For us, the snow presented a problem I hadn't planned on—Lauren's schooling. I doubt that more than half of Kettle Valley's students made it to the schoolhouse those early months of the year, but Lauren simply wouldn't stay home. She'd made her first close friend.

"Stop at Mama's on the way down and warm up," I ordered. She had pleaded all morning to go, though the icy wind rattled the house like teeth. "And if it looks bad this afternoon, just stay there and I'll come for you." I gave her extra mittens and a scarf nearly as wide as it was long.

"Dana's bringing in her butterfly collection for me to see." She went on and on.

I wasn't thrilled that out of all the little girls in Kettle Valley, this was the one Lauren had chosen to take up with. Not that

Dana Small wasn't a nice enough child—she minded her manners and was clean—but her daddy was one of those end-of-times preachers over at Cupper's Mill. Even Granny, for all her religious ways, had thought those Cupper's Mill folks too righteous for their own good.

I could not deny her Dana, though. Even after these many years, I missed the friendship I'd had with Ivy—hard to forget someone who was happier just because I came into the room. Mama still spoke of the times she and Hazel Blicker had shared, and still fussed over the family Hazel had borne. Besides, though I no longer fretted over Lauren's every move, I wasn't completely sure that what had happened with Herman wouldn't again. A special friendship with a girl her age—something so ordinary— seemed a blessing.

On the days where the snow clouds hovered or the mountain was shrouded in fog, Lauren knew to stay down at Mama's after school. More than once I came down in the driving snow, just to enjoy their company in Mama's snug little house. Days sometimes went by before the weather broke and we could go back up the mountain to Alvin. Lauren would miss him something fierce, and even I felt out of sorts, not being in my own house with all my things. So as soon as we could, we always headed home. Twas on a day in late January, the year still dark and new, that we reached the house and heard voices coming from inside.

"Who is it?" Lauren asked me. Since I'd stopped midwifing last summer, we had few visitors.

"We'll soon see, won't we?"

Inside, the house was bright with shining lamps. Both candles were lit above the mantel board. A man was warming his hands before the stove.

"Union!" I called. I'd never thought to see him again, after that night so long ago when Ivy had been with us.

He leapt forward in great steps, hugging me so tight that I

was breathless. "Here you are!" He put me down and spun Lauren around. "You were just a baby when I saw you last."

"I'm thirteen now," Lauren said, seeming a little dazed, her hair in her eyes.

"Well, you're a fine-looking lass," Union said. "And you got your mama's eyes." He tipped her chin back and winked.

"Thank you," she said, her voice cool, but I saw her touch the skin where his hand had been.

"And my Elizabeth." He hugged me again. "So you're Alvin's woman now." He held me a few feet from him, his face mock-sad, like a clown's. "About broke my heart, hearing that. Not fair that my baby brother should have had you and that Ivy woman both." He kissed me suddenly, on the mouth.

"How you been, Union?" I said, my mouth burning, as though it too remembered the kiss we once had shared. How hopeful I had been then, just barely a woman, hungering for a man who was more myth to me than mortal. I tried to recall the last time someone had touched me, looked at me with such feeling.

"Fine and dandy." But he had aged in the years since I'd seen him. His hair was still thick, but it was streaked now with gray. His eyes and mouth had deep lines about them, laugh lines some, but also the look of a man who had lived a hard life. I felt a pang of sadness before I pushed such thoughts from me.

"You all eat yet?" I asked, looking for the first time at Alvin. He shook his head, and I could see the anger in his eyes. Jealousy, too, which made me glad. I turned back to Union. "I got some sausage I can fry up, and some buckwheat batter left from breakfast."

"That sounds fine." He sat down at the table, drumming on it with his hands. "Can't recall the last time I had me some cakes."

"We ain't bedded down your horse," Alvin pointed out.

Union waved him away. "You take care of that, won't you?"

So much the older brother. I smiled a little, seeing Alvin's face flush red.

"What brings you home?" I stirred my buckwheat batter while the skillet heated.

"I'm looking for a wife." He winked again at Lauren, who was sitting next to him. "I've traveled this whole blasted land and ain't seen any to suit me, so I thought I'd best come home and find one here."

"A wife?" I was so surprised by the news that I just stood there, spoon still in my hand.

"I'm getting old, Elizabeth. A man starts to feel his age, wants a son to tell his secrets to." He crooked an eyebrow at Lauren. "Or a daughter. I'd like a daughter if she was as pretty as you."

Lauren blushed.

"I thought you loved Katie Barnes," I said.

"Ain't she dead?"

"Yes . . ."

"Well, then, she won't do at all, will she? Got to at least have a woman with some life in her, don't I?" He leaned over to Lauren and said in a loud whisper, "Course I might not have hurried back here if I'd have known that your daddy got to Elizabeth here first."

A rush of want started in my belly and ran up my body so strong I put my hand down on the stove to steady myself. "Ow." Union jumped up, taking my hand in his, running his fingers over the burn.

Alvin came in from the barn then, his eyes flickering back and forth from Union to me. I freed my hand and put dinner on the table. While we ate, Union told us about his travels—tall tales, no doubt, seeing as how he always had the last word and final laugh. They were big, bold stories, full of life—panning for gold in Alaska, living in a house made of sod in Kansas "which was colder in winter than Alaska any day." Arizona had been his favorite—he'd worked on a Mexican's ranch. When he broke into a smattering of Spanish, Lauren made him repeat dozens of words until she could say them, too.

Was after nine when I hustled Lauren off to bed. She didn't want to leave—Union was telling her a story about fighting some tramps in a boxcar—and only by promising that he would finish in the morning did she agree to go. I didn't blame her. I could have sat there all night, listening, waiting for those moments when Union would let his eyes run over me, and the longing rose up again.

Soon after midnight, Union grew weary. Alvin seemed ready to outsit us all, and I knew that neither of them was going to move until I'd done so myself. "I think I'll turn in," I announced. I opened a chest and took out a pile of quilts for Union's bed. "These ought to keep you warm enough. There's a featherbed too, to make the floor softer."

"Lord, honey, it ain't like I've had something this fine to sleep in for some time."

"Good night, Union," I said.

Alvin followed me to our bed, and we coupled together like two dogs in heat, scrapping and fighting. His hands gripped my arms so tight I knew there would be bruises, and I welcomed them, as I did the salty taste of his blood when I bit the flesh of his shoulder. We rolled on the bed until the covers were off and our naked bodies felt the chill of the night air. We moved against each other, lifting ourselves higher and higher, daring the other to follow. We never said a word, letting our bodies speak for us. Once I cried out, but he clamped his hand over my mouth.

I was furious with myself for having spent my youth and fertile years pining for a man who didn't care if I lived or died. Furious that he had taken my hand the day of Ivy's funeral and brought me to his home. That he was a man whom I had once loved so much, only to find so wanting. A man who had taught me what it meant to love, but had given me none.

Alvin fought me, too—punishing me for lapping up Union's silver tongue, for not being Ivy. What distant kindnesses he had shown me over the years fell away from him that night, leaving only the bitterness and loss that he had always felt in my presence but kept in check, wanting a mother for his daughter, a woman in his house.

Wasn't any way that Union could have been in that house and not heard Alvin and me. We were past caring as the bed banged against the walls and the slats of the floor creaked and shook beneath us. Not even the thought of Lauren was enough to keep us still.

When we came out into the main room the next morning, Union had already started the fire. He was sitting in a chair, his head bent and heavy-looking. He seemed to have aged overnight. His eyes were rimmed with tiredness, bloodshot and thick around the edges. The longing I'd felt for him last night was gone, leaving only a faint memory of a man who, like me, knew what he had lost. I wished that we'd been able to give each other what we needed, all those years ago. I might have made you happy, I thought. Maybe I would have been happy, too.

"You don't look well," Alvin said. He did not trouble to keep the satisfaction from his voice.

"I forget," Union said, a small smile on his face, "just how tiring traveling is."

At breakfast, there was chatter-talk. Lauren would ask about the West and Union would answer her. He finished the story about the fight in the boxcar, but the thrill was gone in the pale light of day. We all sat side by side, as chaste and respectful as Adam and Eve before the fall. I had taken my fill of the Denniker men.

Two weeks later Union ran over to Maryland to marry a

woman who was half his age. Wasn't long before they were headed for California, off on some adventure. Hannah had been Lauren's schoolteacher, a woman known for reading poetry. "A romantic streak," folks said, not surprised when they heard the news. Her hair and eyes were light in color, and her nose was very thin, but more than one person commented on how much we looked alike.

We lost a lot of folk that winter, what with the cold. Hard to get a doctor in, when the roads are frozen over. More than one poor soul died drunk or foolish, but some were truly tragic. Young Mrs. John Teller had bundled her baby so closely to her body that when she arrived to her mother's, the baby had smothered at her breast.

Some just weren't strong enough to withstand the chill, including Mrs. Doc. We'd been hearing off and on all year that she was doing poorly, so when Mama told me that she'd passed on, I wasn't too surprised. What did catch me was how upset the news made Mama.

"You're taking this kind of hard," I said. She was pacing back and forth, rubbing her thin arms.

Mama took out a handkerchief and put it to her mouth. "Goldie Woodley was a good woman," she said. "Doc should be thankful he had her."

That might be, but this seemed a little strange—Mama mourning Doc's wife. Of course Mama wasn't her strong self right now—hadn't been all winter. The cold couldn't be good for the cough that she'd had since October.

"You taking care of yourself?" I asked. I didn't know how old Goldie Woodley was, but I figured she hadn't been much older than Mama.

Mama nodded, but didn't stop pacing. "Goldie was real nice to me, when I went to study with Doc. Took me into her own home and treated me like a sister. Even your granny commented on it. She said a woman that could have another in her kitchen was worth more than her weight in gold."

"How's Doc taking it?"

"He's grieving. She's been sick a long time, so he was prepared."

"And he never loved her."

"Oh, he did."

I shrugged. I knew that you could reach a point where the man next to you found comfort only in your warmth and cared little for the person who offered it. I wondered if Mrs. Doc hadn't lain there at night beside Doc and realized that she'd gone and made him up in her own mind.

"There are many different ways to love," Mama said. "I'd be foolish to sit here and say that Doc never loved her."

"But he loved you."

"He loved me in a different way." Mama tucked the handkerchief up her sleeve. The pies she had baked that morning were packed in a large basket to take to Philippi. At the door was a satchel that I figured held some extra clothes.

"Your uncle Donald should be here any minute," she said, standing by the window and looking out. "He's just bought a new automobile and is dying to show it off." Maybe this explained her jitters, as rides in automobiles were a rare treat then, even to go to a funeral.

"I'll be at your uncle's until the service. It's on Saturday. You think you'll be there?"

"Most likely." I saw her relax a little. "They set a time yet?"

"Probably noon."

Just then I heard the car horn and I could see the dark shape of the automobile through the branches of the trees, square and sudden, as though someone had built a little house right there on the road.

Mama stooped and picked up the satchel, but she wasn't

steady on her feet. Her hands, clenching the baskets, looked small and wrinkled, like old-lady hands, for all she was barely two years past fifty. The sharp May wind blew in the open door.

"Let me help you," I said, and we walked out to the car together.

I came home to find Lauren sitting in a chair, her colt-like legs and narrow feet tangled in the rungs. She'd braided her hair, pulling it away from her face. She was crying.

"Don't tell me you're all shook up about Mrs. Doc, too." I grabbed a quilt from a chair and wrapped it around her.

"What?" Lauren's face was shiny with tears, but under the damp her skin shone with youth. I could hardly believe she would turn fourteen this fall.

"Doc Woodley's wife died yesterday." I went over to the water bucket and poured a cup. Every midwife knows that the best way to stop a woman from giving way to tears is to fill her up again.

I realized, holding that cup in my hand, that I had just thought of Lauren as a woman. "Here, honey." I pulled out a chair and sat down across from her. Seems like most of my life had been spent sitting in that chair or in its twin, down at Mama's. "Something happen at school?" I thought maybe she and Dana Small had had a falling-out.

Lauren's mouth trembled. "I've done something awful."

"Couldn't be all that terrible." But even as I spoke, I was running through my mind's eye all the trouble that a young woman could get into when the zest of springtime raced about her body.

"I healed a baby," Lauren whispered.

"What?"

"I healed a baby over at Cupper's Mill."

"What were you doing over at Cupper's Mill?" But part of

me knew—had been waiting for years to hear her tell me
something like this. "You were supposed to be at school."

She looked shamed. "I know. I should have . . . I mean, I
never meant to do this." She spoke so earnest-like that I nodded without thinking. "Dana's daddy was having this revival,
and it was all she could talk about. She made it sound so exciting that I just had to go and see for my own self."

I knew the pull of a revival, having sneaked away from the
Homestead once or twice to go myself. The service was a stew
of high emotions—the crowding of bodies, the reaching of
hands, the lifting of voices, all wanting wanting wanting.

Those same hands would now reach for her. I could see
them, plain as day, angry when my little girl couldn't give
them what they wanted.

I ran my hands through my hair. "Tell me what happened."

Lauren frowned. "Wasn't at all what I thought. The church was
crowded with people. The singing was cheerful enough, and
people said that they were happy, but they weren't, not deep
down. They were all there so they could ask for something."

Yes, I thought. Yes.

"Folks were crying by the end of it, and even after we were
outside I couldn't seem to get the sound of them out of my
head. Then I saw this woman there, on the steps. You couldn't
tell by looking, but she was crying inside. I could hear her. At
first I thought it was the baby crying, but it wasn't."

A baby, I thought. Of course it would be a baby.

"I could feel how pained she was, so I walked over to her.
All this pain coming off of her just washed over me—like I
was standing in the creek. And I reached out to touch her but
I couldn't." Her lip trembled again. "I couldn't bring myself
to touch her. I was afraid I would reach out and there would
just be, well . . . nothing."

I didn't understand. "I thought you said you healed a baby."

Lauren seemed to be seeing the woman all over again, as though she were next to the table where we sat. I could feel the hairs on my neck and arms prickle.

" 'What do you want?' the woman screamed at me. By then I could tell that she was holding a blue-baby—hardly growed at all."

My body recoiled. I'd seen only two blue-babies born in my lifetime, and they were awful to see. Doc Woodley told me once that they had holes in their hearts, but knowing what was killing them didn't mean there was a thing you could do.

"I told her I wanted to help and she said that there wasn't nothing that I could do. That God was killing her son and that she hated Him for it. And I knew then that I could reach out my hand and the baby would be better. I knew this." She'd stopped crying. "We tussled a bit, and she called me all sorts of names. Folks ran over, thinking we were fighting, because I kept reaching for the baby and she kept pulling him away. I had to touch him, Mama. I couldn't turn away once I knew that I could heal him."

"Of course you couldn't." No one knew better than I how Lauren would take a burden upon herself, if she thought it would ease another.

"I . . . I touched the baby, putting my hand on his little chest. I don't know what happened next."

I reached out to take her hands in mine.

"He was pink, Mama. Bright pink and fidgeting and kicking."

"Doesn't sound so terrible, helping someone like that." I wanted to make her feel better, but I knew that things now were forever changed.

"The healing part wasn't," she said. "Only afterwards, people were crowding around me—people started touching me— Dana's daddy started praying over me and I ran home, cutting

across John Teller's field and through the orchard so they
wouldn't find me. Some folks tried to follow me, thinking that
I could heal them too."

"Could you?"

"No." She looked stricken. "It isn't like that at all."

"What *is* it like?" If I knew perhaps I could prepare us all
for what would come.

"I don't know exactly," Lauren said, her words coming
slowly. "Like I said about the woman—there's all this noise
coming from them that keeps getting louder and louder, until
there's nothing else but that sound."

"Are you scared?" I recalled such a feeling myself, when a
baby was coming out too fast, too hard, splitting wide open
the woman that contained him. The roaring that came from
inside my own head.

"No," Lauren answered. "It's just strange." She pulled a leg
up on the chair and rested her chin on her knee. "What's scary
is knowing it's going to hurt. When you touch the person."

"Hurt? Hurt how?"

"I don't know." She thought a minute. "You remember last
fall, when I cut my thumb with the kitchen shears? How I
didn't think it hurt until I looked down and saw all the blood
pouring out? It's like that—doesn't hurt much when it hap-
pens, but thinking about it seems to hurt just awful."

I was at a loss, completely furious. How dare God give my
daughter such a gift to make her bleed.

Lauren must have seen this on my face because she tried to
reassure me. "When I'm done, though, it's a good feeling.
After all the noise, the world is quiet."

"Do you hear this crying often?"

"There's always someone crying, Mama," she said. "You
know this."

I did, and felt helpless against such endless sound. "Then
how do you know what to do?"

"I don't know. But if the crying gets too loud, I just know I have to stop it."

I wanted to know if Herman had cried, and how a little girl of six had known what to do. But just then I heard something outside the door and I jumped up to answer it. The yard was empty, and there was only the wind banging the gate against the barn.

"Wait here," I told her, and went to secure the lock. I knew that crowds would be here soon. Perhaps were already coming.

She was still sitting there when I closed our door behind me. I went and put my hands on her small shoulders. "Finish your tea," I told her.

"What's going to happen, Mama?" she asked.

I kissed the top of her head. "I don't know," I told her. "But I'm right here. Nothing will happen without it going through me."

THIRTEEN

I sent Lauren to Mama, down in Philippi. "If you go by the west side and through the orchard, you should be all right." I was folding her clothes into a carpetbag. She started gathering up her little treasures—a poetry book she'd won for reciting the most lines of Shakespeare, a photo of Mama and me, standing out by Kettle Creek. She understood what I couldn't bring myself to say—that she might not be coming back.

As I watched her go, she seemed so small, loaded down by the bag and the lantern she carried. If I could not take these most basic of burdens from her, how did I think I could protect her from the world? I knew we had to get her away from here—she was too easy to find—but what then? If she was called to heal then people would always be looking for her, asking for more. I couldn't help but picture a life of dreary boardinghouses where we feared knocks at the door, meeting strangers in the streets.

Even now, the story of Lauren at Cupper's Mill was being told, spreading from one hollow to the next. Soon the story would be twisted into tales that had nothing to do with

Lauren as a girl, but as some sort of freak, just as Alvin had foretold. She would be shunned as much as sought.

I can admit now that I was afraid—afraid of leaving home. I pictured the Great Plains, too flat and empty to offer a place to hide. I saw mountains with snow, chilling us even in summer.

I dreaded telling Alvin, for my own qualms would pale beside his own. I knew he loved his daughter, but I also knew, more than anyone, how much he loved his mountain. Blood might be thicker than water, but the earth would drink them both and not bother to note a difference. Would Alvin go? For more than ten years of my life I'd lived with this man, and I simply didn't know.

The knock at the door was loud, or so it seemed amid such quiet. My first thought was that something had happened to Lauren, so I ran to open the door.

There was a woman there, a stranger in a dress sewn with coarse black thread. She wasn't getting a baby, but I could tell by looking at her hips and breasts that she had borne several. She was hurting bad—I guessed that her womb had never shrunk, and now pressed heavy inside her belly. That such a woman would come to me now was like some horrible joke.

"I don't do midwifery anymore. I can't help you."

"I'm searching for Lauren Denniker."

Of course she was. For every woman who had sought Mama and me out over the years, there would be a hundred looking for my daughter. Who were we, with our herbals and skills, when a woman could be made well at the touch of a hand?

"I heard she can heal. I live over at Cupper's Mill. Folks are saying she healed a baby."

"I don't know what you're talking about." I tried to shut the door but she pushed forward. "Lauren isn't here."

"Where is she?" The woman placed her hands just above

her privates. Her face twitched with pain, and I hated seeing
that.

"She's in Kentucky." Kentucky seemed far enough away.
Doc Woodley's wife had come from there, which was probably
why I'd thought of it. "We sent her on the train."

The woman bowed her head and began to walk away, her
body stooped. Soon she would be as bent as an old woman.

"Wait!" I called. "I can't heal you, but let me see if I can find
something." I went over to the herbal chest—I hadn't opened
it since last summer. I poked my fingers into the drawers, testing the dried leaves and twigs for potency. The sweet joe-pye
seemed strong enough, and I folded the last of it into a square
of white paper. Then I emptied a cupful of ox balm into a jar
and added a bit of snakeroot.

I found the woman leaning against the rough walls of the
cabin and I handed her the paper and the jar. "Take these in
tonics, as often and as strong as you can stand without heav-
ing. If you start to vomit, you're taking too much. Some folks
do better if they drink it cold."

The woman took the herbals and tried to put some coins
into my hand.

"No." I pulled away. "I told you, I don't do this anymore."

"I won't take them," she said, "if I can't pay." I nodded then,
tired suddenly by this whole exchange. I had helped her, yes,
but I'd denied her Lauren. By protecting my daughter, I added
to the misery of the world, and that was an ugly thought to
have to bear.

Alvin came home while I was in the midst of packing.
"Where's Lauren?" He washed the coal dust from his hands in
the bucket we kept just inside the door.

I tried to read his face to see if he knew about Cupper's Mill. I didn't know if I would feel better knowing that he did or if I wanted to be the one to tell him.

"She isn't here."

He looked about the room, seeing the clutter spread everywhere. When he said nothing, I knew he'd heard. "I'm gonna ask you one more time. Where's Lauren?"

I tried to prepare myself for his anger.

Alvin banged his fist against the table so hard the lamplight flickered. "Where is my goddamned daughter?"

"A place where she won't hear you speak like that," I shot back.

"I'm her father, and I'll speak any way I want," Alvin yelled. "They're talking about her on the streets! She had no right to go and do something like that—"

"This isn't about rights."

"What? She couldn't help it? Like she's some sort of animal? I didn't raise her to be a sideshow act."

"You didn't raise her at all!"

"My daughter is a freak!"

With that, I became so angry that I could hardly see. I had to grip the table in front of me else the fury would knock me down. "You called her that once, when she was a little girl, and I should have struck you then for saying such a thing. But I didn't, because I couldn't half take all that was going on then. I was scared for her, too, you know. And I loved you too much. . . ."

Alvin dropped into a chair. "You don't think much of me, do you, Elizabeth?"

I shrugged.

"You know, when you first came here, I could hardly stand to look at you." He ran his hand over his eyes. "What did I know about raising a little girl? I couldn't even stand to be in the room alone with myself, and here I was, my wife dead, my daughter mute."

"What does this matter?"

Alvin paid me no mind. "Then you came. You, who loved me so much you seemed to burn with it." He looked more rueful than angry. "You'd been after me for so many years that I told myself that bedding you wasn't wrong." This might have been truth, but I didn't like hearing it spoken so bluntly. "I told myself that I could give you that, for coming up here and taking care of Lauren. For taking care of me."

"You needed more care than I could give you," I muttered.

"So did you."

Then came another knock at the door. We'd been so caught up in our past that for a moment I'd forgotten what was to come.

Alvin flung the door wide. There was a man this time, older, but not yet aged. His skin was yellowed, thick as parchment paper, and his eyes were rheumy. I figured he was dying of liver-growth. "I'm looking for the girl."

"She ain't here," Alvin said.

"Where is she?"

"Pittsburgh," Alvin said. "We've sent her away."

I watched the man's face fall and he shambled off. Alvin slammed the door, his hands trembling when he pushed them against the wood.

"Why Pittsburgh?"

"We have family in Pittsburgh, and I was thinking of going there."

I shook my head. "I'm taking her to Union." The thought had only come to me right then, but I knew it was a good one. If we were to wander, surely Union would show us how.

"California?" For the first time, he seemed to pay attention to the carpetbag on the table. "Where are my things?"

"I didn't know if you were coming with us or not."

Instead of yelling, his whole body seemed to wilt. "My fault," he said, muttering this several times. "My own damn fault."

"So you coming or not?" I hoped I didn't sound as ungracious as I felt. Having him would be a help, but I knew he couldn't make me feel any less alone.

"Yes," Alvin said. "I'm coming."

I went back into our room then, throwing his clothing into a sheet. I could tie the ends up like a hobo's pack. He followed me.

"Do we have to leave? Can't we protect her here?"

"She's a Denniker. We live on Denniker's Mountain. They'll be coming for her and we can't keep them all away." I held a stocking in my hand, wondering where the other was.

"So we'll come back after this brouhaha dies down, then?" He sounded hopeful.

I took a deep breath. "She has to heal people. If you'd heard her talk, you'd know this. Same as you were born to be Alvin Denniker, she has to do what she's been called to do. Best I can do is try and protect her from giving too much."

"Oh, God," he said, pressing his hands upon his head. "She down at your mama's?"

"No, Mama's at Uncle Donald's. In town. I sent her there." He looked at me, and for the first time I saw he approved. I'd done better than he'd expected.

"I watched her leave," he told me. I was glad then, proud of him even, for coming to me instead of following her. He had protected his daughter from his own fear. I took this as a sign that he would protect her always, out there in the world.

Between the two of us we were soon packed. I added a few little things—Ivy's linen square of embroidery, faded now after all these years. Some good soap. A tin cup Lauren had drunk from since she was a baby. When Alvin wasn't watching, I wept over these things, wiping my tears on them as though I could charm them to keep us safe.

I had to leave so much behind—Mama's candlesticks, Lauren's favorite willowware plate. Alvin's birch cups would never survive such a rough journey, and only by putting them aside could I ever hope to see them again.

As soon as dawn broke, Alvin and I loaded our few bags on the horse and climbed onto its back. We took what little cash money I'd earned the last year I'd midwifed, then on our way to Philippi, we stopped at Mama's and I took the can of money she kept behind a loose brick in the fireplace. I dipped my fingers in Kettle Creek, listening as hard as I could. I wanted to carry the sound in my ears forever.

The sun was up by the time we made our way through town, but no one was about yet. Uncle Donald's house was dark, though we'd no more than curbed the horse before Mama was out on the porch with Lauren. She had her arm around the girl's shoulders. I knew that Mama was ready for whatever was to come, even if I was not.

"We took the money," I told her. "Under the brick." I held up the metal can.

Mama nodded. "I have some more here, from Donald. You'll need whatever we can spare."

"Thank you," Alvin said.

"There's a hamper of food in the kitchen," she said. "I'll just be a minute."

"I'll come help you," Alvin said, and I knew by the way Mama hesitated that she was surprised.

I turned to Lauren. "Are you all right?" I put my hand to her forehead, checking for fever.

"I'm fine. But I need to tell you something," she whispered. "You can't come with me, Mama. You have to stay."

"What?"

Lauren looked towards the door, where Mama and Alvin had gone. Her face flooded with color, and I worried again that she would take sick. "We should wait inside too," I started to say, but she took a deep breath and cut me off.

"Trust me, Mama. You need to be here."

"But, Lauren . . ."

"Please, Mama. Trust me."

"I can't . . ." All that night I'd fought with myself, drawing on anger and fear and my own will to keep moving. Now all of that vanished, leaving me weak and small. Was Lauren saying that I couldn't protect her? Did she not want me with her?

"This isn't the end, Mama. I'll come back. But right now you need to stay."

I'd raised this girl from babyhood. I'd given her what was best in me, and she'd always given back that and more. I'd spoken proudly that I'd deny her nothing. Sending her away without me was the hardest thing I've ever done. "You promise to come back?"

She hugged me. "Yes." I held her tight, breathing in the very smell of her. I can't do this, I thought. I hugged her again twice more, as though I could seal the feeling of her body into my own. Then I stepped back and let her go.

"I'll be staying here," I said, my voice clear and steady.

Alvin's eyes darkened, but Lauren put her hand on his arm. Then I looked at Mama, and instead of seeing disappointment I saw only relief. Gratitude. I began to understand. Lauren knew something about Mama—she knew that Mama needed me more than she. My being a daughter was more important to her than needing a mother. This I could accept.

About a month later I had a package in the mail. Bunch of papers, so official looking that I caught my breath, sure they were bad news. But they were only deeds—all marked with Alvin's X, signing Denniker's Mountain over to me. Perhaps Lauren had put the idea in his head. But as this is my last memory of Alvin Denniker, I like to think that he made the decision all on his own, for me.

FOURTEEN

After Mrs. Doc's funeral, I stayed with Mama for a week. Between fussing over her and worrying about Lauren and Alvin, I must admit I did neither of us any good. I woke every time Mama coughed or sighed, and then sat up the rest of the night imagining people crowding about Lauren, and Alvin unable to keep her safe. "Go home," Mama finally told me, when I hadn't slept in three days. "You'll do better in your own bed."

So, alone, I went up the mountain. My bag seemed light and small after Alvin and I had carried so much down. There wasn't a scrap of food in the place, and I spent the next two weeks restocking and cleaning. I scrubbed the wood of the walls and floor, trying to get the stench of coal oil from the place, the grit out between the boards.

The house felt bare, not only of Alvin and Lauren but also of all of their little bits and pieces, like Alvin's pipe and Lauren's tortoiseshell mirror. The cupboards seemed huge with only my things in them. I put Lauren's blue willowware plate on the mantel board where I could see it.

Being outside was easier than in. I planted a large garden,

more than Mama and I could ever eat. For the money they could bring, I sold off most of the chickens and the horse and the cow. Out in the barn I found Alvin's old boot—the one he'd lost last winter, worrying us for days.

A mountain in springtime roars with wind. At night, the wind dies down to a low-pitched sigh, not unlike the sound of a woman crying.

By the summer of 1930, Kettle Valley had grown quiet without the scream of the shift whistles and the tumbling of the coal tipple. Creeks began to run clear and grasses sprouted between railroad ties. I learned that many of the heartiest and most potent herbs thrived amidst this industrial decay.

I would never be the birthing midwife that Mama was—just seeing a baby on the street was hard for me to bear—but that didn't mean I had no use. Granny's teachings were still with me. I took to wandering throughout the valley, finding choice spots for shepherd's purse, ox balm, and spikeweed. When folks came looking for Lauren, they, at least, did not go away empty.

The best days were when Lauren's postcards arrived, one about every three weeks. Each showed a photograph of a town they had stayed in—London, Kentucky, Kansas City, Missouri. "Salt Lake City is a stark and beautiful place," she wrote. "Daddy and I went to the lake, where they say no person can ever drown. They sell little vials of the water, and I bought one for you and Nana, because I knew you would both want to see for your own selves."

I would take these cards down to Mama's and we would both exclaim over them, rubbing the pencil marks into smudges. Perhaps because I was watching her so closely, I remember how well and strong Mama appeared that summer. Her cheeks were pink, her hair shiny with health. She never coughed now. I wondered if Lauren hadn't been wrong.

We visited together every few days. Often I joined Mama on her front porch after a day walking the mountain ridges. We talked about Lauren, our gardens, herbs. "You recommend something for pleurisy?" Mama asked one night. She'd made wintergreen tea, which we drank cold to ward off the heat. "I've tried snakeroot and the last of the wild jessamine."

I thought a minute. "I have some button-willow bark. Who you treating?"

"Earl Wilson, over on Little Laurel. He's set on marrying Anne Tucker this fall, and those Wilsons never did have the health God gave a flea."

"Hard to believe she's marrying. I remember the day she was born. And you can tell just by looking how fond he is of her."

Mama put her hand on mine. "You sound too old, Elizabeth. A woman of thirty-two ought not to talk that way."

I felt quick tears in my eyes, but I held them back. I swallowed the rest of my tea until I had my voice under control. "Speaking of courting, I notice Doc's been coming around here quite a bit."

Mama actually blushed. "We're thinking about marrying. End of summer maybe, though no matter when we do folks will say it's too soon. There's his children to think about, and you."

"I'd be glad to see you married," I told her, and I would be.

"I don't like the idea of you up on the mountain all alone."

I didn't like that idea, either, but I pushed it from me. "Well, I happen to like the notion of you being mistress of that grand house over in Philippi. Folks say the front porch is the largest in the county." Mama turned to me with such hope in her eyes that I leaned over to embrace her. That I could give her my blessing filled me with gratitude, and a taste of happiness that I savor to this day.

Both Mama and Doc did their best to include me. Doc even offered me a place in his home. They were both so kind that it was easy to put on a brave face all through the festivities and pretend I wasn't so empty inside that I wondered if I shouldn't ring like a bell.

Days now often found me sitting on the famous porch in Philippi instead of the little one by Kettle Creek. I liked watching the cars and people walking by. From time to time I stayed overnight, but even though there were only three of us in that old house, I felt crowded somehow. The town was too noisy at night. I always returned soon to the mountain.

Mama seemed happy, but more and more, folks in town were turning to Doc's sons for birthings. She was too far now from the coal camps that remained open, and she made fewer and fewer calls. "I'm becoming a lady of leisure," she joked once, but I could tell this bothered her.

Doc knew this too, and he did his best to keep her busy. He had a Hupmobile, a bulky box of a car with side curtains that snapped down. Mama was crazy about riding in it, and soon we were spending our days driving about the state, stopping when something caught our fancy. If I sat in the backseat as prim and proper as a maiden aunt, I enjoyed the ride just the same.

"A grown woman ought not to love gadding about so much," Mama said. This particular day we were in Fairmont, where the Normal School trained teachers. Doc had spent the afternoon talking with those who might come to Barbour County.

"You and me and a road before us—what is more thrilling than that?" Doc wiggled his bushy eyebrows over his glasses.

"Nothing," Mama said, and he took her hand. I turned my head and watched the houses flash by. Fairmont was full of stately ones, but I waved to a woman sweeping the porch of a cozy brown bungalow.

"There's a carnival ahead," Mama said.

Doc slowed the car. "You want to stop?" Then, as though he remembered I was there, he turned around. "It's up to you, Elizabeth."

Now, I'd been to plenty of carnivals over in Philippi, but who can resist one at dusk, when the lights are flashing in all their gaudy glory? Doc had already pulled over.

"That's a mighty tall Ferris wheel," I said, as we climbed out. The mountains weren't so close here, and the wheel looked huge against the darkening sky.

"No way I'm riding that." Mama crossed her arms.

"Come on, you chickens." Doc slipped his hand beneath her elbow. "What's the point of stopping if you won't even ride the Ferris wheel?" The seats of the giant wheel were big enough for two, and only two.

"I'd like a caramel apple," Mama said.

Doc rolled his eyes. "And you wonder why your teeth rot." The words didn't sound romantic not at all but there was something about his knowledge of her teeth that made me feel more lonely.

We walked under the shadow of the Ferris wheel, then over by the merry-go-round. People bustled about us—women with children and young men taking their girls out for a lark. Old men watched brazen young flappers strutting about with their short skirts and bobbed hair. There was even one wearing trousers.

Carnival clowns mingled with the crowd, some on one-wheel bicycles, some juggling. One was doing magic. Electric lights sparkled, spelling out FREAK SHOW in yellows and blues. I had once dreamed of Lauren trapped in such a place.

More than four weeks had gone by since her last postcard, longer than ever before.

Mama nudged me. "Remind you of anyone?" She pointed to a picture of a woman so fat her thighs looked like the round bodies of sows.

After a moment, I caught her joke. "Birdie Brown."

"Who's that?" Doc asked.

"Birdie lived up on Hudson's. She was a huge woman," Mama told him. "Was so large that no cabinetmaker dared build her coffin for fear of her busting free. So they up and buried her in a piano box."

"A piano box? Surely I would have heard of that."

"She never left home, after she got so big. She cooked every-thing with white sugar when the rest of us were making do with brown."

A clown bumped into my arm, and I stepped back. He fell in front of me, so gracefully that I knew it was a trick. When he stood, he juggled three bright blue balls, which he kept in the air even as he fell down again. "You might say ex-cuse me."

He started juggling the balls in one hand, lifting his other so that it hid his face. Slowly he dragged the hand down, his rubbery mouth now a bright red frown.

Mama clapped her hands. Doc tipped him a nickel. I rubbed my elbow, although it didn't hurt.

"Nothing makes an impression on you, Elizabeth," Mama chided me.

"Well, that might," I said, trying to make amends. Across from us was a man so thin that his eyes looked too round against his face. He held a torch in his hand, which he slowly lowered until it moved past his lips, entered his mouth, and plunged into his belly.

"How do you think he does that?" Mama asked. That was Mama, always needing to know.

"Maybe it burns him from the inside out."

"Don't know about you, but all this fire-eating makes me thirsty," said Doc, and we headed over to the food stand. He got his fizzy drink, and Mama her caramel apple. I had a cotton candy, which melted on my tongue.

"So are we going in?" Mama asked, peeking around the corners of the freak show's tent flap.

"I'll get the tickets." Doc walked over to the booth.

The tent air was thick and warm inside. I could feel people breathing on my neck. I was pushed along by folks around me, as though caught in a river current.

"Look at him," someone whispered behind me. "Him" was a man who walked on his hands as if they were his own two feet. He slowly dipped his legs until they came down over his shoulders and his toes brushed his chin.

"My stars," I heard a woman say. "He's gonna bust himself in half." Then he stretched himself long again, and the crowd surged past.

Next was a pig with five feet, an old, fat, and contented sow. Then came a cow with two heads—the second one shriveled and hanging like a trunk-shot squirrel from a man's belt. You could still see the half-open eyes, a nose, and a mouth with teeth.

"Now you know that ain't real," said a woman beside me. She was dressed in fancy clothes—a city woman.

"I delivered a cow with two heads," Mama told the woman, who now stared at us as though we were part of the show. "You remember that, Elizabeth? That cow of Jake Switzer's?"

"He's the sort of man who would have a cow with two heads," Doc muttered. I'd forgotten that Jake had once been sweet on Mama.

Next in line was the fat woman. Her legs swelled beneath her like she was sitting on a great white cloud of flesh, but it was her eyes that got me. They were blank and hateful, staring back at us while we gawked at her. "Let's move on," I said. I could see the end up ahead, a square of light.

We passed a dark-skinned man with a great horn poking through his nose and carvings all over his face. There was a woman with a beard longer than old Ebenezer Meroe's, who vowed not to cut his hair until the second coming. He died with it tucked both fore and aft into his trousers and God still taking his own sweet time.

We were almost to the doorway when I saw the jar.

Inside the jar was a baby. She was swimming in green liquid, like she'd been pickled. Couldn't have been more than the length of my hand, but her fingers and toes were perfect.

"Mama, look." I picked up the jar. My fingers, sticky with cotton candy, streaked sugar across the shiny glass.

"Hey, now!" someone shouted. Mama took my arm and tried to pull me along, but I wouldn't let the jar go.

"If Lauren were only here—she'd make her live."

"Can't be having this now," a man called out.

Then he grabbed me. I felt a push and fell outside the tent. I breathed in and out deeply. I heard Mama behind me, calling. I was shamed then for being such a fool. I picked up my skirts and ran.

When I stopped running, I looked up and saw him for the first time. Sounds silly, put like that, but that's the way it happened. He was standing by one of the ticket booths, surrounded by a pack of raggle-tag kids. The colored lights made his dark hair appear faintly green and made him seem longer and thinner than I was to come to know. He wasn't what anyone but his mother would call handsome, with a heavy brow and bumpy nose, but I liked his mouth, which grew ever more determined as he threw three balls into the air and tried to juggle them.

Several boys booed him.

He tried again, his face wrinkled with concentration. The balls soared into the air once, twice, but then they slipped through his fingers and fell to the ground.

The kids jeered. They were as poorly dressed as the hobo clowns that roamed the fair. Some of their faces, white with hunger, looked almost as made-up and unreal.

Wasn't until I looked at the man's hands that I saw the fingers—or didn't see, as the third finger on his right hand was gone. It was hard to stop looking once I saw it, but he had seen me, and my being there seemed to only make him clumsier. The balls fell into the dust.

"Loser," said a little girl.

I ran over to them. "That's about as rude as can be," I said.

"It's all right, ma'am," the man said. Another girl giggled.

"No, it ain't," I told him. "Not decent for them to be carrying on like that."

"It's on account of his finger," one of the little boys in the back called out. He was dressed in blue knickers and long socks. Town kid, no doubt, well fed and cocky.

"If your mama hadn't snipped your tongue free when you were born, you wouldn't be saying such nonsense." I waved my arms at them. "Now get off from here. Give the man some peace."

"Old bitch," one of them muttered, and I felt justified in giving him a good kick in his seat, tattered as it was.

The man was laughing. He had stopped throwing the balls and shook so hard that I felt my cheeks flame.

"That was beautiful. Absolutely beautiful." He wiped his eyes on his sleeve. "Are you a teacher or something?"

"No." I wasn't sure whether to take offense at the laughing. "I'm . . ." And then I didn't know what to say. I was struck by how little I had to say about myself. "I'm Elizabeth Whitely."

The man gave a slight bow. "Pleased to meet you, Miss

Whitely. I'm David Newland." I wondered if he would hold out his hand to me, the one missing the finger, and what it would feel like. But he didn't.

"You can call me Elizabeth." I blushed then, as if I were fifteen. But this seemed only to encourage him. His eyes crinkled when he smiled.

"I'd be pleased, Elizabeth." He extended his arm, just like men did when they were courting. "Now, for that performance you put on, I'm going to buy you supper."

I kept my arms at my sides. "There's no need," I stammered. I'd never felt more silly in all my life, but I admit that I liked having him look at me. His eyes were dark as chestnuts.

"Please," he said. "Not often I have a chance to eat supper with such a pretty woman." His hand closed over mine.

"Elizabeth!" Mama was making her way through the crowd, Doc following behind.

"Just a minute," I said to David, and went to Mama.

"I was so worried," Mama cried, holding me close.

"That man over there asked me to have supper with him."

Mama's eyes went wide. "That's ridiculous," she said, and then she looked to Doc. To this day, I wonder how different my life would have been if she hadn't looked at him. Just then all I could think about was that Mama had someone and I did not.

"I'm going with him," I announced. I hadn't been asked anywhere by a man in more than ten years. "You and Doc can go on home without me."

"Absolutely not." Mama was shocked. For a moment I enjoyed that she had focused on only me again, but then I felt small for being so petty.

I glanced over at David. He was helping a little boy try to juggle the balls, but he kept checking, to see if I'd made up my mind. My indecision made him nervous, and I realized that he really wanted me to go. He'd been bold enough, asking me, and I wanted to show him I could be bold too.

"I want to do this. I'll be all right. I promise."

I kissed Mama's cheek, and Doc put his arm around her. Then I turned away and walked over to where David was standing.

"Let's go."

FIFTEEN

In all of my thirty-two years, I had never been to a carnival with a man. I'd never walked arm in arm beneath the glittering lights or held someone's hand while we rode the merry-go-round. Never had a man pay so much attention to me that he nearly fell off his great wooden horse.

He tried to play the games, but the barkers wouldn't let him. "You know all my tricks," one of them said, wiping his face on his dingy red-and-white sleeve. "You'd win everything I got."

"I'll pay for my turn," David insisted. "I just want to win a prize for my girl."

His girl. No one had thought of me like that since Horace, all those years ago. I wanted one of those stuffed animals more than anything now.

"Save your money," the man said, and he took a little stuffed rabbit from a hook and handed it to me with a bow.

As we walked, everyone seemed to notice us. Clowns tipped their too-large hats. Women rustled their fancy skirts. David knew them all, from the young girl handing out ice cream at the food booth to the wizened old man doling out the tickets.

He introduced me to the fat lady who told me to "hold on to him, for the little hussies here are just dying to get their fingers in him." We joined her in the supper line, in a big tent behind the freak show. She looked happy here.

The food was good and there was plenty of it, which was nice to see these days. I wanted to try a little bit of everything—the spicy brown meatballs in gravy, the potato cakes fried in lard. There were bowls of soup so thick with barley that the spoon floated on the top. Several men dressed in sparkling costumes chucked me on the chin, told me how pretty I was. Some of the women glared at me, but one of them, dressed like a gypsy, came up to us. She pulled a silver coin from my ear. "Cross my palm with it, dear, and I'll tell you your fortune." She winked at David. Her eyelids were powdered purple and green.

I gripped the coin, knowing it was a trick, but not sure how to play. "I'd be a fool to part with good money," I finally said, and the whole tent burst into laughter. People clapped and cheered.

"She outswindled Jasmine," someone yelled to the new wave of folks coming in.

She patted my cheek. "You keep the coin." I tucked it into my pocket with my stuffed rabbit.

After a while, everyone drifted back to their own seats, as though someone had passed a message that we were not to be disturbed. We were eating dessert—two pieces of blackberry pie with ice cream, but the baking wasn't up to what the cooking had been. "So where you from?" David asked.

I lifted my rubbery crust and smelled the filling before I pushed it aside. There is an art to pie-making that was clearly lost on the carnival cook. I licked the ice cream from my spoon.

"From Philippi, down in Barbour County." I wasn't ready to blurt out every little thing about myself. Don't need to put all your goods in the shop window, as Granny had once told me. "What about you? When you're not traveling with the carnival, I mean."

"I was born up near Somerset, in Pennsylvania."

"I've never been there, but I've heard the name."

"Nice area. Rural. Beautiful to look at. Now I just live all over." He nodded to my pie. "You done?" he asked. I pushed my plate towards him but he was already standing up to leave. People waved to us as we left. Every man, I swear, winked. I felt my face burn bright red, and I was glad to get out into the dim light, where the air was cool, scented with popcorn, caramelized sugar, and cigarette smoke. We walked along the backs of the tents and could hear the barkers luring people into them, just on the other side of the thin canvas walls.

"My family's been in the carnival business for most of my life," he said, putting his hand on my elbow as we stepped over a tangle of rope.

"Your family?" It seemed bad enough that anyone should up and join the carnival, but a whole family?

"My oldest brother's a midget." David was matter-of-fact, as if we all had midget brothers. "He got started young, and he made more money than all of us put together, back in Somerset. He got married here, in one of the tents, like Tom Thumb."

Anyone with the last name of "Thumb" had to be cursed by his daddy, if not God himself. "What's your brother's name?" I asked.

"Henry Newland. We call him Hen." We were walking away from the lights now, down the road a little bit. His arm was around my waist. I could hear the music of the carousel— the tinny ping of the organ and the pounding of the drum. We crossed the field, headed for the woods.

"Is he still here?" I imagined Hen popping up somewhere, like a jack-in-the-box.

David shook his head. "He left the carnival a few years ago. He's a hellfire-and-brimstone preacher over in Ohio now."

I stopped walking. "You're telling stories."

"Swear it. He's a big believer in baptisms, too. Someone gets down in the water and holds him up so he can dunk the person under." I liked David's smile—it made him look a little shy. Alvin's grin was bold as brass. "Of course, Hen has got to do that baptism mighty quick, or he'll be burying the man beneath him."

I know my mouth was hanging wide open like a drunk sleeping off a Saturday night. I kept seeing that midget standing in a river, jostling up and down on the back of a man playing God's horse. The story was ridiculous, but I could see it as vividly as if Hen had been standing right in front of me.

I started to laugh. And I laughed until tears spilled down my cheeks and I couldn't see. I laughed until my legs gave out and I had to sit down at the side of the road. And when I stopped laughing, I opened my eyes and saw David was sitting next to me. "You're funny," I said, and he looked pleased. He took out the balls he'd had with the children and tossed them into the air, juggling them expertly, first with one hand, and then the other.

"Back there at the fair—you could juggle all along!"

He nodded. "I've always been good at making people laugh." He stopped juggling, but his hands still fidgeted as though unsure now what to do.

"What did your folks do before they took to traveling with the fair?" I lay back on the grass. Staring up at the sky, I could have been anywhere—on Denniker's Mountain, in Mama's yard, but here I was in Fairmont.

"We farmed." He stretched out beside me, propped up on his elbow. "My dad wasn't the farming sort, so when he had an offer to sell, he took it." He ran his fingers through the grass between us. "Sold out for a song. Joined the carnival, he and Mom both. They ran the glass pitch for years. My brothers and I grew up thinking everyone picked pennies up off the ground to make a living."

"Are they about, then?" I wondered if I'd met any of them, back at the tent. Surely he'd have said.

"No," he said. "They're all down south now. Told me I was a fool for coming back up north. Listening to them, you'd think it snowed here from September on. But I wanted to see Somerset again. See someplace I should remember but don't."

"What about a wife?"

"I never married." But he'd paused before he spoke. "You?"

I wasn't sure what to say. "I lived a long time with a man, but he's gone now."

Lying down, I could see him up close. I liked the way his ears fell against his head. Granny always said you could tell a man by his ears—too close to the head and the man would be so stingy he'd steal the pennies from a dead man's eyes. But ears that flapped like wings meant you'd never keep your shop bills paid. David had beautiful ears.

"Did you see Somerset?" I asked.

"I did, but there wasn't anything left." He looked away from me for a moment. "I'd saved some money. I think I was half hoping I could come back up here and buy our place back. Go back to living in one place instead of moving around."

"I have a farm," I said. "I mean, it isn't much." I hardly knew what I was offering. "Still, it's a farm. And it's mine." His hair was graying a little in the front, but still thick enough. I wondered what it would feel like to touch.

David reached out with his right hand and gently cradled

my cheek. "I've always wanted to try farming myself. See how I liked it."

"I think you'd like it." I was so nervous I could barely speak.

"I'd like to see you, on your farm." He bent forward, and I was sure he was going to kiss me now. I closed my eyes.

When nothing happened, I opened them again. He was looking at me with such hope, such desire. "I'm looking for a home, Elizabeth. A wife. Not just a place to stay."

I nodded. I leaned a little closer, thinking he would kiss me now. Instead he picked up my hand and one by one, put each of my fingers into his mouth.

"We could grow old together," I said. I would have said anything to keep him touching me like that. "We'll sit on the porch and fuss." Wasn't he ever going to kiss me?

"Don't talk like that," he said, "if you don't mean it."

"I do mean it." Dear God, I prayed, let him mean it, too. "I do."

He kissed me.

The way we were acting was more like sixteen than—well, just then, I didn't know how old David was. I didn't care.

We weren't the first couple to run off to Maryland and get ourselves married. We couldn't stand the thought of waiting, even the few days that West Virginia state law demanded. I'd never seen a man so intent on tying the knot before he'd bedded a woman. All during the wedding—if you could call it that, with the sleepy justice of the peace standing over us—I could hardly keep from touching him. Here I was, standing in a room with a big shiny angel perched over the fireplace, getting myself married. I was the bride, with a ring David had pulled off his pinky finger. It was too loose, but it was mine now, and I would go home Mrs. David Newland and would be that forever more, just because this tall skinny judge in his rusty black suit had said it was so.

"You comfortable enough?" David asked, when we were settled back into his truck.

"I'm fine." Was nearly dawn now, and my eyes were sleepy with grit. Between the two of us, we managed to make our way through the dark streets of Oakland and back to the road that would take us into West Virginia again.

"You hungry?"

"Yes." Supper in the tent last night seemed long ago, as though David and I had been together for ages.

"We'll stop in Kingwood, then?" He pulled me next to him, my face resting against his arm.

"Fine."

"Seems like everything is just fine with you." I could sense his happiness even though for the life of me, I didn't understand how marrying me could make a man feel that way.

As we drove, he began to whistle. I always did like a man that could whistle, and this was the last thought in my head before I fell asleep.

When I woke, I realized we'd driven right through Kingwood and were back at the fairgrounds. The sun shone overhead and the sky had enough blue patches to sew a pair of breeches, so I knew we were in for a fine day. My wedding day, I kept thinking, as if it wouldn't be real if I didn't say so a hundred times.

The fair at late morning didn't look or sound anything as it had the evening before. As we wandered about the place we smelled rotten food and animal dung trampled so fine it rose in a dust that filled my lungs. I started coughing just outside the barracks that David told me had been his home.

"Gawd, but it's awful looking." I was peering inside, trying to imagine David here. Men were snoring on bunks, their breath ripe with wood whiskey.

David shrugged. "I'm going to get cleaned up." Several men stirred at our voices and began to mumble. "You might be better served sitting outside and waiting."

I was happy to leave, but too keyed up for sitting still. I walked along the paths, trying to peek inside the tents that had stood wide open last night. I wondered when the freak show would open. Crossed my mind that the pickled baby was probably just sitting there, alone. Made me sad to think about, and I didn't want to be sad so I kept on walking.

The Ferris wheel stood still and silent, its shadow narrow in the sun. I was so close that I could see the grease between the great gears.

"You want a ride?" David was back, clean and fresh. I wished there was someplace I might make myself more tidy, maybe more like a bride, but I didn't know quite how to ask about something like that. I certainly wanted no part of the barracks.

He pointed upward, at the Ferris wheel. "Come on."

I pulled away. "Don't think so."

"Hey, Helmut!" David called out. When no one answered, he cupped his hand around his mouth and hollered again.

A grizzled old man, so small he might have been a midget himself, came out from under the Ferris wheel, his eyes blinking in the light. He didn't look pleased to see us, but then, he didn't exactly look angry, either. "Crazy fool," I heard him mutter in a heavy German accent.

"We want a ride," David said. "Me and my wife."

We. Wife. The words threw me so that I was still repeating them in my head while the little bench rose into the air.

"Stop," I said, holding tight to the bar in front of me. I

twisted around, watching the ground move farther and farther away. "Oh, my God, oh, my God." My squirming made the seat rock, and just when I thought I couldn't go any higher without passing out, the wheel turned and we plunged for the earth again. I closed my eyes and started humming hymns, trying not to hear the sound of the gears or feel myself hurtling through open space.

"It's all right," David said. He had wrapped both arms around me.

"It ain't." We were going up again.

David held me tight. "Open your eyes, Elizabeth. You're going to miss it all."

I shook my head, but my tongue seemed to be acting all on its own. "Miss what?"

"Chance to see the whole world." He let me go and I opened my eyes. We were at the top of the wheel, sitting like God over the trees and the earth. I could see the mountains in the distance, gray and blue and soft-looking from here, just like they were from my kitchen window at home. When we circled round and the mountains disappeared, there was David, smiling at me as though I'd done something wonderful, and then there were the mountains again then David's smile, around and back again.

"It's a long ride home," I said to him when the wheel had finally stopped. The ground was once again inches from my toes. David lifted the latch and tipped the seat and I was standing back on my own two feet.

"I don't know what stuff you want to take with you, but you don't really need much more than your own clothes."

When David didn't say anything, I began to worry that I'd misunderstood. Maybe David had decided that he didn't want to settle down after all. That would be a fine kettle of fish, since I had no intention of traipsing around with the carnival the rest of my born days. Everything in me was hungering for Denniker's Mountain.

"You coming with me or not?"

David leaned down and kissed me so hard I felt the pinch of it all the way to my toes. "Oh, yes." His eyes blinked, and I thought that he might be crying, but for the life of me, it seemed a strange sort of thing for a man to do.

"So what can you tell me about yourself?" he asked as we drove.

"I suppose you could call me a midwife, though I haven't birthed a baby in years now."

"Why not?"

"Best to just send them to Doc Woodley and his sons. Roads are more plentiful, so folks can reach him. He has a nurse, and he's married to my mama. She's a midwife, too."

"Doesn't leave you with much to do, then, does it?"

I shook my head. "Women come to me for stuff they don't want to bother a fancy doctor over."

"What things?" He sounded interested, which surprised me, coming from a man.

"Oh, regular stuff, like knocking a baby loose or keeping it in there. Some women are anxious to conceive and others would be damned if they do." I worried, then, that I would shock him.

David didn't even seem surprised. "My mother had twelve babies one right after the other until she was too worn out to care about much else."

"Where'd you fall in that line?" Where a person falls in a family often tells you a whole lot about them.

"I was fifth if you count all the babies. Third if you count the living ones."

A middle child has to learn to get along with folks, I thought. Someone that aims to please but knows when to back off. "Must have been rough, smack in the middle of all them kids." I was chattering like a fox. I wished he'd look at me some more, but the road curved too much.

"We were split apart by the time I was ten or so. Circus isn't a place to raise a family."

"Is that where you lost your finger?" I asked, sudden-like. I felt my face get hot.

He didn't seem to mind. "No, it was before that. Raccoon bit me. Bite got infected, turned green, and the doctor was too fond of drink to care for it right."

"That's awful!"

David seemed pleased I was upset.

"Where are we?" he asked, as we came into Grafton.

"Not far." And now I had something new to worry about. What would he think about Denniker's Mountain? Seemed so important that he love it. When he suggested that we stop and eat, I was glad to have a bit more time.

"I told you about the farm, but you have to know, it isn't that much," I tried to explain. David parked the car in front of the drugstore and turned to me, his face serious. He's thinking that I deceived him, I thought. "Mostly straight up on three sides." But instead of speaking, he only kissed me, right there for anyone with eyes who might have been walking past.

"It's your farm," David said. "If I can't farm it the way you want, I'll do something else." He spoke like he was announcing the weather or his plans for the day. The way a man talks to another man. "I plan to do whatever it takes to make you happy."

I wondered if a body could burn up from the inside, without a flame in sight.

·   ·   ·

I put a phone call in to Mama from the drugstore.

"It's me," I said, when she answered. "I'm in Grafton."

"Grafton?" Mama asked. She sounded tired, as though she had been up delivering babies all night, though I knew she hadn't. She'd been up worrying about me.

"I'm married, Mama," I said. "I got a ring on my finger and everything."

"Oh, Elizabeth." There was a pause. "She's run off and got married," she told Doc.

I could hear her breathing on the other end.

"Are you coming home?" she finally said.

"Soon." I might have up and joined the carnival for all she'd known. "I'll be home by tonight."

"I should never have let you go up there with Alvin, all those years ago. Should have clutched you to me like that MacFarland woman did her girl."

I was stunned. "That wasn't your doing." The phone static crackled in my ear. Living in town, Mama was used to talking on the phone, but I felt strange, hearing her and knowing she was so far away. "I would have gone anyway. I was in love. You knew that more than anyone."

"You were so young." I wished I could see if she looked as stern as her voice sounded across the wires. "What did you know about love?"

David was sitting at the counter. He had ordered enough food to feed an army—sandwiches and fried potatoes and apple pie so rich it looked like cake. "This has nothing to do with Alvin," I told her. "Nothing at all." She didn't say anything. "I'll be home soon."

I paid for my call, then joined David at the counter. "She forgive me?" he asked.

"It's me she's not likely to forgive. She doesn't even know you."

"Where you folks from?" the counter boy asked.

David piped right in, "Philippi." As though he had lived there all his life.

"Nice town." I could tell by the blank look on his face, though, that the boy had never been. I'd looked that way myself, when people talked about the towns and cities they had seen.

David nodded. "Sure is."

By sunset, we'd reached the covered bridge, so dark inside that we could hardly make out the great curved beams. Back in the world I had always known, I couldn't help but be antsy over what might happen next. For all the talk there had been when I went up the mountain with Alvin, that would increase tenfold now that I was coming home with a strange man.

"Union army chased Rebels through this bridge," I said. "Came down from that hill behind us."

"Maybe was my own great-grandfather charging down." David strained to peer out his truck window.

"Chasing my great-grandfather," I said. We were driving down Main Street, and I saw people looking at the truck, trying to see who we were. No one knows this is me, I thought, hugging myself with the thought. None of them knew I was Elizabeth Newland now.

"I thought West Virginia was for the Union." David pulled his head inside the truck again. I pointed out the road where he should turn.

The familiar story soothed me as we drove the last few miles. "I got a cousin named Union and one named Robert Lee. Seems like it's that way in most of the families I know." The mountains closed around us and I could hear Kettle Creek.

I was suddenly very tired. "There's my mama's old house—why don't we pull in there? The mountain will be pitch-black, and we're better off waiting to morning."

The little cabin was cold, but I soon lit the stove. "You want some coffee?" I asked. Except for that nap in the car, I'd not slept in two days.

"Coffee's good." David took off his hat and hung it on the hook. He looked around, his eyes taking in every little thing. I tried to see my old home as he did—the worn tongue-in-groove walls and the fireplace burnt with use. I hoped the bedding was fresh enough.

"Come sit," I said, and pulled two chairs closer to the stove.

I don't know who fell asleep first, but when I woke up we were sitting there with mugs half-full of cold coffee. In sleep he looked young and peaceful. As a child, I'd sat in this very room, pretending this was my house. I had been married to Alvin, and we'd had a bunch of babies. Mama would visit us, and we would make fudge or taffy. I had it all worked out.

I listened to David's breathing a moment before I rose and headed out back.

The rain barrel was full, and I hooked my lamp over a nail and stripped down so I could have a good wash. I had just plunged my head under—water dripping all over me—when I heard David call my name.

He poked his head out the back door. "I wondered where you'd gone."

Because I didn't know what else to do, I stepped forward and stood straight, letting the lamp light my body. My skin prickled in the night air. "I was just washing up."

"You're lovely." He raised his hands, offering them palm up. "May I?"

I stared at those hands, with the funny gap on the right one. Then I looked at his face and saw something in his eyes I had never ever seen in any man's before—not one that looked at me.

My own hands reached out and I gripped his face between them and I kissed him as hard as I could. His hands found my breasts, and I tipped forward, leaning into him, until his knees buckled and we settled to the ground.

SIXTEEN

For two days we stayed down at Mama's, not getting out of bed for more than a bite to eat or a drop of water. I took David into me like he was manna from heaven. Don't think I've ever gone so long without wearing my clothes. My body whistled like a dickie bird when he was near.

By the evening of the second day, we'd run out of the last of the coffee Mama'd left behind, and the last bits of food David had brought with him when he left. I did think about staying here, where I could live with David free of memories of having been with any other man. Pleasant thoughts these were, but Denniker's Mountain belonged to me, and my life was there.

"We'd better head on home," I said finally, and saw that David was pleased.

"The road doesn't go all the way." We were winding our way up the mountain in his truck. The engine was loud, startling birds from the trees.

"This is a lovely view." David gazed out over the old Teller orchard. Lovely was a word David used often, I was to learn. Especially about me.

"When I was young that was a bearing apple orchard." The

gnarled trees bent toward the ground like old humped women. "Nothing but grubbing food now."

"Bet it's pretty in springtime. I can't wait to see it."

He would be here in the springtime, I thought to myself. Springtimes, summertimes, and wintertimes, too. "You can pull off under that big pine. We got to walk the rest of the way up."

David shut off the motor and the air was still. "House is just yonder." I jumped down from the truck, making for the path I had known since I was a little girl.

The whole time we walked, David looked around him, sometimes reaching out a hand to touch some plant that had grown up in the last burst of summer heat. As with the apple orchard, I tried seeing my world through his eyes, but to me, everything seemed as it had ever been—the heavy greenery crowding the path, the leaves over our heads colored by fall. Behind us, the mountain ridges fell away in waves, purple and brown in the fading light.

We were almost on the cabin before we saw it—that squat brown mushroom of a house. "Here we are."

David put down his bags and covered his eyes from the last glare of sunlight. "Is this the place, then?" He turned his head, taking everything in. The barn, the well, the slant of the earth where we planted the garden. Then he picked up our things again and waited for me to lead the way.

Inside, the house was dim and a bit chill. Someone had been here and tidied up in the few days I'd been gone. The floor was swept and the old quilt hung neatly over the rocking chair. Firewood was stacked in the grate, and the coal stove had been shined so black I could see my form reflected in it.

Mama, I thought. Of course Mama knew we had been in her little house. Mothers know where their children are.

But I didn't know where Lauren was. Where she had been, yes—the last card had been from San Francisco—but not where she was right now. She might be anywhere, it had been so many weeks now. I wondered what she would think when she came back, finding David here. I prayed that she would say I had done right. That she would still love me, and maybe grow to love David, too.

He was exploring the cabin, picking things up and putting them down—Mama's candlesticks, Lauren's willowware plate. He held everything lightly, but I knew how sure his hands could be. I felt a sting in my belly. My body might never hold a child, but David fit just fine.

He'd put his satchel and leather suitcase by the fireplace and ran his hands over the mantel board. "Nice work."

"Old Caesar's."

"Who?"

Foolish, I suppose, that such a thing bothered me. David, my husband, didn't know who Old Caesar was, him and all his wives. Didn't know a thing about my past, about this mountain.

He'd found the only photograph I had of Lauren, one taken when she was about five. The picture-man had traveled up here on a hot summer day and I fretted that he'd come for nothing, as I knew we couldn't pay him. He'd taken the picture anyway, smart man, and sent it back to me. Then of course I had to have it—Lauren, standing next to the little wooden chair Alvin had carved for her. Her small face was serious. She wore rings on two fingers, a bracelet—cheap baubles Alvin had bought for Ivy at the company store. Her toes were sooty. Took me two months to pay off that photo, but it belonged to me.

"That's Lauren."

"Who is she?"

"My daughter."

"What happened?" he asked, and I could tell that he thought she was dead.

"She went with her daddy." I tried to picture the woman

she must be growing into now, without me by her side. David put his arms around me. I would need to tell him more someday. But not right now. He wanted to comfort me and the strength that he offered felt good.

It was the fiddle that woke me. Woke me from a sound sleep into a dreaming one, where I listened to the flow of Alvin's music and Ivy danced about with baby Lauren on her hip. The gunshots rang out next. In my dream I wondered how Alvin was playing that fiddle and shooting off his gun at the same time, but it didn't trouble me much for all it was out of sorts, the way things often are in dreams.

"Bessie?" I liked hearing that. Wasn't more than a few days ago that I'd never been called nothing but Elizabeth in this house. And here this man I had up and married was calling me Bessie as if we had some secret. David knew nothing of the person I had been. I drifted back towards sleep.

"Bessie?" the whisper came again. I opened my eyes. I could feel Alvin—no, David—next to me in the dark. The fiddle was still playing, and guns were firing like it was Election Day and Fourth of July combined. Metal clanged so loud it echoed through my head.

"What's going on?" David was pulling on his pants. I could hear the snap of his suspenders, even in all that racket.

"They're serenading us," I said, getting my own self up. I pulled my dress over my head. "Hurry!"

"What?" I didn't know if he hadn't heard me or if he simply didn't know. There were so many things that he didn't know. But I couldn't pine about that now.

"Folks must have heard we got married." I slipped into my shoes and tried to straighten my hair. Wouldn't do to have people thinking they'd interrupted our loving, although that was always part of the fun behind a serenade. "But 'deed, I don't see how."

David was looking out the window. "I think the whole world's here." He threw open the door. "Here they come!" someone yelled. The clatter grew louder, and there were catcalls and suchlike. Folks banged on pans with spoons, rattled tin plates together like cymbals.

Every soul I knew seemed to have made the walk up Denniker's Mountain that night.

There was Doc Woodley and Mama, holding a fry-pan so round that I couldn't see her middle. When she saw me, her face relaxed and she waved her wooden spoon.

Luella Porter was there with her rich husband, both of them grinning like fools. They had a passel of kids between them that looked just like their daddy. Marianna Teller was there, with Jacob, the last baby I'd ever caught. Standing next to them were a couple of Whitely cousins I hadn't seen in years, banging pots on pans as though we'd been close all my life. Uncle Russell hooted and hollered—the man who had made Mama so mad that she'd gone and left the Homestead. Aunt Alice watched me, her eyes suspicious, but my cousin Gussie banged a pan as though this were her own chivaree.

I saw Sally Meroe and her oldest boy, the first I'd helped into this world. Caleb Blicker too, his dark girl-bride at his side. He looked pleased as punch—and him a man that had cursed God.

All the Woodley boys were there, standing with their wives and kids. Alice MacFarland Woodley cheered, hooting like an owl, and I realized that though neither of us had ended up with what we'd thought we wanted, we were here all the same.

The noise showed no sign of letting up and I stepped into the yard. "Y'all can go home now," I called, but folks only laughed. No one moved, even when I yelled again. The fiddle

played on and on, "Golden Slippers," lilting through the gunshots and the clatter. There aren't many times your whole
world beats a path to your doorstep.

David put his arm around my waist. Two guns blasted and
I jumped but he held me fast. He waved his other arm at the
crowd.

"When you gonna treat us?" someone hollered. I figure it
was Elroy Teller. He was the biggest hog farmer in the area,
and not many men have the lungs to call like that.

"What did he say?" David asked.

"You gotta treat them. We need to tell them a day to come
back and we'll feed them. It's a party."

David's face broke into a wide smile. "I'll show you off
right." His arm tightened.

"It will cost a fair piece . . ." But David brushed this aside.

He raised his hand, and after a minute the din hushed.
"You all come back on Saturday night, and I'll show you a
party like you have never seen!"

The crowd went wild. Noise filled the air like wind.

Mama came to my side, hugging me close. "Are you all
right?"

"I am." I silently vowed never to worry her again. I was a
married woman now, not some child who needed caring.

Others came to greet us—Hetty Switzer, and Uncle
Donald. My cousin Gussie looked David over and said he was
"fine." I was hugged and kissed by one soul after the other until I didn't think I could stand it.

Once we'd greeted the whole lot, folks began lighting lamps
and heading for home, clanking like the armistice parade at
noonday instead of families out in the dead of night. I could
hear the fiddle—Martin Riggleman, if I had my guess—as they
trooped down the mountain. A couple more shots were fired,
and then the music faded and the air filled again with the shrill
of crickets.

"That was wonderful." David dropped a kiss on the top of my head.

We went back inside, still stirred up by the excitement. "What will we need to do?" David asked.

"Do about what?"

"The party. All those people coming back on Saturday."

I yawned. "Oh, we don't have to do anything, if we don't want. Folks know talk like that is mostly show."

"You mean they won't come?"

"They'll come if we send word round that we're inviting them. You really want to do this?" I tried to imagine all the people in Kettle Valley and even in Philippi coming to this house. Eating food. Drinking, dancing, making merry. I couldn't remember the last party we'd had like that on Denniker's Mountain.

"You a temperance man?" He could be a drunkard, I thought suddenly.

"Never took a pledge, if that means much to you."

"I was just wondering about what to serve. One bunch of folks will be put out, no matter what we do, so we might as well suit ourselves." I tried to think what food I had on hand to give them. I had two hams that should be cured enough. Mama would have to come up to help.

As though David could hear my thoughts, he said, "I'll take you into town tomorrow. We'll buy what we need."

"No point in that. Times being what they are, no one's going to expect much."

David was firm. "I want you to have a nice party. I want people to go home thinking that you weren't a fool for marrying a total stranger." Here was a man who had traveled his whole life. I realized that David wanted to be liked, wanted to make friends.

"Dewey Dalton's got the best still around," I told him. "If you don't mind paying. He bootlegs to Pittsburgh, so you know his stuff is good."

"We'll do that, then."

I almost asked about money—he'd talked about having saved some—but for all we were married, I just didn't feel I could. I didn't know what carnival people made, but it couldn't be too bad, seeing as how there was always work.

Thinking about money made me tired. The mountain seemed too quiet, after all the ruckus. Soon there would be people here again, traipsing about the farm, drinking and dancing to beat the band. "I'm pure wore out."

"Come back to bed." He unbuttoned the front of my dress the way I'd expect a woman to, casual-like. Then he tucked me into bed, and brought me back a cup of water, standing over me while I drank it down. When he had undressed, he blew out the candle and settled down beside me, not touching, just there. "I love you," he said.

I knew he was waiting, wondering what I'd say. Back at the fair, when I said I wanted to grow old with him, I'd been filled with the vision of Mama and Doc. Here, where I had loved and lost another man, believing that I would ever love another took more than my imagination could give. If I reached down to where I held my love for Lauren, for Ivy, for Mama, and even the love I'd wasted on Alvin, there seemed no more to be spared. I'd given away all I had to them, and only Mama was with me still.

I wanted David, but I loved him not. A good woman might have spoken truth and set him free, but I told myself that my want of him would be enough. I knew then and know now that I was lying to myself. No one knew better than I that even the strongest desire fades when the body next to you isn't the one you want it to be.

Alvin, at least, had been part of my own history. David was from nowhere—foreign to me as Ivy had been. I'd grown to love Ivy, but that kind of love would never satisfy David. Or myself.

How could he say he loved me, when he knew me so little? And once he did know me—from the inside out, the way a baby knows her mother—would he love me still? Or would he leave the way all the men I'd ever known had gone—from my father, to Horace, to Union, and even Alvin, too?

"Let me tell you about old Caesar Denniker," I said, and if David thought this strange, he never shushed me. He let me talk on and on, listening to the tales I had been told since I was a little girl. I told him about all four wives, and he laughed to think of being buried among them.

"He sounds like quite a character."

"He was," and I was frustrated. For this was all Caesar could be to David—a story.

"Good night, David." I whispered his name as though by speaking it I might somehow bind us together. For there was nothing that connected us, one to the other. Nothing but a carnival whim and a piece of paper signed by an old man over in Maryland. A few words spoken in the air. Less even than what I had had with Alvin.

David pulled me against him. He reached across my body and took my hand in his. Nothing more than that, just my hand. He was still holding it when I fell asleep.

SEVENTEEN

David took to farming like no man I'd ever seen. He turned that bare and rocky soil into an earth that bloomed. He took his time, and Denniker's Mountain loved him for it. Even during the leanest years of the 1930s, we had plenty to eat. Our sow had eight piglets when everyone else's had none. Our cow gave twice the milk.

Turns out David's specialty was chickens. He liked them, stupid things. Came in one day with a big box of chicks—this was right after we married—and the sight of him standing in the doorway made me recall when Alvin had once done the same. Alvin had talked about how I'd be frying them up in no time, selling the eggs to buy myself some play-pretties—and every chicken in that whole brood had turned out to be a rooster. Didn't get much eating out of those stringy birds, but we sure did laugh at the way they picked at each other, desperate to find something with which to breed. Was a favor, really, to make them into stew.

David made no such mistake. He had no problem asking me or anyone else about the best way to run a farm. So when he brought home his chickens, he knew just what he had. And he cared for them, careful as an old woman. They laid eggs the size of a boy's fist. Course David was heavy-handed with the corn, but since he was growing it, seemed a shame to spoil his fun.

What with all the men looking for work—broken-down men who would wander from farm to farm, mining camp to mining camp, trying to put food on their tables—David became a man people took to watching. By the spring of 1931, I was already hearing about how well I'd done for myself. Even Aunt Annie came around. "I always told your mama that you'd picked up the crooked stick, but in the end, you went and found yourself a good man."

Truth is, everyone loved David. Whenever we went to town, children would crowd around us, watching with open mouths as he juggled whatever was handy—pebbles, coins, buckeyes. Once he made me take off my shoes and he tossed them in the air along with his. The young ones went wild over this, but I didn't like being downtown only in my stocking feet. "What can I make, that you could juggle?" I asked him when we got home.

He thought a minute. "How about some little bags? We could fill them with beans. Give them to the children to take home."

"Child wouldn't hardly get home before their mama would open the bag and empty it into a pot."

"All the more reason to, then," he said. "When the beans run out, we'll try something else."

So that's how David and I came to be passing out little bags of beans to every child that came within ten feet of us. At first I worried that people might think we were getting above ourselves, given how little most had. But instead, allowances were made. One day, when we were on the street, I heard one of the mothers say, "Well, he's a bit odd, but he did used to own a circus." I started to correct her, but David held my arm. He was trying hard not to make a sound and give our presence away.

We said nothing until we'd crossed the street to the next block. I tucked my hand beneath his arm. "You disappointed you didn't marry a circus owner?" he asked as we walked in front of the courthouse.

"I like my clown."

"I'm glad to hear it." We kept on walking.

The only person who didn't seem to take to David was Mama. Not that she was rude to him, never slammed the door in his face or turned her back to him. Nothing like that. And he was always charming as could be to her.

Seems like nothing was right after that telephone call from Grafton. I began dwelling on that conversation until I heard only the bitterness in her voice when she said she'd been wrong to let me go with Alvin. Obviously, I thought, she disapproved of me, of David. I'd taken in a stranger, and she thought less of me for it. Not that she would speak against us—no one could accuse her of acting towards me as Granny had her—but I was stung by her silence.

That was a cold winter for me, sitting with Mama in Doc's parlor, her hands folded in her lap. She would nod her head from time to time, but nothing seemed to catch her interest. Often her eyes would wander, and her face was grim when she thought we weren't watching.

"That's very interesting, Mr. Newland."

"Please call me David," he would say for the tenth time.

"Of course." Not ten minutes would pass before she was back to calling him by his formal name.

I grew angry with her. She spoke to him the way she did to

men who were beneath her—men who went out and bought a new hunting rifle, when their wives hadn't enough buttons to keep their dresses closed.

"Are you all right?" I asked her one evening after she had gone nearly a half hour without speaking. We were in Doc's kitchen, putting away what was left of the dinner the cook had made. Roast chicken, we'd had tonight. Last week we'd eaten duck, as though every meal was Christmas.

"I'm fine, dear." She opened the icebox door and I felt the rush of cold air. "The icing hasn't set on the sponge cake."

"You act like you're Mrs. Doc." This was unfair, since I'd never known Mrs. Doc to be anything less than a good woman. But I wanted to push Mama into saying something. Even her yelling at me for being rude would be better than this cool unconcern.

Mama took out the cake only to drop it on the floor.

Doc rushed in then. He saw Mama and me kneeling on the floor. "I'll get it, Maisie," he said, and helped her to her feet. She began to cough then, and couldn't make herself stop.

"You'd best go home, Elizabeth," Doc said. David came in the kitchen then, all of us crowded there, watching Mama try to breathe.

"Come on, Bessie." David tried to take my arm, but I wouldn't move. Mama had taken coughing spells before. I waited for her to tell me she would be all right, but instead she only nodded when Doc repeated that I should go.

David led me out of the house, my arms and legs as stiff as a doll's. "What's going on?" I asked him.

"Won't make things better, you catching cold, too." He helped me in the truck. I was sure that Doc had said something to him, perhaps while Mama and I were in the kitchen. I pestered him all through the evening, but he kept his own counsel, and at bedtime I was so angry at his silence on the subject that I ignored him by staying in the big room until he'd gone to sleep.

Doc came up late the next morning. After a fretful night I'd risen at dawn, going out to pick all the tender dandelion greens I could find. I was cooking them up when Doc knocked.

"How's Mama?" I looked behind him, disappointed that he'd come alone. I was worried clear through now, for I knew that Mama would never have sent Doc if she could have come herself.

"Where's David?"

I motioned for him to sit down. "He went over to Joe Teller's—he's thinking about taking on a bull and wanted to talk to Joe about it."

Doc nodded. "Your David is a good man, Elizabeth. Your mother and I want you to know that."

Doc didn't know it hurt me, him saying the words I wanted from Mama herself. "I'll get us some coffee."

"You need to know some things, Elizabeth." He spoke in his doctor's voice. I knew then that I was right to be afraid.

"Your mama has holes in her lungs."

I put my coffee cup down on the table. I heard the ring of the wood, sturdy and hard. It was my hands that seemed no more substantial than fog on a mountain.

Doc pulled out a handkerchief and wiped his upper lip. He took off his glasses, wiped them, and then put them back on. "I had hoped," he said, clutching the handkerchief, "that I could heal her. But she just gets worse."

He began to cry, thick tears that rolled down his cheeks and seeped into his mustache. "I'd do anything for her. I knew when we married how ill she was, and that we wouldn't have long. But I could take care of her at least. I could, God help me, give her something for her pain." He shook his head. "I know that's why she came to me—because I could help her bear it in ways she couldn't ask of anyone else."

"That isn't so," I said, nearly undone. "Mama loves you. She's loved you as long as I remember. And anyone who's seen her these past few months can tell that you've made her happy."

Doc reached out then and patted my hand. "Bless you for that." His shoulders straightened. "There is still some time."

Some time, I thought. "What does that mean?"

"I don't know. A few months maybe. Perhaps a year. As long as I can give her." He stood up. "Her herbal chest is out in my car, and some of her books. She wanted me to bring those to you." His voice thickened again. "I won't send her away, no matter what the county health board wants, but she can't do any more birthings."

We walked down the mountain to his car. How can we be so calm? I wondered. Without speaking, Doc carried the small chest and I shuffled beneath the tall pile of books. I hugged him before he left, this man who felt as dear to me as any father I might have had.

Later that afternoon, I opened one of the black ledgers at random. Mama's handwriting filled the pages—pencil marks asking as many questions of the text as there were other marks to know she'd found the answer.

I remember leaving the house and heading down the mountain, but I don't know when I started running. I was feverish with fury—at Mama, for not being able to heal herself when she had helped so many. At Lauren, for going out into the world to heal strangers, when her need was greatest here. She wouldn't even be in one place long enough for me to write her to come home.

When I reached Kettle Creek, I didn't stop but plunged in. The water was cold and the current strong. I was tossed about like a twig until I came up, sputtering like a cat.

David was coming on the creek just then, and he saw me struggling. He was laughing, thinking I had taken a spill into the creek.

"You think this is funny?" I yelled.

"You should have seen yourself." He flung himself back, arms and legs waving.

Looking back on it, I know that if I looked half as silly as he did that he had every right to tease. But right then my anger was like a bruise and he was pressing on it.

"God damn you," I screamed at him. He rose, shocked and hurt.

"Bessie . . ."

"Get away from me." I wanted to bang on his chest with my fists. It would be better to hurt someone—anyone—rather than feel the way I did.

Now that Mama no longer had to keep her illness a secret, she seemed to improve a little bit. Nearly every morning, David would bring me to Doc's house. I had taken to scouring the hills for herbals that might ease her pain in any way. Some days, she would be as gentle and patient as she had always been. Other days, her white face and barking cough echoed in my ears and I could hardly wait until I could get away. I was a poor excuse for a daughter then. Over the weeks of that spring I learned to hold my anger against myself until I felt it always covering me like a thick, heavy coat.

At home I had taken to ranting and crying by spells. David was better to me than I deserved. I fussed at him over the smallest things, picking fights for no other reason than that he was there.

"Are you all right?" he asked me one night when we were in bed. I had screamed at him earlier, for kicking over the slop pail when he'd brought in some coal. Kitchen would stink of rotten food for a week.

"Please leave me alone," I answered, turning on my side.

"You still angry?"

"No," I said, trying to keep my voice level. "But you keep asking me that and I'm gonna be."

"What can I do?"

"Nothing!" I sat up. "I said I ain't angry!"

That got to him, for I felt his body begin to twitch up and down until laughter burst from him like a preacher's call to glory. "Oh, no. You aren't the least bit angry."

"I'm sorry." I lay back down, pulling the covers to my chin, wiggling my toes beneath the sheets. His warm body seemed to draw mine against it.

"You know, Bessie, not everyone is going to disappear on you. Sometimes the best way to let someone go is by creating a new life."

"What?" I asked.

"All those babies you caught and you never thought about taking one home for yourself?" His tone was light, but I knew David was asking me for a child.

"You want babies?"

"I like babies." He was confused.

"I don't want no babies."

He said nothing.

"I said, I don't want no babies." Louder this time.

"You mean that?"

I turned away.

From that night on, when David reached for me, I'd pull away from him. Slide from his arms and roll myself tight into a ball. Wasn't always easy, what with his hand on my bare arm, his toes touching mine. In all my life, I'd never denied a man who wanted to be loving me. I couldn't but think of those tales boys told about being filled with poison if they got all riled up.

"This isn't right," he said one night. I'd moved so far from him that my fingers clutched my side of the bed to keep from falling off. "You know it isn't." I felt a moment of glee, at finally angering him. He grabbed the quilt I'd wrapped around me and pulled, stitches snapping.

"Way it is." My words were meaner than I meant them to be, as though I'd become hard clear through. I pulled the quilt back and tucked it under me, shoving a corner into my mouth, sucking on the wool and cotton batting.

David stood up. "I don't like this," he said. I pushed the quilt off and twisted until I was kneeling, my hair tumbling about my face. I saw his expression change.

"You're so lovely," he said. "Please, Bessie. I can't stand being near you, not able to love you." He held out his hands.

I slapped them away. "I hate your hands."

"My hands?" David pulled them back. "What's wrong with them?" And he held them up. "How can you say you hate my hands?"

"Ugliest hands I ever seen," I hissed. "And a man's hands only tell you about the rest of him."

I wondered if he was going to strike me, and I crouched, waiting for it. But instead all the strength seemed to go out of his body in a great whoosh. He sat down on the bed and started pulling on his boots.

"Where are you going?" I felt fear jabbing my insides like a cold poker.

"Out." I heard the swish, swish, swish of bootlaces being pulled and fastened. I heard the zipper of his pants, and the rustle as he pulled his shirt over his head. Then he was on his feet and out the door, the light of the moon briefly flashing his shadow before everything was dark again.

I waited for the roar of the truck, but there was only quiet. After a while, I got up and tiptoed outside. The yard was empty.

I found him in the barn, curled up in the haymow like a colt. When I knelt before him, he opened his eyes and they showed such joy that I couldn't help myself. I reached for him and took him deep inside of me until we both lay there as still and empty as shed snakeskin.

EIGHTEEN

I remember talking to a woman in the fall of 1931, the day David came looking for me and wouldn't leave us be. Don't recall the woman's name, which means she had probably come for food and not for something to keep a baby in her. The 1930s wasn't the time to be bringing babies into the world.

Still, David had no business standing there and watching us. I'd made this clear. When I was with a woman, he was to stay away. No woman is going to talk if a man is looming over her. I tried telling him with my eyes that he should go.

Instead he sat down on a rock, kicking his feet against it.

I was so furious that I could hardly concentrate on the woman at all. When she had gone, I stomped over to the rock. "Don't you know better than to spook a woman by sneaking up on her? That woman wouldn't say nothing to me after you came."

"You have company." David was unfazed by my anger.

"So? You gonna let me talk to them this time?"

"Not a them." He cleared his throat as though about to announce something. "A she."

I shrugged. Most of them were.

"It's Lauren," he said.

"Lauren." As though I'd never heard such a word before. "Lauren," I said again. "Lauren's home!" I ran for the house.

She stood on the front stoop, her hand shading her eyes from the setting sun. Her yellow hair blew about her face. "Lauren!" I called out. She'd been gone only a year, but for a girl of fifteen, a year can make all the difference. She'd grown tall, slender still, but not so thin. As she moved across the porch to lean against the rail, she might have been Ivy, who had stood so, waiting for me.

She saw me and began to wave. I could see her face now, the bright blue eyes, the soft chin. Not such a different face after all. Then there we were, the two of us together.

I cooked everything she loved—beefsteak and baked beans, apple dumplings for dessert. As I worked, she told me of all the places she had been. Didn't seem possible that a body could have been so many places in so short a time, but she described the crowded buildings of great cities all through the empty Great Plains. When David had finished the afternoon chores, he joined us, adding his own stories of places they had both seen. Between the two of them, I felt as though I'd been just about everywhere there was to go.

Soon the stove made the kitchen too hot for three, so I shooed them out into the main room to set the table. Lauren seemed to have taken to David just fine. I scraped the last of the mashed potatoes into the good bowl, the one with the gold rim.

David was quiet at supper, and as much as I enjoyed us being all together, I hungered to have Lauren to myself. When he announced he'd do some reading in our room, I nodded my thanks.

As soon as he had closed the door, I asked about the healings. The names and dates tumbled out of her, one after the other.

"How do you remember them all?" I asked her.

Lauren grinned at me. She went over to her satchel and pulled out a black leather ledger same in every way to the ones I had sitting on my shelf. "I write them down. I write everything down."

She sat with the ledger on her knees, talking about a humpbacked woman she had helped stand tall. A little boy with a clubfoot who now ran as fast as anyone.

"And how are you?" I finally had a chance to ask her.

"I've learned that I can't help more than one person at a time, which means I'm always turning someone away. I feel badly about it, but one night in Kansas I tried helping three men in one night and I fainted." She looked down at the ledger and brushed her fingers over the names. "Daddy had to carry me back to the house where we were staying."

"But you're well enough now? No more fainting? You look so fine, honey." I didn't want Alvin or anything else to intrude on us just yet. "I like the cut of your dress. The dark blue color." I wondered who had bought the dress for her—it was good quality, nice shape. I told her about Mama marrying Doc, but not about her illness. I talked about the people I'd helped, who came to me for herbals.

"Tell me about David."

"I met him at a carnival." I'd learned that the details of my story were enough to satisfy.

But Lauren wasn't fooled. "He seems to love you very much."

I waved this away.

"I'm serious. I can tell by looking at him that he thinks you hung the moon."

I blushed, for I knew I hadn't been a loving wife. More often than not I would come from Mama, face sore from holding back my tears, only to let my anguish pour over David like water. Too many nights I'd held my body away from his, waiting until he grew angry, too.

"The farm looks great," Lauren said. "Better than when Daddy kept it."

"How is he?"

Lauren pulled at her dress. "He's fine. Watches me like a hawk most times, but he let me come back here."

"So you gonna tell me about her?" I'd known since I'd seen her dress.

Lauren looked startled, then a little uncomfortable. "She's nice, Mama." She obviously didn't want to say much. "She's real sweet."

"How old is she?"

"Maybe thirty, thirty-five." She hesitated, then said it straight out. "She's getting a baby. It's almost her time now."

There was nothing I could say to that. My own ache felt so close to my skin that I wondered if it didn't show.

"I'm glad you're here," I said.

"I had to come," Lauren said. "I knew you needed me."

I nodded. Now that Lauren was here, Mama would be all right. "Did you know about Mama? When you told me to stay?"

"Not exactly. I didn't know what was wrong. Just that something was."

"She's dying, you know."

"I know." But she spoke in a small voice, turning away from me.

"Soon as it's daybreak, we'll go down to Philippi. You can help her, Lauren."

"It doesn't work like that." She spoke so low I had to bend forward to hear the words.

I took her by the shoulders, made her face me. "Mama's dying. Don't you hear me?"

Lauren's lips trembled but she held my gaze. "I hear you, Mama."

I dropped my hands and took a deep breath. Lauren sat hunched in the chair. I felt a little shamed for making her look so, when she'd been so radiant just hours before. "Come on." I took her hand. "At least you'll be in your own bed again."

She followed me to her room. Together we changed the linens, and I opened the window a crack for some fresh air. The room was cluttered, as if I hadn't believed she would ever come home. I should have kept it nicer.

She didn't seem to notice. She stretched out on her bed so that she filled the whole thing. "I'm glad to be home, Mama. You have no idea how much I missed you." She spoke again like a woman, but she'd pulled the covers over her chest, grasping them with both hands, as she always had when she was small.

I kissed her forehead. "Oh, I might."

David had waited up for me. After I undressed and climbed into bed, he said, "Were you ever planning to tell me?" He'd kept a candle burning and his face was filled with shadows.

"What?" I was keyed up yet, having Lauren home. I'd had too much blackberry wine.

"That the girl out there isn't your child."

"Lauren is my daughter." I was stung.

"I told her she had beautiful eyes, and she told me that they were her mama's eyes." He seemed nervous. "I know your eyes, Elizabeth."

I'd gone from being Bessie to Elizabeth. As soon as I told him everything I would be no one at all. He would leave me. Lauren would leave again, as I knew she must. And without healing, Mama would die.

"They her daddy's eyes?"

I could have lied then. Said Lauren had made a mistake. I could have told him he was imagining things. Easy to see that was what he wanted to hear.

"I'm barren."

David's head lifted. "What?"

"I'm barren. Lauren isn't my daughter by blood, but I didn't lie. She is my girl."

"Are you sure?" His face was stricken, ghostly in the dim light. Here he'd waited all this time, no doubt filling with righteous anger, and I'd made him pity me instead. "About the babies, I mean."

"I'm a midwife, David." I sounded cold. "You think I wouldn't know? You think a woman don't know when her monthlies stop flowing? Do you think she forgot what that blood meant?"

David reached out and touched my face. "I'm sorry, Bessie," he said. "I wish you'd told me."

"Why?" I jerked my head away. "So you could have found someone else?"

"No . . ."

"You got yourself a broken woman," I cried out. "You're tied to a woman who can't carry on your line."

David closed his eyes and settled back into the bed. "I have a son."

"A son?" I was shocked. "Where is he?"

"He's down in Carolina with his mother. Must be half grown by now, I guess."

"You didn't tell me?"

David sighed. "You aren't the only one with secrets."

I wondered how many more we'd kept from the other and whether it was better or worse for a couple when you'd gone and given voice to them all. "You have a son," I repeated. I could see him now, a younger David. "Does he know where you are?"

"I don't know what he knows."

"Mama had a baby and that man never knew me." I saw his hands clench the covers. "You know how many babies I've brought into this world that didn't know their daddy? You know how many babies I've knocked loose on account of men leaving their women all alone?"

David didn't twitch a muscle at all. "You want me to go back to a woman who told me I wasn't good enough to father her child when she'd found me good enough to take into herself?"

"I don't know what I want." I slapped the bed with my palm. "Our marriage legal?"

"Yes. Of course it is." He looked so fierce and protective then.

I pulled my legs up and wrapped my arms around them. "So here we are—me your barren wife. You who've sown your seed."

"Bessie . . ."

I turned away from him.

"Bessie." A whisper this time. "I love you."

"I know." I wished this was enough.

I'd hardly dozed off before I heard the knock. David stirred, but didn't wake. I couldn't help but think that Alvin would have been up and on the porch now. But then, Alvin never grew used to the people coming to find me on his mountain.

I knew what this knock meant. Doc had come for me. I made my way through the dark house, my dress tangled about my arms and twisted over my neck.

Mama was dead.

I stumbled on a chair and felt the pain racing up my thigh. I focused on the doorway, seeing the lantern light through the bottom crack. I'd been too worked up at bedtime to remember to braid my hair, and I grabbed the lengths of it in my hands as I opened the door.

Caleb Blicker was standing there.

"Good Lord," I called out. I was so relieved I almost fell

down. "What do you want?" I could smell the waves of whiskey coming off of Caleb's breath.

"It's Missoura," he said, his voice slurring. "It's her time."

"I don't help with babies anymore." I started to shut the door, but he leaned forward.

"You got to." Caleb reached out for me and I stepped back. He fell in front of me, hugging my legs. "You got to come." His hands were warm on the back of my legs, and for a moment I allowed my hand to settle on his hair.

Then I slapped at his ears and shoulders until I was free. I realized I was sweat-soaked, freezing to death out here with Caleb Blicker. "Get up, man." I hit him a little harder than I needed to, really. "Get up, I say."

To my surprise, when he rose his face was prim with a dignity he'd never have found while sober. "I know you claim not to do this no more, but it would mean a great deal to me and Missoura if you would help her." His voice was deep and inviting—as solemn as a preacher's ought to be but seldom ever is.

"Besides," he added, "your mama said to fetch you."

"Mama sent you?"

"She's there now, with Missoura. She wants you."

Of course Mama would go, I thought. Mama would go in Hazel's memory, no matter that she had been dead going on fifteen years. She had no business wandering about Hudson's Ridge—she shouldn't be out of bed at all. I would have more than a few sharp words to say to Doc the next day. "I'll need a minute to prepare."

"Take your time." He could afford to be gracious. This was how men were, once they'd gotten what they came for. After all, it wasn't him nor me waiting for the child to leave our body and come into its own.

I found Lauren awake, sitting on her bed. "Caleb's wife's birthing. Told him I'd go help." She began to dress.

I hunted up my bag and rummaged through my herbal chest. I packed fine silk thread, the last spool Mama had owned, and the faded piece of felt where I'd always kept my needles. I fretted over not having any ready sterile cloths, but Lauren handed me a pile of pretty white quilt blocks, and some large swatches of fabric left from my good green dress and a pink one she'd worn years ago. The cloth was as clean as such things could be. I was nervous that I'd forget something, the way I'd been the night Lauren had been born. So I packed as much as she and I together could carry.

I told David I was going on a birthing and he stirred then. "Mama's there," I said. "She needs my help."

"Of course," he said. "What can I do?"

I kissed him. "I'll want some coffee when I get back. But until then, just get some sleep."

Caleb had passed out on the porch, snoring in the way only the truly sotted can. I slapped his face a few times, but he wouldn't stir. His idiot grin and rosy cheeks made me angry, thinking of his woman waiting on the mountain.

"He'll freeze out here," I told Lauren. "We have to move him."

"I'll get the door, and then we can drag him." With her pushing and me pulling, we managed to get him inside. Lauren disappeared a moment and came back with a wool coverlet taken, I noticed, from her own bed. I wondered what sorts of blankets the Blickers would have in their cabin, so I picked up another old quilt and draped it over my shoulders, just in case.

"What will David think when he wakes?" She was grinning.

I couldn't help but smile, too. "Caleb can explain himself."

A light snow blew over us as we walked, but falltime leaves still fell around us when the wind blew, making the path slippery. Jesus tells that the poor are always with us, and maybe this explains the many babies that they bear. I recalled when Mama and I had followed Caleb to where Hazel lay. How she and I had gone again during the influenza. Now Mama was dying, I thought. Lauren was with me, but only a little while. Alvin was gone. Hazel dead. Caleb . . . well, they say that God is kind to drunks.

Dawn had broken across the face of the ridge, and the Blicker house looked shabby in the weak light. The gray wood was lost in the ashy grit of sky and earth. The boards sagged as we crossed the porch. I stomped my cold feet on the doorjamb, as my hands were filled with the supplies. "It's Elizabeth Whitely," I called out from habit. Bessie Newland had never delivered babies.

The woman who opened the door was so dark-skinned that only the tip of her nose and a great swath of cloth covering an enormous body were visible. "I am Missoura's ma. And I am much obliged to you for coming."

My lantern filled the small front room with light. I saw Missoura stretched out on the bed.

"Where is my mama?" I opened my bag, spreading out an old sheet at the foot of the rumpled bed.

"Out back," the woman said, and at the same time, Mama came through the door dragging a bucket of water so heavy that she couldn't walk without trouble. Lauren ran to help her. When Mama caught sight of her, I watched the joy bloom on her face. I stood there, waiting, as they hugged and kissed. Mama held Lauren's chin, and told her how grown up she seemed. Then the woman on the bed let out a moan and Mama turned away.

I wondered if I had seen the miracle. Surely Lauren had healed Mama.

But then Mama coughed, moving quickly from the bed. She took her handkerchief and wiped her mouth. I saw bloodstains there. Nothing had changed at all.

"Elizabeth," Mama called. I could hear the bubble of water boiling on the stove. I could see Lauren's mouth trying to say something.

"Elizabeth," Mama said again, sharper this time. "I need you."

Mama was sitting in a chair at the foot of the bed. I rushed over to obey her. "You'll need to be my hands. I don't trust mine inside of her."

Her hands, I thought. Mama's hands.

"Elizabeth," Mama called a third time, her voice as hard as I'd ever heard it. Then the woman on the bed let out a howl and I went to her. The years seemed to melt away. I might have been sixteen standing there, or twenty, or twenty-five. My fingers moved about the girl's body, taking note of what might go wrong. Granny had known me so well. I would always be a midwife—not because of what I did, but because of who I was.

"How is she?" I began to spread out my birthing supplies on a piece of starched sheet.

"Been at it a long time." Missoura's ma sat down in a chair next to the bed.

"You're going to be fine," Mama said, her voice soothing and confident.

Missoura was pretty, I'll say that, but Caleb always had taken up with pretty women. Her dark hair, no doubt a gift of some kin sent west to the Nations, was soft and curled. Her wide eyes were as blue as mine. Her skin, covered with birthing sweat, shimmered warm and deep in the lantern-light. She couldn't have been more than seventeen—barely older than Lauren—and I felt motherly towards her, as I never had to any other woman I'd helped.

"She's going to be just fine, yes, she is." I was in charge now. I smiled down at Missoura and washed my hands in the steaming bucket at the foot of the bed. "Bring the lantern closer." This to the mother. "And I'll need hot water in a sterile basin by my feet." This to Lauren.

Missoura's birthing parts were as pink as any woman's and I couldn't help but laugh. "All women are red enough where it counts," I muttered Granny's words under my breath. Mama's mouth twitched and I knew she'd caught the joke. I slipped my finger about the birthing tube, swollen with water, testing for strength and stretch. The skin held taut, but was easy enough to bend. When I slipped my hand inside, I could feel the muscles grip. "You're doing fine." There was little else to do but wait.

Using nutmeg butter, I stretched and bent the hard ridge of skin around the opening, hoping there would be no tearing and no brilliant red flow of blood. Lauren had threaded the needle just in case, and had run the metal through the candle flame, then soaked it in boiling water.

"Where Caleb be?" Missoura asked.

"Last I saw him, he was passed out inside my house." Mama frowned at me and shook her head.

Missoura's ma snorted. She was rubbing the girl's back. "Leastaways he made it that far."

By full daylight, Missoura was pushing. The baby would crown into my palm and then retreat back again. Missoura had given up on being brave, and screamed as loud as a woman can. She kept pushing, but that baby would come no farther.

"It's breeches," the ma said. "Missoura here was breeches."

"It isn't." I'd felt the crowning head enough to know. My own head was hot and stiff, pounding as though something were trying to be birthed out of me. "It's the shoulders. They can't make it through." Lauren kept the water at my feet clean and hot. Mama stood a moment, then ran her hands over the girl's belly. She nodded.

"What do you mean?" Missoura's ma had rubbed her

daughter's back until the light brown skin was blotted with red streaks.

"It's too big." I could hardly say the words around the growth of fear in my throat. Mama was telling Lauren to fetch Doc, but I knew there wasn't time. "Can we turn it? Deliver it upside down?"

Mama shook her head. "If it's the shoulders, it won't matter."

I looked over at Lauren. "I'm no midwife," she said quietly. And I turned my back to her. She couldn't heal Mama. She couldn't help me now.

Doc could cut her wide open and take the baby out through the belly, but no midwife would dream of such a task. I might save the baby, but would surely kill its mama.

"She's pushing again," Mama called out, as though I couldn't feel it with my own hand, hear it in Missoura's screams.

From deep inside Missoura came a popping of bone. Her pelvis was splitting apart like chopped wood.

"I need to break the shoulder." I scrubbed my hands in boiled water again. The skin was bruised and cracked around the knuckles. I knew it would pain me tomorrow something awful, and I thought about that hurt as I reached into the birthing tube, wanting to be gentle.

"You ain't going to be breaking no bones in my little girl." Missoura's ma reached for my arm, but Lauren was quicker and held the big woman back.

I was reaching up, thinking only of the baby's bones. My fingers needed to be at just the right place, my body and Missoura's body and the baby's body, all one and the same in that moment.

I felt the snap, and then the stillness, as though we'd all breathed in at once. My hand slid free and the baby slithered out on my lap.

The baby was dead. I could tell by looking at her that she'd been a sugar baby, riddled young with the disease that had eaten away at Granny. Baby hadn't been alive for days, weeks maybe,

and her skin was blotchy with rot. I hated seeing that poor shriveled form, knowing that if I'd kept watch on Missoura, as a midwife should, the baby might have been saved.

"We were too late." My voice, though a whisper, sounded
too loud for that room. Missoura's hands stretched out, then
fell back when she saw the blue-gray little girl, one broken
arm dangling. She burst into tears, pressing her face into her
mama's leg.

I felt surrounded by death. Mama on my right hand, the
baby in my left. My own barrenness inside of me.

I put my head in my bloody hand, holding the baby up in
the other.

"I don't want it," I heard the girl say.

"Take it away," the mother hissed.

"Course you want her," Lauren insisted. I raised my own
head just in time to watch Lauren take the baby from my arm
to hers. The baby began to cry.

NINETEEN

Not two weeks passed before Mama died in her sleep. From the Blicker house, Lauren had run ahead to tell David to bring the truck. When we got to town, Doc was standing on the porch, heedless of the cold. He'd no doubt been waiting there all night. He started to scold Mama for leaving, but his words faded when he saw David carrying her up the steps.

We all went into the downstairs bedroom Doc had made up for Mama months before. David set her on the bed, and Doc knelt beside it. "Maisie." I'd never seen him so stricken. I recalled the stronger, younger man he'd been, rushing to save Mama during the influenza outbreak. This old man couldn't help her now.

"I had to go, Jack." This was all she could say before the coughing overtook her.

"Go in the parlor," Doc ordered us. I didn't move. "Go on, Elizabeth." He stood up and put his hand on my shoulder. "I can help her. Now let me do so." I went as far as the doorway before I turned. Doc had taken a needle and a vial from a cabinet. Mama was still coughing. There was blood splattered across the sheets.

It's like a birthing, I thought. After a point there is nothing to do but wait.

He kept her full of morphine, which eased her. She dozed a lot, and the medicine gave her headaches so bad that we kept the room in darkness, no matter the time of day.

Doc made me up a cot so I could sleep next to her. Lauren took one of the rooms upstairs. She was the one who made sure I took a bite of food, that I dressed in clean clothes. I asked her again if she could help, but she shook her head. "She won't let me."

"What do you mean?"

Lauren thought a moment. "She has to want me to heal her. And she doesn't."

David came to town each evening, after he'd taken care of the stock, and sometimes I would sit with him in the parlor, giving Doc and Mama a chance to be alone. But mostly I never left her side.

"Your David is a good man," she told me once. Doc had just given her the drug and she was clearheaded for a minute.

"Everyone loves David." The words sounded sad, even to me. I tried to be more cheerful. "Even Aunt Annie approves."

Mama managed a smile. "Well, that should settle things then." She closed her eyes.

I slept that night beside her, waking to find her body still. I'd thought for sure I would know the moment that it happened. That I'd feel something, somewhere, in my body to let me know she'd gone. But I didn't.

Years ago, back in Old Caesar's day, midwives often sat up with the dead. Granny had still done this, when I was growing up. Said lots of folks could use a steady voice and a gentle hand at the end of their lives just as their mamas had needed one when they were first coming in.

I would have liked a midwife then. Someone to guide me through the pain. But there was no one to come. There were no more midwives after me.

We'd laid Mama in Doc's parlor, because we knew folks would come to call. I'd scrubbed my skin until it hurt, and all day I felt it burn against the heavy wool of my dress.

"What can I do?" David asked.

"I don't know," I told him. "I wish I had something to do myself."

Lauren had cleaned Mama up, dressed her in fine clothes. I fixed her hair. Doc handed me some sheets trimmed in lace, and I was pleased we had something so fine to give her. We spread Great-granny's log-cabin quilt over her. I'd stared at that quilt for so long now that I could see it turning over on itself, see the light blues cavorting with the yellows and the dark greens. It was a winter quilt, thick and heavy, filled with wool and cotton so soft that the tiny stitches in it looked like the dimpled hands of an infant.

All that day I sat there. I sat there all throughout the afternoon, while folks I'd known and some who were strange to me called to pay their respects. I watched Aunt Annie come in, wailing like a lost child. She threw herself upon Mama's body, joined by women who pulled her back to her feet and comforted her.

Men, dressed in their dark suits and boiled shirts, nodded at Mama when they passed. Then they gathered on the porch, telling stories about her to anyone who came by. Several held children on their knees, who listened, asked questions, then peeked inside with awe.

Every person who came brought food—I could smell ham and turkey and beans and gravy. Cakes and pie and puddings were all waved under my nose, but I turned away. "You're being unfeeling," Aunt Annie said. David took her arm and drew her back among the crowd.

There was so much noise. Why was everyone so loud?

All that night I sat there, smoothing the quilt when someone rumpled it. Perhaps the weight of it would keep her there, stretched out across the bed—I remember thinking that. When folks had gone, Doc joined me, him on one side, me on the other. He wept then as only a woman is supposed to weep.

We buried her on Denniker's Mountain, next to Ivy. Doc fussed a bit, wanting to keep her in town, but it just didn't seem right, to place her beside Mrs. Doc. And I wanted her on the mountain, near to me.

Again, the people came. I stood at the grave, holding the shovel, unwilling to let anyone take it and cover her up. Every time John Teller tried, I turned away from him. I was growing more and more upset until David stepped forward. "Let me," he said. He held out his hands, and I gave him the shovel.

Doc headed down the mountain, for his empty house, and Lauren and I began to climb towards our own. I hadn't been home since Caleb Blicker had called for me.

We didn't speak. I went into David's and my room and sat down on the bed. I felt utterly alone.

Lauren brought me a cup of tea. "I'm sorry, Mama."

Over and over these past two days I'd heard those words— I'm sorry, I'm sorry, I'm sorry—until I'd wanted to cover my ears from them. But Lauren's words meant so much more.

"Why didn't you heal her?"

"She never wanted me to." She lit the candle by the bed, and I could see her clearly.

"Help me, Lauren. I need to understand this. But I don't." A ghost of the anger I'd carried for so long now stirred. "You healed that baby. You heal strangers. You heal everyone but those who love you." I wondered if the words sounded as bitter as I felt.

"I wanted to heal her. Just like I wanted to heal you, all those years ago. But I couldn't."

"What was to keep you from reaching out, taking her hands and making her well? That woman at the church, who pulled her baby away. That didn't keep you from healing."

Lauren sighed. "I don't know why some people claim not to want healing, but seek it anyway. The woman was there because she wanted to believe that God would do something for her. Nana didn't believe at all. To her, miracles don't happen."

Wanting, believing, looking, finding—these words mattered little. Mama was still gone. "Why did you come back, then?" My voice broke. "Why did you let me hope that when you came home it would be all right?" I couldn't keep the tears back. "What am I going to do? You'll leave again— there's no way Missoura won't talk about that baby. And once you go, then who will I have?"

"David," Lauren said.

"Who will I tell things to? Who will listen to me?"

"David loves you."

"I don't love him," I told her. "I've tried."

"You've been afraid. All those years with my daddy, and now you have a man to love you the way a woman needs to be loved." I could feel the bed shift as she stood up. "It's good, Mama. Let David give back to you the love you gave away."

"What do I do when he decides he'd rather have a woman who will bear him children?"

"This has nothing to do with babies." Lauren touched my face. "You're already pregnant, though you don't know it yet." She tipped her head, studying me, the way Mama used to do. "Maybe four months or so. Should feel the quickening any time now." She grinned in that familiar way. "That summer, when you wanted my daddy's baby, you asked me to heal you and I couldn't. I've always heard you crying, Mama, but a baby with my daddy would have been no miracle at all. But now . . ." She reached out her hand. "I didn't come back to heal Nana. I came back to heal you."

Her hand was before me—the rough edges of her skin, the ragged nails I had known all the years of this girl's life. I was Lauren's mama. Nothing in this world was strong enough to keep me from taking that hand in mine.

I went out into the main room, only to find it empty. Feeling light-headed, I headed for the lean-to kitchen, suddenly craving a drink of cold water. My body was waiting for him—ears pricked, eyes watching. And soon he came.

"Lauren said she was going to get your things from Doc's," David said.

We are alone, I thought. There would soon be little time in our lives to be alone.

I fixed my eyes upon his face—this man who was my husband. There was the graying hair and the small scar on his cheek. I watched his mouth move, the shape so firm and gentle.

"Lauren said you wanted me?" He looked hopeful.

I gathered his right hand and lifted it to my mouth. I kissed the four fingers, taking each knuckle against my lips and holding it there for the slightest moment. I closed my eyes and pushed my tongue against his palm and tasted the salt of his work.

"What is it?" he asked. His eyes are so dark, I thought, and in them I could see something that moved me. Something I had always known in my mind, but had never believed in my heart.

"You love me?" I wanted my ears to hear what my eyes could see.

"I love you," he said, his voice rattling like coal rushing through a tipple. "I have loved you for so long. . . ."

I put my hands on his shoulders. I felt him quake beneath my touch, but when I leaned into him, he did not fall. He caught me and held me against him.

"I love you, too." This was a joy to say. I kissed his face, feeling the lines carved into his skin, flooding now with tears—his or mine, it mattered not. I unbuttoned my dress and placed his hand upon my belly. His eyes went wide when he felt the kicking there. "I'm getting a baby."

"But you said . . ."

"I love you."

His arms came up under me, settling me down upon the creaking floor where a hundred Denniker feet had stood. I wanted him to share in the love that Lauren had given me—that Mama had given. I knew that this was what they wanted and what I wanted, too.

I've never told anyone about that evening—about David and me making love on the floor just after Mama had been buried—until now. I've never been one to worry about the judgment of others, but even I could see this might be carrying things a bit far, looking at it from the outside. But knowing the whole story, there might be some out there who are able to understand. For like all miracles, mine is known only as I experienced it. For others, there is only faith. Some hope is good, too, and without love, no story I tell will matter a whit to anyone.

Evelyn, knitted in my womb, was a miracle in her own right. And she was only the beginning.

The Psalmist tells us to lift our eyes upon the hills, from whence cometh our strength. Here, on the peak of Denniker's

Mountain, I felt the need of something greater than even these hills, which have been my home, my shelter, and my sustenance. I wanted to give something back to this man who had loved me from the first. Who knows me every day.

More was asked, and more was given.

I named him David, after his father.

EPILOGUE

Come each springtime, before Decoration Day, I make our candles for the year. Of course candle-making isn't a one-day job, and not one you can begin in May. To make them right you have to gather the milkweed in the early fall, before the end of harvest, when the fluff is long and fine but won't yet blow away in your hand. A good milkweed wick will burn a clean bright flame.

I walk along the edge of the creek to gather my pods. Not much living around that creek anymore, for the mines are open again. Some days the water is bright orange, and stinks of brimstone as though it came from hell itself. And who's to say that it doesn't? Over in the next county I hear tell of a mine that caught fire and has been burning twenty years. With all the coal under there, the flames ain't likely to burn out until the end of time.

Evelyn comes with me to gather the silk. Evelyn, who hasn't known anything but rural electric, is as unfamiliar with milkweed pods as I am with the notion of people flying in the sky. I see the aeroplanes—hear them, too. They roar over this valley, though not so loud as a murder of migrating crows. Even with all this talk of war, there is no doubt in my mind who rules the air, speaking day to day.

Evelyn is disappointed in the small, wrinkled pods. "They

look like rotten potatoes," she says, and wrinkles her nose as if they have a smell.

"They do at that," I tell her, but I am thinking that they look and feel more like a man's private parts emptied of their own seeds. My daughter has never seen a baby born. I hear that in cities even the women who give birth do not see, sleeping through the whole thing.

Back home, we empty my basket on the kitchen table. In our hands, there is the sound of papery shell crackling and then the soft silence of silk falling upon wood.

"It's sticky," Evelyn says. Her fingers are covered with seeds and fluff. Evelyn is a neat child, who makes her bed each morning without being told. She has Mama's red curls, and Mama's gentle smile. She wants to be a teacher, she tells me.

"Why don't you go play outside," I say. She is gone so quickly that I know she's been waiting to get away. Who isn't at ten? In silence, I mix grease with the bits of silk until it is thick enough to roll into long threads the length of my arm. I can smell peppermint, and a little camphor. A touch of ginger too.

When I have rolled a dozen strands, I wrap them in a cotton cloth and place them in the root cellar where it is cool, next to the rows of fruits and vegetables that will see us through the winter. At night, when I hear David snoring in our bed and the humming breath of our children nearby, that is the time I burn the candles. I burn them one at a time, as I read the last letter Lauren has sent, for she writes the longest letters now. I wonder where this day will find her and what is to come.

For candle-making these days, I admit to a little cheating. Mama never used store-boughten beeswax. Old Giles Teller keeps bees on the small fork of Kettle Creek and brings the honey and wax to sell in town. That branch of the Teller clan has always kept bees, and when they stop then I suppose I'll have to give up making candles altogether too.

I melt the wax in a certain pot, one I have used to make candles every year of my known life. Inside is the wax from all the candles we have molded—wax from Mama's candles and Granny's candles mingles with my own.

"Why do we make candles?" Evelyn asked for the first time last year. We were waiting for the wax to harden so we could dump them from the iron tubes.

"Because we always have," I answered.

"But why?"

"And the light shineth in the darkness—and the darkness comprehended it not."

Evelyn shook her head. "I don't understand," she said.

"Watch this," I said. I dipped my finger into the melted wax at the very top where it was just cool enough to touch. The golden liquid glistened on my finger before thickening. When I pulled it off, she could see the ridges and valleys from my skin preserved in solid form.

Evelyn had been impressed. "Can I try?"

I nodded. "But be careful."

Her finger skimmed the wax and she did not even feel the heat enough to wince. The tip of her finger sparkled and she was jubilant.

"I did it!" Then she peeled away the wax in one piece, and revealed the tiny bowl, fitted only for her.

"Can I keep it?"

"For now." Evelyn placed the bowl on the windowsill and then ran off, leaving her print behind.

This year I make the wax bowls alone and remember.

"There is nothing like candlelight."

I can hear Mama's voice as clear as a hammer, sounding in the January chill. "Some light chases the darkness away, but candles remind you that the darkness is still there, all around you."

Now I am the one who is ten years old. "I don't like the dark."

"It's good to appreciate the light," Mama told me. "And while you don't need to make friends with the dark, we should acknowledge that it is there. This way we can rejoice in the light without fearing that it only keeps the dark at bay."

I don't understand, but I pretend to. I watch her take the candles from their iron molds. I like to hold them in my hand. They are long and slide through my fingers.

Back in my own kitchen, standing over my cooking stove that turns on and off, I shake the batch of candles from their molds. I pack them into old cigar boxes, and store them in the root cellar, where it is very dark. There are plenty of candles there already, made in years past. My family is ready, just in case. The war breathes down upon us. Who knows what might happen?

I keep one candle on the table. Alone, it looks small and delicate, like a root exposed to the air. I take a match and light it, then set it in the window. The sun has already dipped behind the mountain. The air is growing cool.

Soon David will be in from the barn, wanting his supper. There is a bit of pork for him, and plenty of biscuits and gravy to go around for the kids and me. Our bedsheets were washed today and smell like warm sun and mountain air.

Soon Davy will burst into the kitchen, hungry, busy, loud, telling me of his play. Evelyn will help me set the table, where we will sit down to eat. While we do not ask a formal grace, I will whisper one to myself, hearing the words in my head. Thanks to Mama, blessings for Lauren, prayers for Union and Alvin, too. I think of Ivy, and Granny, and Old Caesar. I remember all those who have gone before me so my world might be.

ACKNOWLEDGMENTS

This novel could never have been written without the story-telling tradition of my family—especially that of my grandmother, Colleen Riggleman Moran. I would also like to remember my other grandmother, Virginia Kuhn Wilson, and my cousin, Goldie McCrobie Louk.

Two stories used (very liberally) came from friends—thank you Robin Quackenbush and Michael C. Smith.

The research on Appalachian and American studies was invaluable, especially: *Albion's Seed* by David Hackett Fisher, *Death and Dying in Central Appalachia* by James K. Crissman, *Land of the Saddle-Bags* by James Raine, *History of Barbour County, West Virginia* by Hu Maxwell, *History of Preston County, West Virginia* by S. T. Wiley, *Southern Mountain Speech,* by Cratis T. Williams, *The Wolfpen Notebooks* by James Still, *Images of America—Barbour County* by Barbara Smith and Carl Briggs, and *A West Virginia Mountaineer Remembers* by Homer F. Riggleman.

For books on birthings and women's health, I recommend: *Listen to Me Good: The Life Story of an Alabama Midwife* by Margaret Charles Smith, *A Midwife's Tale—The Life of Martha Ballard* edited by Laurel Thatcher Ulrich, *The Midwives Book: Or The Whole Art of Midwifry Discovered* by Jane Sharp et al., *Mormon Midwife* by Patty Bartlett Sessions and edited by Donna

Told Smart, *Infanticide* by Maria W. Piers, and *Mother Nature* by Sara Blaffer Hrdy.

All of the herbals in this book are time and place appropriate, but our understanding of their potency and power has improved a great deal the past few years. Many are now considered dangerous, especially for pregnant women. For more information on herbals, both old and new: *Eve's Herbs* by John M. Riddle, *A Field Guide to Medicinal Plants* by Arnold and Connie Krochmal, *The New Holistic Herbal* by David Hoffman, *The Old English Herbals* by Eleanour Sinclair Rohde.

Writing may be a solitary profession, but being a writer needn't be. I've been encouraged by many writers from the Appalachian Writers Workshop. I would like to especially thank Silas House, who has believed in this manuscript and this writer since the beginning.

The Internet makes finding community easier—I've enjoyed the Speakeasy message board, hosted by *Poets & Writers Magazine*. Thanks to everyone there, for the good conversation and unstinting support. Laura Ruby, Anne Ursu, and Lisa Tucker have been my friends throughout this journey, and I don't know what I would have done without them. Readerville.com, run by Karen Templar, has also been very welcoming. Here I met M.J. Rose, who is certainly the most generous.

I have had great fortune finding my agents—first Pam Bernstein, and now Mel Berger. Many times I've relied upon them to hold my hand and stiffen my spine. I could not have made my way through the publishing process without their wit and wisdom.

My experience with The Dial Press should put to rest all rumors that editors are anything but passionate about the books that they publish. My thanks to Susan Kamil, for always treating my characters like real people. Thanks also to Zoë Rice, who worked with me one sentence at a time, and Margo Lipschultz, for answering every question.

But, as always, I come back to my family. Thank you Brennan, for creating your own stories to tell me even as your mother created hers. And every good thing within me goes to Karl. Nothing in my adult life has been accomplished without Karl Laskas by my side.